EVIL RUNS

A Novel

Vince Milam

Published internationally by Vince Milam Books

© Vince Milam Books 2015

Terms and Conditions:

The purchaser of this book is subject to the condition that he/she shall in no way resell it, nor any part of it, nor make copies of it to distribute freely.

All Persons Fictitious Disclaimer:

This book is a work of fiction. Any similarity between the characters and situations within its pages and places or persons, living or dead, is unintentional and co-incidental.

www.vincemilam.com

Acknowledgements:

Editor – David Antrobus

Cover Designer - Slobodan Cedic

Be sober, be vigilant; because your adversary the devil walks about like a roaring lion, seeking whom he may devour. 1 Peter 5:8

Chapter 1

Cole Garza still relished the walks through his town, more so now that the cowboy boots sat in the closet, replaced by comfortable walking shoes. It might not fit the sheriff image, but it sure made for better walking. The cowboy hat stayed—functional under the Texas sun—as well as the .40 caliber pistol and sheriff's badge. A genuine smile towards citizens on these morning meanders, heartfelt and sincere, softened his bird-of-prey focus—a legacy from Comanche blood of four generations past.

Experience had taught him to believe in the general goodness of people, to not get your shorts in a knot over chosen lifestyles, give folks a break, and maintain a quiet environment. He kept it simple. Don't harm others, and don't take what isn't yours.

Violent actions toward the innocent were a whole different ballgame. In those cases, he had been known to become, as the locals called it, "ballistic." On the rare occasions he'd drawn his firearm, it was done so with the utmost seriousness.

Rockport rose to a classic summer morning. A Gulf breeze kept it to the mid-80s, seagulls called, shrimp boats eased their way through the small harbor, and sport fishermen headed out for redfish and sea trout. The summer sun would soon overwhelm, but the early daylight reflected fresh possibilities.

Cole smiled, nodded, and said, "Mornin'" to a dozen folks before he dropped into Shorty's for a late breakfast. As was typical, he had arrived at work earlier, before daylight. The dark mornings afforded time to reflect on events both minor and of greater import as he checked the previous night's activity report and outlined the day. A short prayer followed, asking for safe endeavors for the people of Aransas County. A request for guidance and understanding used to be included. That had ceased several years ago.

"Dang light on the corner still ain't fixed," grumbled Shorty as he poured Cole coffee.

Rockport had eleven stoplights. The one at Shorty's corner blinked red in a semipermanent mode, sufficient to make traffic from all directions pay attention.

"Not my department." Cole laid his hat on the counter and reached for the stevia. He'd had to badger Shorty to get the natural sweetener. Shorty saw no point in it, at all.

"Well, when someone gets killed roaring through there, it'll damn sure be your department who gets to scrape up the body parts," said Shorty.

Cole smiled into his coffee and glanced sidelong through the diner's front window. One of Millie Gustafson's many green-collared rescue dogs ambled through the intersection, unmolested by traffic.

"Good grief, Shorty," said one of the regulars. "Scrapin' body parts? We're tryin' to eat, here."

Shorty wiped wet hands on the apron stretched across his belly. "Speaking of which, the regular, Sheriff?"

"Yep. Please." Regular breakfast consisted of huevos rancheros—fried eggs on corn tortillas covered with ranch sauce and melted cheese, with pooled grease at the edges. The stevia provided small solace as a gesture to better health.

He sipped coffee and glanced around the room at mostly regulars. A far corner held a large, bald, angular man—pale as a corpse. He stared at Cole and as their eyes met, the man lifted his coffee as a greeting, accompanied by a strange tight smile that the eyes did not reflect. Cole nodded in return, which should have ended the lifted-cup-as-greeting ritual. Instead, the stranger extended a long and hairy index finger on his free hand and pulled down the skin below one eye. The exposed portion of the eyeball showed brilliant purple. With crystalline clarity, the voice came unspoken and sibilant—resonating in Cole's consciousness. *It shall come hot and bright; pain, screams, suffering.* Their stares locked; the world distilled to that frozen moment. Cole's heartbeat hammered in his ears. The stranger released the skin and lowered his cup. The tight-lipped smile remained.

What the hell? thought Cole. He pushed off the counter to stand, felt fear wash through him, and turned back to the counter, breaking eye contact with the stranger. He stared at the surface of his coffee, unblinking, with fingers pressed white into the counter. His neck hair tingled and his gut knotted. The Gulf breeze cracked open the screen door where it hung suspended until the gust died and the door quietly shut.

"You heard what those loony bastards in DC are doing now?" This came from a regular customer. The loony bastards in DC had always done something. Rockport seldom felt any of it.

"I know what they ain't doin'. They ain't fixin' that damn light," said Shorty, which brought general laughter.

Cole barely heard any of it, twisted with indecision and rising anger. *Enough*, he thought. *Enough. You just showed your back to something bad wrong.* He turned as he stood to go talk to the man in the corner. The pale stranger had left.

He moved food around on his plate, too uneasy to eat, and tried to scan the *Rockport Pilot*, Aransas County's community newspaper. Time passed, shoulders relaxed, and the question of whether that voice really happened began to present itself. *Maybe*, he thought. *Maybe not.*

In the newspaper, the city council were arguing over bike lanes, some proclaiming the need to formalize that mode of transportation. He wouldn't allow his deputies to hand out any tickets to bicyclists, and suspected some on the council saw that edict as a revenue opportunity lost. They likely knew his opinion on the matter, so he wasn't asked to attend the council meeting.

When Shorty moved along the counter to refill his coffee, Cole asked, "The guy by the corner? Tall, thin, bald guy. Know him?"

"Gives me the creeps," said Shorty.

Cole cracked a smile. His sense of disquiet had subsided as he rationalized the encounter with the stranger as a mixture of one weird dude and his own imagination. "Everyone north of Dallas gives you the creeps, Shorty."

Shorty snorted. "Been here a few days. Staying at the Breeze Inn. Fanny said he gives her the creeps, too." Fanny Ulrich ran the Breeze Inn. "Must be foreign."

"Or from north of Dallas," said Cole.

Shorty grunted, swatted at a fly with the greasy towel he kept tucked in his apron, and headed off to service customers, wiping the faded and cracked linoleum counter as he moved.

"Fishing this weekend, Sheriff?" asked a regular.

"Hope to."

"Heard they've schooled on Parson's Flat." An area about five miles by boat from Rockport across the thirty-inch-deep waters of the Laguna Madre, redfish often schooled there to feed.

"Thanks," said Cole as he slid off the swiveled chair and put a five-spot on the counter. He grabbed his hat and said to no one particular, "See y'all."

"Adios" and "See you" came back from several people. Outside, the first waves of the daily summer bellows began to fire.

Chapter 2

Oyster shells crackled under the tires of Burt Hall's rattling pickup. He parked on the back lot, joining half a dozen other vehicles. The truck door creaked as he slid out and fished for the killing tools behind the seat. The white sun baked and a hot Gulf breeze carried salt and fish, masking whiskey sweat and body odor.

He removed a two-gallon gas can and the club. He'd stolen the club—known as a salmon priest—from a fishing boat out of Juneau. Two feet long, its hard hickory handle carried a weighty, solid brass knob on one end. Designed to dispatch salmon when removed from fishing nets, Burt intended a different use.

"This will do." He caressed the smooth handle and tested the heft of the brass knob. "This will have the pissants flopping."

He moved with power and conviction, strength and courage—all new and all good. He'd show them.

"Transgressions, Burt," the tall stranger had told him last night. "Transgressions and calumnies."

"What?" Burt squinted through smoke.

The tall stranger tried to smile back. He lacked eyebrows, eyelashes, or any visible hair, except for the backs of the long fingers. There, the hair showed coarse, black, and thick from top knuckle to fingernails.

"They refuse to understand. They have all done you wrong. A complete lack of respect," said the stranger.

The stranger's voice was deep, quiet, and foreign. You damn near had to lean into him to hear. He'd walked right up to Burt and offered to buy the booze if he could sit. The stranger gave a fellow a bit of the willies but, hell, free booze was free booze. And it turned out he listened, and that was a helluva change. Burt was so damn tired of people not having enough respect to listen.

"Pissants. The lot of them." Burt stared into his whiskey at the ramshackle bar. "The pissants don't show me a damn bit of respect."

The weather-beaten structure smelled of stale beer, smoke, and urine. It sat near the commercial fishing docks, frequented by deckhands who drifted through the fishing town as regular as the tides. A neon Pabst sign provided much of the lighting, and the handwritten sign behind the bar proclaimed No Credit—Don't Bother Asking. A fishing boat passed by the bar's open windows for a night run and created enough wake to cause other tied-up boats to bump against the old docks. The slight impacts reverberated through the floor of the bar. The wind freshened enough to keep the mosquitoes at bay and Patsy Cline cried "Crazy" on the jukebox.

"That's right," said the pale stranger. "Pissants. Doing extremely wrong by you. The whole lot of them. No respect. No love, Burt."

"Love? Hell, my own mother don't even like me."

Mom had fiddled with the inheritance and planned to cheat him. A man could tell these things. She wouldn't produce the will as she clung to life at the local nursing home, and had mentioned a couple of times something about giving to the Salvation Army. The brother and sister had passed on and now she owed him. He seldom visited Mom because all she'd do was bitch about some damn thing or the other. And now she smelled bad—a sweet, sick smell. It was disgusting.

All that work fishing in Alaska as a young man had bought a small shrimp boat on the Texas coast near the family. Shrimp were harder to harvest now and more Chink bastards had moved into the game. Christ, a man damn near had to work every day to make ends meet, and now the nasty old bitch might give his money away to someone else.

Burt's yellowed fingers removed the unfiltered cigarette from the side of his mouth. He spat tobacco flecks at the floor as a cockroach scuttled past the table, and looked for the cheap stamped-metal ashtray.

The pale stranger slouched to Burt's level, bony elbows on the table and his chin rested in the hairy nest of crossed hands. He made a slight gesture with one of the fingers. The ashtray scooted across the table and stopped under Burt's cigarette. *Neat trick*, thought Burt. *This guy's alright.*

"But you do fear them, Burt. All of them. You are afraid. I can tell. I see a fearful little man."

Burt's fist slammed the cheap table. "I ain't afraid of a goddamn one of them!"

The stranger sat taller and became more animated. "Oh, you fear them. I can tell. I can always tell."

"Pissants! Pissants! Afraid of them? They goddamn better well fear me!" Flecks of spit flew across the table.

One long hand crossed the table and encompassed Burt's curled fist. "They need to fear you. They need to pay. You have the power to make them pay." The stranger smiled wider, eyes furrowed with conviction.

Burt nodded, captured by the stranger's eyes and a sudden flow of animal energy. Then he too smiled. The new friend confirmed everything. He deserved respect. They owed him, big time. They would fear. The pissants would pay.

Chapter 3

A nurse stood outside the back door of the nursing home, engaged on her cell phone. She had not bothered to turn at the arrival of the pickup. The oyster shell parking lot lay firecracker hot and the nurse had started to sweat.

Burt edged behind her and with a quick backhand stroke of the salmon priest crushed her skull. The open air carried the sound, muted and hollow. Her body crumpled to lie on her back, one leg folded under the other. As he opened the back door the voice on the fallen cell phone carried on. High circling gulls called.

The back entrance led to the kitchen where the head cook was preparing lunch. The cook paid no mind when the door opened and continued to hum "Oh Happy Day." Burt delivered a blow to the cook's neck, fracturing vertebrae. It caused instant death. The cook fell and pulled the large pan of half-prepared lasagna to the floor with him. He paused to stare at the victim. "Stay there," he said, cackling as he moved on.

He exited the kitchen and strode along a hallway where three wheelchair-bound residents collected and gossiped around a Coke machine. Burt paused and listened. Something about a new resident. A retired banker. A pissant. Two of the group thought the new resident looked handsome. The third bitched about all bankers. All three laughed and teased each other, like it was some kind of goddamn happy-time. They paid no attention to the footfalls that headed their way on the polished hallway.

He knew where to go. To see Mom. To take care of business. A hot, intense force consumed and empowered him.

He slowed long enough to jerk each of the three frail residents from their wheelchairs and onto the linoleum floor. It was so unexpected, so bizarre an action, that none of the three emitted a sound. Then, collectively, they cried for help. *Good luck with that*, he thought, raising the club and driving it downward repeatedly.

He unscrewed the cap from the gas can and continued toward Mom's room, pouring a trail of gasoline. The fuel pooled on the hard floor and collected in a ragged line.

A staff member screamed, "Call 911! 911! Quick!" and ran down the hall behind Burt to see if she could help the brutalized residents. He watched her over his shoulder. *Well, then, join the party, toots*.

He emptied the gas can at a hallway intersection, dropped it, and stood still. The salmon priest drifted against his leg, back and forth. So easy. So goddamn easy.

"Not a good time to be afraid," said the tall stranger, apparently waiting for him. Not spoken, the words entered Burt's consciousness loud and distinct. "They hate you. They see you as a scared little man. You are not afraid, are you?"

"Do I look like I'm afraid?" He grinned at his new friend and extracted a lighter. "Pissants."

"Make them pay," said the friend. The unspoken words came clear and intense.

A door at the right turn of the hallway flung open as two staff members started to enter. The tall friend uncurled a hand, palm extended. He never took his eyes off Burt. The door slammed shut on the staff members.

He leaned over the pooled gasoline trail, flicked the lighter, and set it ablaze. He cocked his head at the elevated screams of the staff member behind him. The tall friend had vanished.

Fire alarms blasted throughout the nursing home. He headed to Mom's room and encountered two more residents. One used a walker and the other a cane. They saw him approach, turned together, and attempted to flee. He strode at a normal pace and roared over the noise, "Afraid, are we? You goddamn better be afraid. Run! Run, you pissants!"

The resident with the walker turned at the sound of his now close-by voice. She raised the walker as a lion tamer might raise a chair and confronted him. The other resident with the cane continued to flee.

He killed them both with vicious overhead blows. Blood and brain matter splattered on his shirt.

The open door to Mom's room showed her on the bed, sliding her feet into sandals. *The Price Is Right* played on the television, the sound overwhelmed by the cacophony of alarms. He entered, covered in swaths of gore, and smiled wide.

"Burt?" she asked, over the din of the hallway. "What the heck is going on?"

He trumpeted, "I'm what's going on, Mom! I'm what's going on!" He gave the brass-headed club a quick flip toss, catching it as he moved toward her.

Chapter 4

The call came on the handheld radio and Cole sprinted the few blocks to the nursing home. He met one of his deputies, R.L. Harris, at the entrance to the single-level building. Smoke alarms screamed and the siren of a Rockport fire engine signaled its approach. A few staff members, one weeping, helped elderly residents out of the building and onto the front lawn. As the residents were laid on the grass, the staff members rushed back inside to save more. The citizens of Rockport who heard the alarms and siren and saw the mayhem and smoke joined the frantic effort to evacuate the building.

Surrounded by this chaos, Cole made a quick assessment and called out to R.L., "Help out here! I'm going around back to see if any more are trapped!"

As Cole dashed around the building he picked up the weird tall stranger blending with the dark shadows of the alley that ran alongside the nursing home. Cole shouted as he ran to the back door, "You! Hey, you!"

The stranger glanced at Cole and popped a large hand open in a peculiar flicking gesture before he looked back down the alley, trembled, and crouched to flee. Nausea swept over Cole, coinciding with the stranger's hand gesture. He staggered, leaned over, gagged, and recovered to hear a scream from an open window.

It was a no-brainer to go inside the burning building—lives were at stake in there. The stranger would have to wait for another time. He committed to the back door, first checking for a pulse from the body of a downed nurse as she lay in a halo of her own blood, eyes open to the sky. Smoke poured from a back window and alarms wailed. *Gotta move, gotta move, gotta move.*

Another man sprinted to the edge of the alley's deep shadows and slammed to a stop, casting a hard focused search. The tall, hairless stranger had vanished.

Think, think, think, and keep moving! Someone had attacked the nurse. The perp, if it wasn't the tall stranger, still lurked inside. People could be saved. A final glance at the new guy standing in the alley gave a quick snapshot of a man very different and very old—pale but illuminated—with '50s garb and a long gray ponytail. No way this guy was a resident of the nursing home. He had the profile of a warrior, ready for battle. *Move, move, move.*

Cole flung open the back door to enter hell. Gun drawn, he checked for a pulse on the downed cook lying next to a deep-dish pan and its scattered ingredients, then led with the .40 caliber pistol out into the hallway. The screech of the smoke alarms, the wail of emergency vehicles, and thick smoke filled the air. All signs indicated that this could only get worse.

He shielded against the fiery hallway with his gun-free hand. The not-yet-on-fire short passage to the right offered an avenue to find survivors when a man came from the left, straight through the flames.

Face covered with blood and bits of flesh, he flipped some kind of club as he walked. The intense heat of the flaming walls and ceiling curled and melted his hair, while his gore-drenched shirt began to smoke.

Cole stood inside the hallway and pointed the pistol at the approaching specter.

"Freeze!" yelled Cole. *Stupid, stupid.*

The man increased his pace and accelerated into a run, prompting his clothing to burst into flames as he headed straight toward Cole.

He fired a double tap—two bullets in rapid succession. Each hit the target's chest, three inches apart. The man slowed, staggered, and fell to his knees.

Then he smiled, freezing Cole. It was the same smile and the same look his wife's murderer had given five years ago. A picture of pure, unadulterated evil.

The dead man collapsed forward, on fire. Flames lapped the walls nearby. Cole kept the gun trained on the fallen body and backed into the kitchen.

Breathing hard, he made a gradual turn, holstered the pistol, and carried the body of the cook out the back door. Sheriff's deputies and firefighters surrounded and led him away from the inferno.

Chapter 5

"Francois Domaine?" asked the Air France ticket agent in France.

"Oui," replied the priest.

"Corpus Christi?" The gentleman behind the counter confirmed his destination.

"Oui."

Such a curious name for a Texas town—Body of Christ. He had traveled to the States several times, but always to either New York or Boston and once to Chicago. Corpus Christi was the nearest commercial airport to some place called Rockport.

It would make for a long flight, but first class seating helped accommodate a short, stocky body and a hip that would, on occasion, throb due to an old injury acquired on the rugby pitch as a youth. Such was life, and so many had far greater issues to deal with.

A miniature tug-of-war ensued over the boarding pass as the ticket agent reiterated Air France's no smoking policy. It made for a great irritant, given the airline people had already admonished him as he stood smoking in the ticket queue.

One remained celibate, abhorred the scandals that had wracked the church, maintained a keen sense of proportion, and attempted to inject style even within the constraints of priestly attire, yet not a single comment from the airline employees on his yellow-paisley silk pocket-handkerchief or his custom Italian shoes. Clearly, the Air France hiring practices had become shoddy. A burden to bear, yes, but he would forgive them.

Francois dedicated life to God. The youngest of five children, he had entered the seminary, fascinated by the study of evil and its manifestations. The research of how evil survived and thrived within God's world created a metaphysical grappling with the age-old dichotomy of an all-powerful loving deity and earth-bound malevolence. Daily ministry bored him; to understand God and the why of evil was his passion.

A path revealed at an early age now culminated in the flight to the wilds of Texas. During seminary studies as a young man, he'd experienced a brief encounter with a creature inside his stoic room at the ancient Abbey de Cluny. The creature had crouched on the margins of awareness as Francois woke in the dead of night. Its presence—its reality—washed the room. He sat upright, flung off the blanket, and stalked the thing, surprised at his own aggression. He knew better than to assume the mantle of battle himself, but instead invoked the name of Jesus Christ and ordered the demon to depart. The apparition diminished and left.

He'd prayed until dawn. Dressed in monastic clothing to greet the day with the other seminary students, thoughts of denial and rationalization crept in. Such physical creatures belied all priestly training. Just prior to leaving the tiny room, he leaned through the stone window to appreciate the new dawn on the Abbey's manicured grounds, as he had done on so many other mornings. The air carried a spring freshness. In the midst of that peaceful reflection, Francois lifted a hand as if burned. There were claw marks on the stone sill, etched. Fresh claw marks.

Although devout and brilliant, he was viewed by the Vatican as an outlier. They allowed him to study and travel, satisfying the arm of the church that kept alive the traditions of exorcism and demonology. The church under Pope Francis had reinvigorated both the actuality of demons and the war against them.

Francois had worked with exorcists and experienced individual possessions. Demons were cast out. It constituted harrowing work, and he gained some measure of satisfaction among the draining physical and emotional processes. Knowledge came with the calm of one who did not fear a fight. The exorcism rituals assumed that the possessed person still had their free will, though the demon may hold control over their physical body. Free will, evil, and the vagaries of that interface caused much reflection.

Still, the element of "the others" continued to haunt him. The creature that visited the room at the seminary, evil that manifested as earth-bound entities, evil that acted and killed—these creatures existed, a worldview on the fringe of church dogma.

Research of this nature created unease among church superiors, yet plenty of evidence buttressed such viewpoints, much of it ensconced among the musty hidden archives of the Vatican. During ecumenical discussions among peers, Francois did not emphasize the esoteric parts of his belief system. There lived among the church hierarchy a few rare exceptions with whom he remained comfortable discussing such things.

Through prayer, he became convinced that God's path for him lay in the confrontation of this evil that walked among us. How to confront it and with what results gave him pause, but did not alter his resolve. He prayed for answers—a guide, probable outcomes, and best approaches. God chose not to edify him on these things.

He read and then reiterated the Rockport massacre to church superiors. They allowed him, after all these years, to pursue his contentions. To find a pattern, a trail, or a path would constitute the initial efforts. He would chase evil. It was an awesome realization.

He acknowledged the human element of hubris on the fringe of his mental makeup, justified, of course, by the inarguable fact that expertise in such areas resided in only a few. The mantle of a solo warrior, a burden to be sure, rested on broad shoulders.

His immediate superior, Bishop Alehandro from Paraguay, showed skepticism yet remained supportive.

"And to what purpose, Francois?" asked the Bishop.

"I do not know."

"And does God lead you in this direction?"

"That, I do know. It is my path."

The bishop sighed. "You know I hold a strong belief toward God's miracles, and the opposite expression does not stretch my faith. But does this path have boundaries? Some framework for God's plan?"

"This, also, I do not know." Francois looked at the ground and stroked his mustache. They stood in a small vestibule, alone. The Vatican, for the moment, carried a sense of quiet and this small hideaway more so. Light filtered through from a small stained glass window. "I carry the power of God, through his son, Jesus Christ. It is all I have for guidance—for direction. Surely it is enough."

"It will have to do, my friend. It will have to do."

Bishop Alehandro blessed him, prayed with him, released him, and observed him walk away with that peculiar declarative gait.

Francois began his first quest.

Chapter 6

Cole stood at the end of a rock jetty that extended into the Laguna Madre. The sun set behind him, and the soft hues of beginning twilight covered the bay. A school of dolphins surfaced, riding the intercoastal canal that cut through the one hundred and thirty miles of the shallow Laguna and allowed barge traffic to pass. Panicked baitfish surfaced near the jetty, chased by unseen predators, and a flock of pelicans, flying a sentinel formation, hung suspended against the Gulf breeze.

This is a tough row to hoe, Lord. Five years. I still don't get it. No answers. Nada.

Martha Garza had gone into Corpus to shop. A young man had confronted her at gunpoint in the mall parking lot and shot her dead. The killer later admitted an intention to continue a remorseless shooting spree. An off-duty cop at the mall ran to the sound of the gunshot and wounded the shooter before he could do more. The authorities allowed Cole to see the jailed killer, pending trial. The young man exhibited no remorse—just a bright, intense look and a maniacally evil smile. Cole chalked it up to crazy. Crazy nonsensical evil.

I saw that look again. I saw it. That crazy bastard at the nursing home. What the hell? Killing helpless old people? In my town. In. My. Town.

Martha's murder had created a crisis of faith. Five years of wrestling with the pain and anguish made for a spiritual observer status. Prayer continued—an exercise in internal dialogue and a hope that prayers would help others. Maybe they did, but it was damn hard to tell. His belief in God remained, but any semblance of a personal walk with a higher power evaporated. Martha was gone. The pain never diminished.

None of it makes a lick of sense. It ties to the past somehow, and that weird tall sumbitch with the hand flicking BS had something to do with it. I'm mad as hell about the whole dang thing but you aren't givin' me diddly-squat to help figure it out.

The verdict delivered death by lethal injection for Martha's killer. The state executing people made for mixed feelings, but he attended the execution two years later to bring what he hoped would be closure. It did not. He raised his children through their teen years and became immersed in their lives. Much admired by the community, he ran uncontested in the sheriff elections.

I'm lost. Plain and simple. How about the big picture. Give me something. Something to hold onto. Because where you have me now is a hard place to be.

The taste of a fresh saltwater breeze signaled an easing off of the heat, and the muted rumble of a Gulf thunderstorm draped the day's end.

Chapter 7

News crews, both local and national, swarmed the town. Microphones were thrust at Cole's face and shouted questions rained. The grand total consisted of twelve dead, either slaughtered or killed by fire. Rockport had never seen anything to compare with it.

Cole holed up and worked the crime. The governor sent the Rangers to help. They told him it was best to face the media now, and to get comfortable with the answer "I don't know."

Rockport's mayor, Adele Remmy, made a point to meet with him several times each day during this maelstrom. She worked hard to establish Rockport as an eclectic destination for both visitors and those looking for a place to live full-time. The fishing—both commercial and sport—provided excellent attractions, along with the winter weather, but she pushed hard to emphasize the growing writer and artisan community.

"Madness, Cole. Madness," she said, entering his office through the now-opened door. "My heart goes out to the victims, but I cannot emphasize enough that you need to figure a way to weave into your press conferences the tranquility of our community and the vibrancy of our arts scene. Hell, everyone knows about the fishing and bird-watching here." Whooping cranes returned to the area every year on their winter migration and attracted nature enthusiasts from all over.

The two worked well together in a relationship he found weird but one in which she apparently thrived. A year ago, Cole and Adele had a brief one-time affair. The implications so weighed on him that the relationship couldn't continue. He had a profound sense of obligation once a relationship became physical and the candor of his deep-felt sentiment caused an unlikely reaction. She chided him for living among the Neanderthals. As adamant as she indicated her desire to keep things casual, it just didn't work that way. They called a truce, never dated again, and kept their professional relationship on positive ground.

But the horror that had currently visited them fell in his court, and his tolerance at the moment for rah-rah-Rockport was at a low ebb. "I'm focusing on the investigation, Adele. I'm up to my ass working this thing, so you're fixin' to be sorely disappointed with my lack of community flag-waving for the press."

Adele sat on the edge of his desk, suspended a hand over a bowl of hard candy, perused the selection, and popped a cinnamon ball into her mouth. She had shared with him, repeatedly, the studies that showed many Americans looking for a vacation destination or to resettle usually bypassed the Texas coast. Fellow Texans and some snowbirds from the upper Midwest constituted most of the influx. She worked hard to change that and enlisted him to turn a blind eye toward some of the antics by the local "artisans." It wasn't a stretch to help her out. He knew those folks might be a good half-bubble off plumb, but they didn't hurt anyone. Adele consistently let him know that this laissez-faire approach toward minor infractions was a blessing to her efforts.

"Alright. I know that. Believe me, I'm glad I'm not wearing your boots," she said. "All I'm saying is that part of your story might include how aberrant this situation is for such a peaceful community. A peaceful, laid back, and artsy community."

He gandered out the window at the satellite trucks of the media, stacked bumper-to-bumper and ready to stream worldwide. "You want a drink?" Cole opened the bottom right drawer of the desk.

"No. And you don't either," said Adele. Cole closed the drawer. "Why don't you let the Rangers report on the investigation and you speak on the normal tranquility of our town. The vibrant tranquility," she added.

The Rangers had come to help. They brought major crime experience and the most modern of technologies, neither of which resided among most Texas rural counties. And help they did, although they stated from the get-go that outward-facing investigative communications belonged to him. Tag, you're it, Sheriff Garza. The Rangers worked the crime, not the media.

"The Rangers have made it abundantly clear to me that I'm responsible for dealing with the news folks. They aren't going to do it," said Cole. "And I wish you'd stop lobbing the tourism thesaurus at me. I'm not that susceptible to implanting."

The mayor joined him in staring at the flock of news people gathered in their town.

"Fine," she said. "I get it. Fine. I'm just saying it wouldn't hurt you to juxtapose the normal tranquility of our town with the horror that took place. That's part of the story. And those people with their satellite receivers extended want a story. That's all I'm saying."

She slid off the desk then turned to take another cinnamon ball candy.

"I'll try, Adele. You have a point."

"Thanks, Cole. Good luck. And by the way, you're a handsome so-and-so on television." She winked and left the office, lips pursed as she sucked the candy, closing the door behind her. A discernible decrease of hallway chatter preceded Adele. Politicians made the deputies nervous.

The work of a madman became the company line. The media accepted it for such a nonsensical horror. Cole emphasized the bravery of the staff and the citizens who'd rushed to help. He mentioned several times how the quiet town of Rockport had never, ever seen anything similar. He left out some details and obfuscated the manner of Burt Hall's death. He became a local hero who had stopped the lunatic from more killing. Someone said his tight good looks and natural reticence came across very well on television. Still, he refused to face any camera except for the twice-daily scheduled press conferences.

Serious questions arose about security at all nursing homes, nationwide. AARP and other seniors groups joined the outcry. These protestations were directed at the big picture rather than Rockport. None of this ameliorated his anger. That murderous SOB did this in his town, to his people.

Cole and Deputy R.L. Harris worked with the Rangers to try and provide motives and framework.

"Check on Burt Hall's prior whereabouts," Cole instructed the deputy. "And I'll find out who the hell that tall, pale sumbitch was."

He came up short on witnesses who had seen the tall, pale stranger at the nursing home. He asked R.L. if he'd seen another stranger with a long gray ponytail wearing '50s garb. At first, R.L. said he had not, but later that day he approached and said, "That fellow you asked about. Long gray ponytail?"

All ancillary activities ceased and he focused on R.L.'s face. "Yeah."

"Well, there's so doggone much going on I haven't had time to think. But I remember now. I remember thinking, how can a fellow that old move so fast?"

"Tell me, R.L. Every detail you can think of."

"Well, I hauled butt toward the nursing home after the 911. The corner of my eye caught someone else running, but he must have taken off on a different angle when we got close. He sorta disappeared. Weird. But I hightailed it toward the emergency call and didn't pay it much mind."

With a nod, Cole signaled for R.L. to continue.

"Not a lot to remember, Sheriff. Except for that long old-man ponytail. And the speed."

"Speed?" asked Cole.

"Ran to beat the band. Flat out moved. And I thought, how could someone seventy or eighty move like that?"

"The face? Did you get a look at his face?"

"Nope. Not a good look. Just enough to see he was old. Really old. Sorry, Sheriff. I was pretty dang intent on getting to the nursing home myself."

Cole nodded again. "Good job, R.L. That may help."

As details arrived, they pieced together Burt Hall's timeline over the twenty-four hours prior to the murders. He had spent a desultory day on his shrimp boat with not much to show for it, according to the records at the packinghouse where the area's shrimp boats unloaded. Then he drank for a couple of hours at a grungy local tavern. The bartender recollected that Hall drank with a tall stranger that night. R.L. highlighted that the bartender's meth habit made for a mighty unreliable witness.

They had a name. Cole had called on Fanny Ulrich at the Breeze Inn about the pale stranger.

"Mercy, yes, I remember him," Fanny said. "Gave me the heebie-jeebies."

"Did you check his ID?" asked Cole. Fanny tended to skip this with guests.

"Oh, I wish you would!" barked Fanny at her pug dog, Trixie. Trixie had nosed close to a bowl of M&Ms set on a lobby table, accessed from a nearby chair. "I really do, dog."

This led to a stare-down between owner and dog. It ended as Trixie got off the chair and commenced to grumble.

"Did I what?" asked Fanny.

"Check his ID."

"Now, Sheriff, you know I always do that. I've got it right here in the register. And I remember that weirdo showed me a passport instead of a by-God driver's license."

He waited for Fanny to find the name.

"Moloch. Adal Moloch. Wrote it right here. Never seen the likes."

Cole transcribed the name to a notepad. "Do you remember what kind of passport he showed?"

"Not American, that's for damn sure. Blue cover. Lots of stamps and scribbling inside. A foreigner. Now, Cole," Fanny continued as she leaned over the motel counter to cast for rumor fodder. "Did this weirdo have anything to do with the massacre?"

"You mean the recent murders?"

"One or two's murder. This was a damn sight more than one or two."

They stared at each other, neither blinking. Trixie flopped under the M&M-laden table, breathing loudly.

"Do you remember what kind of passport, Fanny?"

Fanny rose from her confidante lean. "I just told you. Foreign. I ain't the United Nations."

He continued to stare, waiting.

"Strange-ass writing on the cover. And some kind of symbol. Maybe a big bird," said Fanny.

"Strange-ass writing?"

"Yes. Strange-ass writing. My foreign gibberish skills are a might rusty," Fanny said.

"Big bird."

"Maybe. Some kind of symbol. Do I get a prize for all this? I could use a new microwave."

"Did you speak with him?" asked Cole.

"Only at check-in," said Fanny. "And that wasn't more than ten words. Weird accent. Fit his strange-ass appearance. He paid cash. Speaking of which, Sears is having a sale on appliances over in Corpus."

He grinned for the first time since the murders. You had to love folks of Fanny's character—independent, hard, and caring where it counted, demonstrated by her regular donations to the local food bank. "How about an elderly gentleman with a long gray ponytail? Seen someone who fits that description?" he asked.

"Sure. Every time our mayor holds one of her art festivals. Ain't exactly a shortage of old hippies around here."

It was worth a shot, although the odds of ID'ing the ponytail guy remained slim at best.

"Next cup of coffee's on me, Fanny," said Cole as he headed for the lobby door.

"How about a couple of M&Ms for the road, Sheriff?"

"And piss off Trixie? No, thanks. Adios, Fanny. Thanks for your help. I mean it." Cole tipped his hat as he left.

Twelve dead, Cole thought. *Nine of them senior citizens. A derelict shrimper on a rampage. No sign of drugs in his system other than a fair amount of booze. A strange foreigner flees the scene, after laying some kind of nauseous force on me. An old man sprinting after the tall foreigner. Why? And with what intent? And why my town?*

Everyone would chalk it up to a madman named Burt Hall. But more lay there. It was an uncomfortable more, but more nonetheless. Time to get back to the office and face the media again. Cole glanced toward the heavens. *Well?*

Chapter 8

Cole strode through the front doors of the sheriff's office building later than usual, and with a slight hangover. A bottle had provided poor consolation last night.

The clamor had died. No reporters and no cameras lurked. Three days had passed since the nursing home murders and the media had moved on, focused on other events.

He said "mornin'" to various members of the team as he headed for his office, looking forward to a day without drama. Quick footsteps signaled that someone followed him. The cowboy hat found its usual place on an old railroad spike that protruded from the wall—courtesy of the previous sheriff—and he turned and sat behind the desk. There, with an air of absolute certainty, stood a round, middle-aged priest wearing a dark suit, white cleric collar, and a brilliant scarlet pocket-handkerchief.

"I am here."

"I can see that," replied Cole, hands crossed across his lap.

"Francois Domaine, at your service."

"Sheriff Garza," said Cole, which evidently signaled the appropriate moment for the priest to light a Gauloises.

"Father, this is a no smoking building."

Francois exhaled blue smoke, raised a hand in a Gallic dismissive gesture, and strode with authority to the window, which he opened with minimal struggle. Cole was impressed. Several years and at least one paint job had passed since that window had last been opened. The move also allowed for a clear view of the priest's form-fitting Italian shoes, complete with small tassels.

Francois glanced at the windowsill and launched himself on it, holding the cigarette outside. "And so. Let us discuss the recent horror. Are you Catholic?"

Behind the priest no satellite trucks idled, bolstering Cole's hope for a normal day. "Nope. Methodist."

The priest raised a skeptical eyebrow. "And yet, your name. Garza. It is Spanish, no?"

"Long story." A discussion of Christian sects with this stranger wasn't on the morning's agenda.

"And so. Then, s'il vous plait, address me as Francois." He followed this with a deep drag on the cigarette and exhaled through the open widow.

"Okay. Francois. Do you represent a grieving family?"

"Only in such a way that is universal. The heat is quite fierce, no?" Francois leaned through the window as if to test this assertion, taking the full brunt of the Texas weather.

The open office door framed deputies and staff going about their duties. Some normalcy had returned. Unbeknownst to anyone, Cole had placed a call to an amazing friend to sleuth this Moloch guy. That phone call would remain private. If a tie-in could be established, he'd made a personal commitment to hunt Moloch down. For the time being at least, the open-and-shut nature of the murders would remain the work of a lone madman.

The priest presented a minor and not unwelcome distraction. "Sir, what can I help you with?"

"Francois."

"Okay. Francois. What can I help you with?"

"It is I that shall help you. A presumptuous statement, oui? But one quite valid. If you would be so kind as to inform me of the killings."

The sound of a passing motorcycle carried through the open window, filling Cole's silence.

"S'il vous plaît. Please." Francois adjusted his seating on the windowsill and cocked his head.

"Everything the media put out just about covers it," said Cole.

Francois maintained an intent gaze and ran a thumb and forefinger along each side of his bushy mustache. His other hand continued to hold the Gauloises out the window.

"Evil, no? The nature of this crime. I have read the newspapers. A madman. So easy. So clean." Francois took another drag of the smoke and exhaled outside. "Completely without insight. Such a description explains nothing. To this, certainly, you can agree?"

"It's the best we can do."

"Ah! The best le système can do! But you, Sheriff. Is it the best you can do?"

Bingo, Padre, thought Cole. *But that's going to stay between me and my friend Nadine.* He had plenty of other things to do. Piles of administrative cleanup remained in the aftermath of the killings.

"Sir, I'm afraid all of this relates to something I cannot discuss," Cole said, standing to show his guest the door.

"Francois."

"Yes. Francois. I appreciate you coming by." He moved from behind the desk and extended a hand toward the exit in case the priest didn't understand that the meeting had finished.

Francois took a final drag of the cigarette and tossed the butt into the outside rosebushes. He turned, closed the window and then, with a fierce intensity, addressed Cole. "Evil exists, Sheriff. True evil. It visited your town. It walks. It is real. I shall assume you have spent the time as sheriff long enough to know such a thing in your heart. But your mind?" Here Francois gave another Gallic shrug and pursed his lower lip. "Your mind may not accept it as of yet. But I have seen it. I have seen evil on this earth."

The priest had an air about him, keen and focused. He exhibited little desire for social niceties or casual conversation. But the peculiar nature of his statements struck Cole as discordant in his small town sheriff's office.

"What does your heart tell you, Sheriff?"

"My heart tells me you just threw a cigarette on my antique roses. A variety called Nacogdoches, to be exact," said Cole. Martha had filled him with a passion for old roses. Their resilience, evidenced by still thriving in old cemeteries and abandoned homesteads across Texas, prompted him to use his own money and plant some outside the office.

Francois looked at the roses, feigned shock, and apologized. "Condoléances, Sheriff. They are quite lovely. Perhaps one cigarette will not devastate them. Now, back to your heart. What does it tell you with regard to the horror?"

My heart tells me I don't understand what the heck's going on, thought Cole. *That look on Burt Hall's face. Moloch and the old man who chased him. My heart's torn in two knowing that somehow it all may relate to my precious Martha. That's what my heart is tellin' me.*

"Look, Father. Francois. I'm pretty doggone busy right now. I'm afraid you'll have to leave."

Francois approached Cole with tight, forceful steps, akin to a bowling ball falling down stairs. "Do you believe in God?"

That type of question, out of the blue, could throw a man off. Plus those three aspirin this morning hadn't stepped on the hangover to any great extent. Bluntness was called for with this forceful round man.

"Yes. I believe God exists. I don't understand God. I think God sometimes screws with my head. I believe things happen and God—for whatever reason—doesn't give a rat's ass about explaining it to us."

"Exactement! And what unexplained elements exist about these killings? What is not fitting? Your perception of this world. What does not fit?"

Francois had moved well within his personal space. Cole returned the favor by leaning into the face of the shorter man and providing what he thought was a pretty darn good badass stare. The priest did not back away one inch.

"I don't know what fits anymore. Things have happened, and I can't explain them. Yeah, I believe God exists. No, that's not helping one dang bit. I can't explain. And I'll bet my bottom dollar that you can't explain either, Father Francois."

"Bon!" Francois stepped back with arms spread wide. Cole thought a hug might ensue from this short block of a man. "Good. Realization. To assist belief, one must first realize." Francois turned and headed back to the window, repeated his earlier motions, and ended up perched on the windowsill. He lit another Gauloises. "Let us continue."

Cole's headache resurrected with a vengeance. This priest was like a bad rash, refusing to leave. "What do you want, Francois? Honestly, what the heck do you want?"

Francois showed respectful consideration of this question. He leaned out the window, took a long drag of the cigarette, and shrugged—communicating that imponderables existed.

"Ce qui est different?" He delivered the question to the rosebushes as much as to Cole. "What is the difference? This time. All your years as le gendarme, what is different? Out of the ordinary? Anything?"

Hauling a foreign priest out of the office by force opened up a PR issue that no one within a hundred miles of Rockport needed right now. He decided to put up with the priest a short time longer and then send him down the road.

"And your expertise with all this? You say you've seen evil. Does that make you some kind of ghost chaser?"

Francois smiled and said, "No. Ghosts and spirits. Another subject. One I understand you Americans are fascinated by. Perhaps for another time." He exhaled smoke again out the window and wiped sweat off his brow with the scarlet handkerchief. "No. I have pursued an understanding of evil my entire life. Not ghosts. Evil as a true force."

Cole remained planted in the center of the room. The priest sat on the sill across from him and smoked, while heat wafted in from the open window. Deputies and staff moved along the hallway, attending to their duties. "Sir, I have my doubts as to your understanding of evil given your life experiences. No offense. You're a priest. I'm a lawman. I've performed this business of mine for some time, seen a lot, and still wrestle with what drives the terrible things I've seen, and how it all fits the human experience." He paused and Francois waited. "I don't mean to insult you, but the life of a priest is a heckuva lot different than that of a lawman."

"A valid point," replied Francois. "Allow me to provide some history. Some context. For many instances, I would agree. Perhaps you will see I possess some rather unique experiences."

Francois gave a high-level overview of his work. He talked of possessions and exorcisms, his research into the nature and manifestations of evil, and his conviction that the human experience included evil external forces.

"It is not my intention to be intrusive, Sheriff. No. It is my intention to pursue a personal endeavor. Your knowledge of the current situation may be of great help. With such matters, I fear great danger for those unprepared. Therefore, I do not seek physical assistance. No. I seek your perspective. Private insights." Francois extended his hands, palms up, as if to receive something.

Cole's chin dropped to his chest and his defenses began to fade under the weight of uncertainty and isolation. Other than the phone call to Nadine to gather intelligence on Moloch, he had dealt with all of it alone. No definitive third-party ties or motives looped back to the nursing home horror. Burt Hall had killed his own mother, for God's sake. But something didn't fit. On a visceral level, something felt wrong. After three days, it had worn on him. Justice had not been fulfilled. He suspected answers might not be available through any normal or rational means. The thought of that dismissive SOB Moloch—flicking his damn hand—in the middle of that mess made for sleepless nights. Now this priest had arrived out of nowhere and clearly had no intention of leaving him alone. But the guy had different perspectives, for sure. There was a strange comfort in that.

He closed the office door. Francois stayed perched on the windowsill. Cole sat on the edge of the desk and let one leg dangle. The giggles of two young girls carried from the sidewalk through the open window, mixed with cigarette smoke and the musk of old-fashioned roses.

"I need to bounce some things off somebody, and do it without getting straitjacketed. Maybe …" Cole hesitated. "Maybe you can, or maybe you are able to—and I'm pretty hesitant to mention it—shed some light on some things. Things that I'd sure like answers to."

Francois remained motionless, so Cole continued.

"I don't know you. And I'm fixin' to trust you with something. Something I haven't talked with anyone about." He was crossing the Rubicon, hell-bent on answers. "Sorta confessional, isn't it?"

"You can trust me, Sheriff. I give you my word as a man of God." Francois took another drag, crushed the cigarette against the outside brick wall, and showed Cole the butt as he tossed it in a nearby wastebasket. "And you can trust me as a man who can relate to your experiences."

Gulls called from the outside salt air, and the sounds of coins as they slid into the soda vending machine drifted through the closed door from the hallway.

"There was someone."

Francois slid off the windowsill and eased toward Cole, as if any sudden movements might spook the sheriff.

"You saw. Your eyes observed?" asked Francois.

At that moment, a clerk gave a cursory knock and stuck his head in the door to announce, "Sheriff, there's a call on line two you'll want to take."

Francois raised both hands, blew out a puff of disgust, and gave the young clerk a glare that caused the door to slam shut. Cole snapped out of his reverie and moved back behind the desk, grabbed the phone, and punched line two on the antiquated system. "Yes, sir. No problem. No, sir. Three hours. Will do." He set the phone down and turned to grab his hat. "I'm afraid I have to go, Father. Right now."

"Again, call me Francois. And to where, might I ask? It is most important, our discussion."

"Austin. It's three hours. I won't be back until late today." A decision made and potential lunacy averted, Cole added, "I believe our discussion has ended. It's all craphouse crazy. There's nothing I can do for you, Francois."

"Bon. I shall see you tonight then." The priest moved with his determined style to the door, apparently unable to grasp the meaning of "ended." Before he exited, Francois spun and pointed a finger at Cole. His round, florid face had taken on a hard intensity.

"You saw. Your heart. You felt. You saw."

A loud, puffed-cheek exhale, rife with resignation and relief, accompanied Cole's reply. "Yeah. I saw."

Chapter 9

As she tromped into the kitchen Nadine May told Mule to move, even though the cat remained perched on a shelf high above racks of computers, servers, and screens. She stopped, leaned back into the main room, and told the cat, "Never mind." Mule flicked his tail.

She rummaged through the refrigerator and pulled out food items well past their expiration date, or that looked suspicious, and dumped them in a trash bag. The cleansing left three diet sodas, a brick of Irish butter, Portuguese sparkling wine, goat cheese, a jar of caviar to go with the cheese, and some sesame crackers. A serious grocery run lay in the near future. Empty takeout containers strewn about the place found their way into the trash bag. She counted them in threes, an OCD trait she accepted as part of her makeup and no big deal, since lots of folks had worse little defects. The synapses still fired on all cylinders. That's what counted.

The imminent arrival of guests constituted an event so unusual it required substantial preparation as to where they would sit and what hospitality she would provide. Cole had called and that was better than good. The recent Rockport events poured through both the media and her more reliable sources. Cole had shown up on TV. She thought he cut a fine figure for the camera, but he wasn't exactly hell-on-wheels when it came to verbosity. His phone call had provided a cool new puzzle to solve about some guy named Moloch. More importantly, the call reignited the opportunity to connect as friends, and maybe build on that to create something more.

She hadn't known Cole when Martha was alive, but had worked with him twice since that tragic event and had established a personal relationship. On one of those occasions, she helped him, the Rangers, and federal agencies when drug smugglers began to focus on Cole's part of the Texas coast. Assigned by Homeland Security to assess and gather information for the newly formed task force, she traveled to Corpus Christi.

Cole ranked high in the looks department, no doubt, but it was his quiet strength and touch of sadness that especially intrigued her. He probably thought of her as a friend and professional compatriot, which made no sense whatsoever given the overt signals she'd sent in his direction expressing her keen interest. At least she thought they'd been overt. Surely he had picked up on them, although maybe not, but either way another opportunity lay ahead with his visit due in the next forty-eight hours.

Nadine managed to get by within social frameworks, but getting by still left bumps and byways—frustrating for someone used to excelling at any endeavor. She loved life and all of its components, although her apparent inability to adjust to social signals drove her crazy. No matter how hard she tried, her responses to subtle changes within interpersonal settings often came out off-kilter. It made for a chink in her armor, and self-awareness of the issue failed to lead her to any satisfactory solutions. Frustration at others' misperceptions of her would boil to the surface regularly.

Over dinner in Corpus Christi with members of the task force, someone asked her, "Any idea where they may try to land and unload next?"

"I've done some predictive modeling," she said. "Next Thursday night. Late. Port Lavaca. Man, my skin feels salty here. I wonder if that's good? Two boats. Five or six people, total. Coke, mostly. Some heroin."

One of the feds joked, "Any idea about their style of clothes?"

Nadine stared at him for a moment, digesting the request. "No. Do you need that? I can run some heuristics and give it a shot. Or shall we just assume it won't be Armani."

Everyone at the table laughed good-naturedly.

She had asked Cole about his life and interests. He'd replied modestly that he was nothing special—"plain vanilla." She shared how she grew up a tomboy, aced every test she ever took, went one year to college to satisfy her PhD parents, and wore out several boyfriends.

"Are you married?" she asked during the conversation.

Cole explained his circumstances. She filed the information, piecing together probabilities on how such a tragedy affected your worldview.

"Still figuring it all out," Cole finished. "I can't get the higher purpose."

Nadine decided on a pensive look for Cole at that comment. Pensive provided neutrality. Any conversational gambit regarding spirituality never ended well for her. One exasperating experience after another in that realm had taught her to craft a neutral response as the best social strategy. A higher power in the universe? Sure, she knew odds pointed in that direction. Hard data, on the other hand, was scarce at best, and all of it wrapped in alternative explanations. And those type of spiritual conversations, she had come to realize, led to false impressions about her—impressions that she viewed everything through analytical eyes. That wasn't entirely true and there was no point in bringing that subject up either, since that led to conversations during which the other person's eyes grew wider by the second, and once that train left the station it was nigh on impossible to pull it back. Man, people were strange.

At the end of the meal, she said to Cole privately, "Plain vanilla. Maybe that's what I like about you." She felt that was safe and solid. He didn't appear to carry any major defects or strange baggage or peculiar habits. A normal guy, a straight shooter—appealing qualities all.

The task force disbanded after that last big bust. At eleven forty-five on Nadine's predicted Thursday they boarded two boats that had just arrived in Port Lavaca. They arrested five men. They found two hundred kilos of coke and fifty kilos of heroin.

Hands on hips, she surveyed the living room of the garage apartment and squeezed three times. A past boyfriend had called her rawboned, which in that part of the world meant a swimmer's body but more angular, with sharper edges. Those hip bones were pretty pointed, but a quick assessment of ribs and butt revealed nothing protruding beyond reason. Besides, some heads still turned when she entered a crowd dressed to the nines, which admittedly had become more and more rare an occasion.

She owned the large house and unattached garage with its overhead living quarters. The house provided far too much area for her to fool with, so she rented it to a doctor who worked at the nearby Texas Medical Center.

"This place is a mess, Mule. I blame you." The cat rolled on his back and stretched a back leg. "You look like a furry ballerina when you do that."

Years ago she completed extensive work on the one-bedroom garage apartment, adding layers of physical and electronic security. Its interior held a mishmash of computer equipment, printers, backup power supplies, charts, graphs, and printed photographs.

Nadine loved to help catch the bad guys. Her professional endeavors provided personal satisfaction and brought deep admiration from her clients and law enforcement teammates. Once on an assignment, she would forego food and sleep for long stretches, focused intently on solving the puzzle and stopping the evildoers. A client at the FBI had once told her, "Nadine, you may not be in a class of your own, but it sure doesn't take long to call the roll."

She thought maybe it was karma or some cosmic circle that would cycle Cole back through her life. She knew she tended to put men off for some God-only-knows reason. Her looks department was okay and maybe better than okay. She had learned affectations such as massaging egos and listening to horrifically boring stories as if they were the most enthralling things imaginable, all accompanied by attentive facial expressions. But men scooted away at the first opportunity. It was a drag, but she couldn't just douse her uniqueness. Cole came across as different. He didn't appear threatened by her mental acrobatics. He laughed when she hoped he would. She discerned from him some true affection toward her.

Music, she thought, handling another garbage bag. *Music to straighten up by*. A few keyboard strokes later and Andean flute music came through hidden speakers. Mule watched. She went back into the middle of the room to assess and then back to the keyboard. The music changed as Susan Tedeschi began to belt out "Rock Me Right." That was much better and she hummed along. She shook the plastic garbage bag to open it. One, two, three times.

Chapter 10

The Texas Rangers make claim to the oldest law enforcement body in America, although folks up in Boston and New York would argue the point. Rangers seldom number more than one hundred and fifty, spread across the state. They have no prescribed uniform, supply their own weaponry, and wear the star-in-circle badge crafted from a five-peso Mexican coin. These things have not changed since the 1830s.

Bruce "Jeeter" Johnson was approaching retirement as head of the Rangers. Among his many duties, supporting small rural law enforcement entities was a constant. Several of his Rangers had helped on the investigation of the Rockport murders.

The call to Cole to hustle over to Austin happened because the governor had just called him. The governor explained he'd received a call from the US State Department, asking if he'd help out. Prior to that, the department had received a call from the Vatican. These domino diplomacy proceedings happened on a routine basis, were a pain in the ass, but no red flags flew over the sequence of events.

The Rockport murders wrapped up simple and clean, always the best way. Those mullets in the media had hauled ass to cover some celebrity's exposed tit or some damn thing so that part was wrapped up as well. This added twist from the governor shouldn't affect things. The Rangers' immunity from politics didn't extend to state budgets, and lending a hand as long as it didn't have to involve any of his Rangers held little risk and even a potential upside during budget season. Johnson would wipe this diplomatic booger on the sheriff of Aransas County.

Three hours after the request call, Sheriff Garza arrived at the Austin Ranger headquarters. The unwritten rules prompted this. Garza reported to the citizens of Aransas County, not the Rangers. But every county sheriff understood you did not say no to the head Ranger for a reasonable request, due to the fact that the Rangers always helped small-town law enforcement folks when needed, and made a point of crediting local law for solving crimes. Sheriffs were elected. Rangers weren't.

"Good to see you, Cole. Thanks for hustling over. How are the kids?" He'd perused Cole's personnel file over the last hour.

"Fine, sir. Fine." Cole occupied the proffered leather chair, branded with an outline of Texas. Lyle Lovett sang in a low volume on hidden stereo equipment. The overhead fan emitted a slight squeak every slow rotation. He'd asked maintenance twice to fix the damn thing.

Johnson sat, boots on desk, crossed his hands behind his head, and said, "You know what flows downhill, son? And I'm not talkin' water."

"Yessir."

Johnson knew that would put the sheriff on high alert and damn sure get his attention.

"The governor wants you to help a man coming from, now get this, the Vatican. Beats all. We've had to deal with potentates and such before, so tossing some help toward the pontiff shouldn't be a big deal."

"The Vatican?"

"Yep. International diplomacy. Something to do with that mess in your backyard. Now, Cole, two state concerns have sprung from this as well. Something the governor made crystal clear to me." He moved his boots off the desk and pointed toward the corner cabinet. "Pardon my manners, son. Can I get you a drink?"

A moment's hesitation, and then, "No, thanks. If you've got any coffee handy, that would work. I like a cup after a long drive."

Johnson moved to a coffee setting on an old madrone credenza. Five cups with the Ranger badge on display stood next to a stainless steel carafe. Above the credenza hung an oil painting of a West Texas landscape. It wasn't signed. Johnson didn't want folks to know it was his work.

"Cream and sugar? This cream is the real deal—we get it from the Blue Bell ice cream folks in Brenham," said Johnson.

"You bet. Thank you, sir. Any stevia handy?"

Johnson paused in mid-pour. "What the hell's that?"

He watched Cole squirm a bit before answering, "It's a no-calorie sweetener. Natural."

"Cane sugar from East Texas is pretty damn natural. You on a diet? Hell, you're about as big around as my leg." Two hundred fifty-four counties in the state, each with an elected sheriff, and good money could be bet this one was the only one who would ask for some newfangled sweetener.

"No, sir. No diet. A little sugar would be great."

Johnson handed Cole his coffee and continued. "Like I was sayin'. This Vatican thing has kicked off some state concerns. The governor wanted to make sure I understood that it's election season. And South Texas is big-time Catholic. Concern number one. During election season, the administration is a big fan of the Vatican. Sabe?"

Cole took a long sip, swallowed, and nodded. George Jones replaced Lyle as background music.

"And since it's election season, it was also pointed out to me that old folks vote. Boy howdy, do they vote. It's damn near an annual milestone for most of them. Which brings us to concern number two."

Cole nodded again.

"If any questions come up during election season about the mass murder of old folks, the governor would like to assure these senior constituents that no stone has been left unturned during the investigation in Rockport."

Cole finished off his coffee.

"Is all this jelling for you, son?" asked Johnson.

Cole looked at the assortment of Ranger memorabilia hanging behind Johnson's desk. Framed ancient photos of Bigfoot Wallace, Rip (Rest In Peace) Ford, Lone Wolf Gonzaullas, and John Coffee Hays festooned the wall.

"I think I've already met him," said Cole.

"Met who?"

"The Vatican's guy. A priest. Francois. He dropped by my office this morning."

This was a positive development and movement in the right direction. "Good. Good. Then the ball's rolling."

Johnson belted back the remains of his coffee. "I'll back you on this, Cole. Whatever you need. I mean that. The governor has set aside funding for this little soirée. Within reason, of course. But you have to keep me informed. I know I cain't make you do that. So I'm askin', plain and simple. This is my fifth governor, and I've never gained an appreciation for any one of them crawling my ass."

"Well, sir. You know I will. And I appreciate the offer of assistance. But I could still use some clarity," said Cole.

The head Ranger leaned forward and waited.

"The Vatican sent this priest. Asked for cooperation. But that doesn't explain why he's here."

Boots up on the desk again, no rush, and it would be unfair to expect this county sheriff to get the bigger picture. "Hell if I know, Cole. 'Bout half the time we never do. I could go up the chain to the State Department, but those Hunyaks aren't going to tell us a damn thing. We just know that they've asked for cooperation from the 'local authorities.' That would be you."

Johnson had less than fond feelings toward the US State Department. In his earlier Ranger days he had been assigned to the town of Marfa, in Presidio County, to assist the very large and very empty counties near the Mexican border. Quite a few ranchers in that part of the state owned small single engine airplanes that they flew as part of overseeing vast rangeland. On several occasions, a plane had been stolen and flown into the wilds of northern Mexico. Johnson would saddle an old horse, cross the Rio Grande, and disappear into those roadless mountains for a week or two. Then he would fly the stolen aircraft back to Texas, with his saddle and tack stowed. The folks in Marfa often wondered what became of those old horses. They were certain of what became of the thieves. The State Department went ballistic when they got wind of these exploits. Johnson told them to kiss his butt—it was a matter of "hot pursuit."

"It still doesn't make sense. So it's tied to the nursing home murders. Why is the Vatican interested in that?" Cole asked. He held up his coffee cup and stood, pointing at Johnson's cup. The Ranger handed it to him with a "thanks."

Cole poured for both of them and handed Johnson the now-steaming drink. Something clearly wasn't sitting right with the Aransas County Sheriff.

"About that drink, sir. It might go good with this coffee," said Cole.

Johnson had no problem with that. He ambled over to the corner cabinet, produced a bottle of bourbon, and poured two fingers into Cole's mug and one into his.

"The doc says I shouldn't consume so much coffee or booze," said Johnson as he leaned back, took a sip, and looked out the window. College students were tossing a Frisbee around the park across the street. "I'm retiring before too long and, contrary to my doc's advice, may just hang in a coffee shop all day. With a flask. Maybe start smokin' weed. Me and ol' Willie. Turn into a Texas hippie."

"You may not fit the image, sir," Cole said, grinning.

"Well then, a hippie with lots of guns."

They both laughed, and then Johnson got back to business. "Maybe he was sent to support the local Catholics after the murders. Not outside the realm of possibility. Good PR. And maybe he wants to go fishing. Whatever it is, just cooperate with this fellow. Make him feel engaged. I would appreciate it, Cole. And don't forget about the keep me informed part."

They chatted about mundane matters while they finished their drinks. It evidently created a respite for Cole, this idle story-swapping, and there was no need to rush the time.

Eventually Cole stood and Johnson came over, hand extended. As they shook, Johnson nodded—a brotherhood of lawmen nod.

"Keep me informed, son," stated Johnson for the third time. The last thing he and the Rangers needed was to be blindsided.

"Will do, sir. The Vatican. Mercy, I hope this won't get weird." Cole retrieved his Stetson hat from the adjoining chair.

That was a piss-poor way to end a meeting in Johnson's book. "Keep any weirdness tamped down, Cole. Tight. At a minimum, keep it between you and that priest."

"One last thing," Cole said. "I've asked Nadine May for help. To look into a possible accomplice. It's a stretch, I admit. That funding set-aside may be needed if she decides to bill us. You never know."

That little bit of information would make any man's ass tighten. Nadine made him nervous. His Rangers had worked with her over the years. She made all of them nervous. "Is that necessary?"

"Yep. It's a tenuous connection with a strange man. Maybe nothing. But no stone unturned, etcetera," said Cole.

"Tight, Cole. Tight," said Johnson. "You've just increased the circle fifty percent. Now it's you, the priest, and Nadine. And Lord knows what Nadine is liable to get up to."

Cole started toward the door, looked back, and smiled. "Lord knows."

Chapter 11

The fishing guide was nonplussed. Over the years, he had seen it all. This round gentleman approached him with the air of a person more than a few fries short of a Happy Meal, but such was the life of a fishing guide.

This client wore white linen peasant pants, rolled to his knees. Sandals covered sockless feet. The ornately embroidered white Mexican shirt offset the bright kelly-green scarf used as a hatband for a plain straw sombrero.

"Welcome aboard. I see you didn't bring any fishing tackle, but I've got plenty," said the guide, and pointed to several rods and reels standing in rod-holders on the boat.

"Au contraire, Capitaine," said the client, and pulled from his pockets a new stout oyster knife and a bottle of Tabasco. "In fact, I am well equipped."

The fishing guide tilted his head, and the client tilted back, at the opposite angle.

"To the place of oysters, mon Capitaine!" exclaimed the client as he moved with an unexpected agility from the dock to the small boat.

"You want me to take you to an oyster bed?"

"But of course." The client settled in the comfortable passenger seat, lit a cigarette, and added rose-tinted clip-on sunglasses to his frames. "Aller! Let us be gone!"

***

Later that evening, Cole settled into Jimmy's outdoor bar overlooking the Laguna Madre. The heat had let go and the light had begun to soften. He removed his hat, put his feet on one of the two empty chairs at the table, and ordered a Shiner beer. It arrived icy cold, the bottle sweating. It had been a strange day.

"Bonsoir." Francois plopped on the remaining empty chair. Attired in all-white pants and embroidered shirt, he wore a bright green scarf around his neck. He appeared sunburned and happy.

Cole took a long pull of the beer and gave himself a bit of time to accept the inevitable. "You look different."

Francois adjusted his round glasses and looked at himself to inspect and verify Cole's statement. "Oui. I have made a decision."

"A decision."

"Oui. I shall sojourn incognito."

Cole exhaled and looked past Francois across the three miles of the Laguna. On the other side, the sands of San Jose Island took on a pink hue.

Francois lifted his chin at the young lady who served food and drink to the porch's patrons—a universal signal that brought her over, smiling.

"You look thirsty. What'll you have?" she asked.

"Pernod, s'il vous plaît."

Cole arched his eyebrows. This would be interesting.

The young lady continued to smile, moved alongside Francois, and placed a hand on his shoulder. "Honey, you've stumped me. You'll have to tell me what that is."

"Stumped?"

"Yep. Stumped."

Francois looked at Cole with an expression suggesting he needed assistance.

"How about a beer, Francois?" said Cole. He looked at the waitress and continued, "Another for me and one for him. Thanks."

Francois produced a Gauloises, and wafted it to and fro in front of Cole.

"Yes. You can smoke here."

Francois fired the cigarette, leaned back, crossed one sandal-clad foot over a knee, exhaled smoke and looked at the sky. An osprey glided from the shore side over the water, then dived. It broke the water surface with extended talons, and flew back to altitude, grasping a small mullet.

Head still lifted skyward, Francois asked, "And the communiqué from Austin?"

"The Vatican made a call to our government. It passed downhill to me. I'm to provide assistance. Now that you're incognito, maybe I shouldn't share that."

Francois gave a shrug and waved one hand, expressing, "Oh, well."

"If we agree to cooperate, we should return to the question of what you want from me," said Cole as he took another sip of beer.

Francois used his free hand to stroke his mustache. "A serious question, to be sure. Allow me to answer. But first, shall we dine?"

Life had an overarching pace, individual events had their own pace, and clearly this priest had his own unique set of timing and priorities. They ordered the flounder, rolled in a batter of egg, cornmeal, and very cold beer, then deep-fried. Slices of onion received the same treatment, and the meal was served on a large platter with two separate plates. Francois asked for the wine menu, glanced at it, and gave the laminated wine list a light slap on the table. The waitress took this as a sign he wanted to order and approached.

Preemptively, Francois stated, "You may decide, Mademoiselle, for I am unfamiliar with such a selection. The wines of France would seem to be unavailable at this establishment." This was accompanied by a look of deep pain and resignation.

"We have a nice Texas albariño. Would you like to try that?" she asked.

"One must make do. Oui. S'il vous plaît."

The food proved excellent, the wine bright and crisp. They ate, exchanging small talk and backgrounds. Cole told of growing up in Corpus Christi, how his father had owned a small furniture store and they'd lived a solid middle-class life. Raised by a loving mother, his childhood filled him with good memories.

At eighteen, he joined the US Marine Corps. Honorably discharged, he headed for the oilfields of West Texas and made good money as a roughneck on the rigs. In the oil town of Odessa he met Martha. They got married six months later and Martha became pregnant. They both saw the oil patch as a poor place to start a family, so they moved back to Corpus.

Sheriff John Nash—a fishing buddy of Cole's dad—hired him as one of the deputies for Aransas County, so Martha and Cole moved to Rockport. A short ten years later, Nash retired and the people of Aransas County elected Cole sheriff. Martha had been very proud of him. They had two children; Lisa, now a student at the University of Texas, and Jeri Ann, who worked at a Lubbock insurance company and, in Cole's view, shacked up with some full-time professional student at Texas Tech.

He touched on Martha's murder. Francois wrinkled his brow and muttered a soft, "Mon Dieu!"

Francois spoke of his childhood, his calling, and his background within the church's more esoteric arenas. Cole absorbed it all and seldom asked for clarification, knowing this was information from the heart. It told him a lot about the Frenchman. Francois explained that he saw God in everything—the first crocus blooms of spring, the laughter of a pretty girl, the death of a friend. God was all and everywhere. "Perhaps I should have been a Buddhist," he stated between bites of flounder, then clarified that unlike Buddhism, he saw the power of an active God in our lives. He conveyed that since a very young age, he had been tuned to power, and it had become a sixth sense.

Francois explained his belief that it was a denial of faith to see evil as a metaphor for bad things. Satan and his kingdom were real. And as a reality, one must understand the enemy's power as well as the enemy's limitations. He claimed there existed limitations, although he couldn't state their boundaries when Cole enquired.

The priest gave it a shot to differentiate between demonic possession and other physical manifestations. It had to come to this, but it didn't make it any less weird for Cole. Apparently, Satan and his acolytes walked among us. Francois had no doubt about this. This fell into a spiritual gray area for Cole, but there wasn't much point in arguing with the priest's declarative belief.

For Cole, the entire ecumenical conversation was uncomfortable. Personal belief systems were best kept private and the whole spill-your-guts thing on God and Satan dang sure didn't fall under the job responsibility of Aransas County Sheriff. There would be no faith-based reciprocating on his part. On the other hand, Francois was a priest and it should probably be expected from him. Besides, the beer and wine helped smooth the prickly edges of his discomfort.

"And so. To the question, what do I want?" said Francois, as he emitted a light burp and leaned back to light a cigarette. "It is not what I want, mon ami. It is what God wants."

How nice to be so sure, thought Cole as he nodded back.

"I am on a path. This path requires me to confront evil as evidenced on earth. I am to seek it, recognize it, and address it. To what exact end has yet to be revealed. But it is my path. This I know." Francois paused and leaned forward. "I shall tell you what I do not want. I do not wish for you to participate in my pursuit. My quest. It will be most dangerous. I, alone, am called. Yet, I do need your cooperation. Information. Sentiments. Observations. This is—to answer your question—what I want, Sheriff."

Cole sat back, lifted his arms, and stretched. His shoulder joints popped. *A week ago, priest, I would have written you off as a wingnut*, he thought, *although the jury's still out on that one.*

"Alright. Some ground rules. And call me Cole."

Francois nodded.

"This must remain very private. I need your word that this will not leak, nor do you intend to write a book, nor—God forbid—make some kind of dang movie. If I see your ass on TV, there will be hell to pay."

Francois opened his eyes wide, offended. "This should not be considered a trivial pursuit. This involves no notoriety. All of this has nothing to do with the credit or the fame. This is a most serious business, Sheriff."

"Cole."

"Oui. Cole. I am shocked at such an assertion. Shocked!"

Cole displayed two fingers as the waitress passed by. She returned with the beers. Cole continued. He saw no point in responding to the priest's indignant reaction. Most serious business, for damn sure—there had been a mass murder in his town. Getting to the bottom of that event took precedence over any other consideration, including hurt feelings.

"You and I need crystal clarity on that. Very private. What you report to your superiors in Rome is your business. I understand those folks are very discreet. I'm talking about here, now, in Texas. Discretion."

"But of course!" exclaimed Francois. "You may wish to recall my vocation as a priest!"

"Right. The whole incognito thing threw me off."

Francois adjusted his scarf, muttering in French.

Cole had no idea where all this would lead, but secular matters such as how to keep his job and not have the head Ranger on his butt needed addressing. It could all possibly fit a plan formulated on the drive back from Austin. When Nadine located Moloch—and she would—this whole "help the Vatican" thing could provide administrative cover to hunt Moloch. It just might work out. The priest needed to understand the discretion aspect in no uncertain terms. The two stared at each other, eyeballing a mutual pact.

The slight smell of creosote floated from the pilings that supported the outdoor deck. A laughing young boy dashed from the main restaurant. Mom, calling him "jelly bean," hurried hot on his tail and scooped him up. Both laughed and giggled as Mom carried him back inside.

"Do you believe in your heart that this madman acted alone?" asked Francois.

Here was the big question. Cole knew that once that bridge was crossed there was no turning back. A strong belief in justice, however delivered, stirred inside him, and if he revealed his gut feeling to the priest then they would be yoked together. What he had seen so far pointed to positive traits from the Frenchman. The man had focus, determination, and it would appear no small amount of courage. Trust remained the bigger issue. But

Cole wanted justice and, deep inside, some spiritual answers. This priest could help. So he crossed the bridge.

"No, I don't feel he acted alone," said Cole. "There was another man."

"Yes! Describe him if you please." Francois shoved plates and beer bottles aside and leaned his forearms on the table, eyes piercing. "Such as strange habits, actions that seemed out of place? A feeling, a sense?"

Cole began to dump. If it had to be him and Francois, then they'd best get some answers. He filled Francois in on details and perceptions. He told of the stranger and Burt Hall at the honky-tonk the night before the murders, his peculiar uneasy reaction when he met the stranger at Shorty's diner, how he responded with nausea to the stranger's hand gesture, and the look on Burt Hall's face when Cole shot him—the exact same expression his wife's killer had worn, years before.

At all of this, Francois sat and absorbed. His lack of incredulity or questions proved a measure of comfort and Cole began to feel a sense of building trust.

"We're driving to Houston tomorrow. I have a name of the stranger and I have a friend who can help us find the man behind the name. If anyone can, it's Nadine," said Cole.

"Yes? The name?"

"Moloch. Adal Moloch."

Francois sat back, stroked his mustache and paused long enough to light another smoke. "I know this name. Most ancient."

Cole hesitated for a moment before he continued, digesting Francois's acknowledgment of the name. "One more, Francois." The priest tilted his head, focused on Cole's face. "A very old and very peculiar man. He had powerful athletic movements. Like some Special Forces guy. But old. Very old. I have nothing on him. I saw him for less than two seconds, but he appeared to pursue Moloch. I sensed that. Deadly serious pursuit."

Francois drummed his fingers on the table. "Most interesting. I shall store that for further consideration." Francois drained the remains of his beer. "And so, one more thing for you as well."

Cole waited.

"This I must ask. Moloch. Are you so sure he was a man?"

The muted conversation of two sport anglers as they compared the day's fishing drifted from parked boats at the nearby marina. Laughter came from inside the restaurant. Life went on, in so many ways, simple and pure. Cole yearned for that feeling.

"I'm not going there, Francois. Something bad wrong with Moloch, for sure. Something out of the ordinary. But he walks, talks, and breathes. Let's find the sumbitch. And if it comes down to it, I'll bet he bleeds."

Chapter 12

The two-hundred-mile drive to Houston took four hours. They hit congestion thirty miles from Nadine's place, and ground through the traffic of America's fourth largest city. The air conditioner stayed on max the entire time. The trip had not started well. Cole would not let Francois smoke in the car with the windows up.

"And so I shall lower this window," said Francois after they departed.

"Fine. Enjoy the weather."

The window rolled down and allowed the fetid heat of a Gulf Coast summer afternoon to fill the car. Francois immediately started to sweat and closed the window.

"Mon Dieu!"

"Yep."

Francois dressed in khakis, huaraches, and an orchid-pink dress shirt. He rolled up the shirtsleeves and raised the collar to surround his thick neck. A pack of Gauloises showed through the thin material of the shirt pocket. His socks, visible through the huaraches, matched the shirt. Cole wondered where the heck he got those socks. A rattlesnake-skin belt purchased in Rockport supported his ample midsection. He had told Cole it filled a rare hole in his sartorial arsenal.

Cole called Nadine a second time soon after the first call. He was concerned that bringing a priest would be met with her disapproval.

"He's here to find something about the murders," said Cole. "It's a bit undefined, but Jeeter Johnson asked me to cooperate. So I'm dragging him along to Houston if that's okay."

"No worries," said Nadine. "I just hope he won't inhibit our intercourse. But bring him. Hope he doesn't mind my little Buddha statue. Mule likes that tiny fat guy."

He chewed on that, unclear as was often the case with her overall meaning, then said, "Well, anyway. He's a good guy. A little different, but a good guy. I'll see you day after tomorrow."

The two men drove in silence while NPR interviewed authors on the radio. Cole contemplated Francois's attempted introduction of a new reality. Life experiences had led him to a worldview of good people versus bad people, with gradations of both. Evil as a tangible item stayed contained in the individual—some folks were bad and their actions evil. There was not much need for more analysis than that.

A bad person performing an evil act had committed Martha's murder. It was the same with the nursing home murders. Francois kept tossing out some kind of demonic possessions or demonic entity as a prime driver and normally Cole would dismiss this out of hand. It had no basis in his belief system, other than niggling doubts left over from childhood. *That dang movie*, he thought, remembering *The Exorcist*. But life was experiential, and you couldn't just chalk up something to a possession, although Moloch pointed to something unknown. And the exact same perverted smile and facial countenance on both Burt Hall and his wife's killer gnawed at him.

Moloch knew fear, regardless of his nature. Before vanishing from his sight, Cole observed abject terror and deep hatred in Moloch's face—a cornered animal attacked by a stronger animal. Moloch had fled—not from the crime or from him, but from that old-man stranger. None of it fit normal behavioral patterns related to a crime scene. Something different was going on. To bring all this up with Francois during the drive to Nadine's place would open the door to more confusion and alter the focus on acquiring concrete facts about that tall pale SOB.

As they approached Houston, Cole gave Francois background on Nadine. He tried to explain in a digestible format how people might construe her as different. She had always been infatuated by computers, the languages of software, puzzles, and games. Her analytical mind frightened those who chose to get close. When the Internet and all its tendrils bloomed, she dove in lock, stock, and barrel. She had found her calling. No encryption existed that she could not break, no firewall she couldn't breach, no system she couldn't hack, and no information she couldn't find. She carried a Top Secret clearance.

The main house had ionic columns and a porte cochère through which they drove to park in the shade of a huge river oak next to the garage. Francois couldn't wait to smoke and lit one as they ascended the peeling wooden stairs to Nadine's apartment.

***

Nadine flung open the door and admonished them to hurry before the cold air escaped. She stood in flip-flops, shorts, and an old Colt .45s T-shirt. As Cole approached, she panicked a bit, not sure how to greet him. Cole removed that concern when he gave her a big hug and a "How're you, Nadine?" She hugged back and patted him on the back as he entered.

"That's Francois," he tossed over his shoulder, followed by "Howdy, Mule." She thought it was a nice touch to remember the cat's name. The guy was authentic, no doubt.

Francois stood before her. "Mademoiselle. Francois Domaine at your service." He gave a slight bow.

"Can I have one of those?" she asked, pointing at the lit cigarette.

"But of course!"

As he reached for the pack of smokes, she grabbed him by the arm and led him inside. The insulated metal door closed with a heavy clank.

"I know you fellas are thirsty after that drive. Drinks? Ice tea or adult beverage? How was traffic? Francois, sit anywhere. You're a priest? Can I call you Francois? I like your socks."

She turned and flip-flopped into the small kitchen while Cole relaxed in a comfortable chair and signaled for Francois to do the same. She paused long enough for an answer and to watch Francois inspect the couch and its resident, Mule the cat.

"Oui. Francois will be quite adequate."

"Adult beverages, please," Cole said.

"Cole, I haven't seen you for almost a year. Tell me about the kids," she said as kitchen cabinets opened and slammed shut in her quest for glasses.

"College appears to suit Lisa. Jeri Ann still hangs with the bum in Lubbock," said Cole.

"Jeri Ann may not agree that her beau working toward a PhD constitutes bum status," came back from the kitchen, followed by, "there they are."

Francois settled on the opposite side of the couch from Mule and viewed the mishmash of computers, monitors, servers, and assorted blinking lights while she poured. He held one hand under the cigarette as a portable ashtray.

Nadine carried in three Flintstone jelly glasses and a bottle of Maker's Mark bourbon—the latter stored in the freezer with a handful of mint from under her stairway shoved down the neck and mixed with the liquor. She always believed it made for a nice cocktail on a hot summer evening. She balanced on one foot and used the other to sweep documents off the coffee table in front of Francois. His long ash and lifted palm prompted a rush back into the kitchen to return with a vintage Tiffany silver ashtray.

"Wilma, Fred, and Bam-Bam," she said. Nadine figured two fingers each of the Tennessee liquid ought to do it unless this priest wanted something different. If that was the case, she had wine cooling in the fridge.

Cole got Fred. Francois stared at the offered Bam-Bam glass, and then with quick, sure movements placed the cigarette in the ashtray and accepted the drink. He took a long and loud sniff of the bourbon, gave a grunt of satisfaction as he took a first sip, smacked his lips, and settled back, giving Mule a look with every bit as much attitude as Mule conveyed toward him. This was good to see, since the priest and Mule both needed to find personal demarcation even if it resembled the Maginot Line. The grunt of satisfaction struck her as a nice touch.

Nadine sat at her computer console and swung the chair around, planted her now flip-flop-less feet on the coffee table, and began rummaging through a Folgers coffee container filled with small bottles of nail polish.

"I suppose I could have offered something other than bourbon," said Nadine. "I have some wine."

"No, don't go there," said Cole. He smiled at Francois. The priest responded with a shrug.

"It's good to see you, Cole. It really is. First time in Texas, Francois?"

Francois adjusted himself on the couch and said, "Oui. I have purchased a belt."

She gandered at the snakeskin around his waist. "Nice. Are you celibate?"

"Oh, Nadine," groaned Cole.

"It is part of my calling," said Francois.

Cole rolled his eyes and cleared his throat. "Those murders were a bad, bad deal, Nadine. You and I aren't going to see worse."

"Meadow Green or Mystic Purple?" she asked, and lifted two small nail polishes from the container, then took the proffered cigarette, already lit by Francois.

"And this Moloch character. I just don't know," continued Cole.

"And the effect. To what effect?" asked Francois, as one hand gave a broad sweeping gesture, directed toward Nadine.

"Analytical but passionate. Vulnerable but in control. Right, Cole?" She didn't take her gaze off the two bottles of polish.

Cole appeared undaunted by the other two's conversation and said, "This isn't the usual crime story. Not by a long shot. Something is going on. Some connectivity I cannot get my head around."

"Pourpre. Purple," said Francois.

Nadine pursed her lips. "Yup. I think you're right."

Francois took a sip and said, "For such lovely feet, one may wish to improve on those." He pointed with his chin at her Walmart flip-flops.

"Folks, this is serious. Nadine, pay attention please," said Cole.

She heeded Cole's admonition to a small degree. "I've got nothing on Mr. Moloch yet. But I will, bucko. I will," she said, shaking the purple nail polish and waving her other hand in the general direction of all the computer equipment. "Retro. Very much a throwback to simpler times," she said to Francois, pointing at the flip-flops.

"We've got mass murder, ostensibly by a madman, and some guy who fled the scene who had talked with said madman the night before. Moloch has something to do with it. But I don't know what," said Cole, and took a hefty slug of bourbon. "So quit worrying about your dang toenails, please."

"These are strong," she said, holding the cigarette with her thumb and first two fingers. "French?"

"Oui. And the sheriff is correct, Mademoiselle. This will not reside among normal pursuits. It will not manifest from our reality. It is spiritual in nature."

"All those dead people aren't part of our reality?" asked Nadine. She leaned over to start on her toenails. "You guys hungry? With fresh purple toenails, I fully expect two fine gentlemen such as yourselves to escort me to dinner."

"A meal would be most satisfying," said Francois. "Regarding our reality, no—the true perpetrator does not exist in this reality. The sheriff has of yet not come to such a defined realization, but I do have hope that will change soon."

Her auburn hair obscured her face as she bent to the task. At Francois's comment, she turned her head and looked hard at Cole.

"Francois has a different perspective," Cole confirmed, and went to pour another drink.

She sat back, put her polish down, and took a small sip. From the freezer, the liquor had a syrupy consistency. Nadine processed within multidimensional frameworks. She didn't ascribe to neat boxes of cause/effect, nor discount outlier alternatives. Abstract concepts such as evil remained far-fetched possibilities, but that did not disqualify them as motivators of human behavior. They were, after all, possibilities. She had backtracked motives and rationalizations on dozens of bad people who did—or tried to do—horrible things. Cultural motives, economic motives, religious motives, personal motives—these things she interfaced with actions and outcomes and forecasts. But active spiritual interference fell outside her few mental constraints.

The priest likely wanted her to consider possessions; implanted evil from a source she could not see, hear, or feel—proposing some spiritual force related to centuries of Christian dogma. She bent back to her task and applied nail polish. *Does Cole really buy into this possession stuff?* she wondered.

The air conditioner hummed. Mule purred. Nadine took another drag on her cigarette and exhaled toward the ceiling.

"Everything is real. That's why it's everything. It exists," she said. "Outside our reality? Well, I'll tell you both what's outside our reality. Something that can't be explained. A dozen dead people at a nursing home can be explained when you toss some sick bastard into the mix. Or multiple sick bastards. I've tracked their type before. Believe me, they are real enough."

Francois took a long drag and gave Mule a momentary glance. Smoke blew from his nostrils as he looked at Nadine. "No, mes amis," he said with a soft and serious voice. "No. This is evil. With no dilution, no elements of this good earth. Evil. Pure evil."

Chapter 13

The sounds of electronic equipment mixed with the smell of mint, whiskey, and cigarette smoke. Francois waited and wondered if this peculiar woman was as good as the sheriff had led him to believe.

Nadine shifted position, causing her office chair to give a mild squeak. "Francois, before I try and wrap my head around this, I have to understand what this is. Admittedly, I live inside a murky world of obfuscation and misdirection. But at the end of the day there exists an informational reality. Something tangible, based on what we know. Now, you're telling me that this man, our Adal Moloch, shouldn't be treated as a normal human?" asked Nadine.

"I'd like a bit more information on that myself," said Cole.

Francois had prepared for such a conversation. The drive to Houston with the sheriff had passed without such an interchange—to be expected given the radical adjustment in the latter's worldview. But now the sheriff had an ally in this strange woman. Francois knew that adjusting realities, paradigms, and foundational footing could not be accomplished quickly. A bit more of a challenge, perhaps, with these Americans, infused as they were with absolutes and surety, but one must address such matters in the appropriate timeframe.

"Bon," said Francois. He finished his drink and clapped his hands once as he stood. "Bon. An excellent conversation. And in grand concurrence with Nadine, one we shall have over a meal, n'est-ce pas?"

Nadine drove them to a nearby Tex-Mex restaurant. She rolled the windows down and kept the AC on high. The two men kept silent as the thick heat wafted over them and sweat dripped down their faces. During the ten-minute trip, Francois chose not to engage her on the incongruity of traveling in such a manner. Some energy must be conserved for more important matters.

At the restaurant, an enlarged black-and-white photo of a Mexican bandit dominated one wall. They were the first patrons of the evening and chose a table in a far corner. Francois inspected the chips and salsa before he dug in.

"Tres Negro Modelo, por favor," said Cole when the waiter arrived.

"What is that?" asked Francois.

"Beer. Mexican. You'll like it," said Nadine, before placing the food order without glancing at a menu. She explained that she was a regular and often sat at a table by herself, perusing her laptop. Her book club also met there. Everyone in the club enjoyed the margaritas.

"What's the current gig you're on?" Cole asked Nadine, to start the dinner conversation.

"As usual, I can't tell you much. Homeland Security. Suffice it to say it involves bad people engaged in bad things. Evil things." She glanced at Francois as she shoveled a chip laden with a strange green sauce into her mouth.

"Ah!" said Francois. "Human evil. Evil of the person. Bon. You have the ability to predict, no? To forecast and follow such actions?"

He needed Nadine to find the trail. He needed a direction and a destination. The information he received from the sheriff was excellent and filled to the brim with possibilities, but this woman's alleged abilities could define a critical aspect of the quest—the location and movement and background of the enemy. The first major hurdle of confirming that the affairs in Rockport were influenced by an evil entity had been accomplished. The chase had begun.

"To some degree. I, and lots of others, have written data mining algorithms. Sometimes it helps. Sometimes not. Random isn't always the friend of data analytics," said Nadine.

"Then maybe that's a good place to start," said Cole. "If your contention is correct that evil walks among us, Francois, do they strike randomly or are specific people singled out?"

The sheriff's tone had an edge. *Could he be thinking of his wife's tragedy?* And now the skeptical look Nadine gave the sheriff indicated the entire non-human contention made her most uncomfortable.

"No," said Francois.

"So then you've discerned a pattern to these events," said Nadine.

"No," said Francois. "By that I mean, no, that is most clearly not a good place to start. And what is this meant to be?" He held a deep-fried pepper for inspection. It had some type of protrusion, making for a most unattractive presentation.

"Ratone. Little rat. Because the shrimp tail sticks out. A jalapeno pepper stuffed with shrimp and Mexican cheese. Don't worry. You'll like it," explained Nadine.

He took a substantial bite. Poor presentation and atrocious name aside, it tasted delicious. A large gulp of beer followed. "Excellent," he said.

"Let's go back to that not a normal human being thing," said Cole.

"You kick off, Padre," said Nadine. "I'm all ears."

These Americans, thought Francois. *No nuance. No first circling the core, absorbing subtleties.*

"Let us start with power," he began. "Not the power of physics, but the power of living beings. Such beings may or may not have visibility, but that, perhaps, opens up a larger discussion for this moment. A discussion with too many variables." At the last comment he nodded to Nadine in recognition of her analytical capabilities. He felt such things must be acknowledged.

"I have studied power, and its effects," he added. "And this?" He gestured at a thin stuffed and folded bread-like substance.

"Cow tongue taco. Eat it with your hands," Nadine said, taking a bite out of hers to demonstrate.

Several more patrons entered the small restaurant and the muted clatter of heavy dishes came from the kitchen. The aromas of stewed meat and spices permeated the small room.

"Yes," said Francois. "To the beginning. At least the beginning of records. And here I shall focus on the unseen forces. Evil power. The Mesopotamians, Egyptians, Assyrians all made references. The Hebrews captured a reasonable classification." He paused to eat, knowing such a discussion required time. The tongue dish was, again, excellent.

He chewed with his eyes closed, finished the last of his beer, and raised the empty dark bottle until their waiter saw it, smiled, and nodded affirmation. Cole turned and displayed two fingers to the waiter. The Mademoiselle hadn't touched her beer.

"The Hebrews. Oui. They knew God. They knew of fallen angels, celestial battles. They knew this earthly realm was only a slice of reality. But the Hebrews today do not mention it. They did document it, of course." He took another large bite of the tongue as his second beer arrived.

Nadine perked up at the word "document," evidently excited by the prospect of tangible information.

"Those documents reside in Israel?" she asked.

"Non. No. And this?" he asked, pointing a fork at an elongated lump wrapped in a cornhusk.

"Tamale. Take the—never mind. I'll do it," said Nadine, and unwrapped the cornhusk from the tamale so he could ingest it.

He held up his fork and one eyebrow.

"Yes. Use the fork. Or your hands. It doesn't matter," said Nadine.

They both watched as he took a bite, nodded, and gave guttural approval. He added some salt and fresh lime to the tamale and took another bite. He chewed and jabbed the air with his fork at the old photo of the Mexican bandit.

"Pancho Villa. Forget that," said Cole. "For God's sake, let's stay on track."

Americans. Francois followed the spicy tamale with a long pull of beer and a small belch.

"Then where, pray tell, does this information rest?" asked Nadine. "Not hungry, Cole? You aren't exactly digging in. You look thin."

"I believe these things may exist in Italia. Perhaps the Vatican archives. Perhaps I have studied them extensively. This would only be hearsay, of course. Une rumeur. Nothing more," said Francois, wafting a hand.

"A rumor," said Cole dryly.

"Oui."

"The Archivio Segreto Vaticano is well known. Nothing all that secret there," said Nadine, referring to the extensive Vatican collection of records open to select academicians and researchers each year. Francois was not surprised she knew of this. The Vatican kept the most extensive library of ancient manuscripts on earth. Much of it came across as arcane to the point of distraction, others thought provoking, and some—unknown to all but a few—described a reality few considered anymore.

"And this?" he asked, lifting a lid on a container of very thin bread.

"Tortillas. Put some of that pork chili verde in one, roll it, and—never mind," said Nadine. She grabbed a tortilla, filled it with pork chunks and green sauce, rolled it and handed it to Francois.

"Ah. The use of the hands again. Such a thing is good. Earthy." Francois thoroughly enjoyed the primitive presentation and lively flavors of the food.

"You must mean the Ignota Libris," said Nadine, filling her own tortilla.

Francois froze in mid-bite and shifted his gaze to Nadine. She raised one eyebrow in response.

"What's that?" asked Cole.

"Ignota Libris. The Unknown Books. Buried über deep in the Vatican. Only special honchos get access. Officially, these documents don't exist," explained Nadine.

Francois wiped his mouth and mustache with a napkin. "There exist not twenty men on this earth that know of this." His voice carried a grave timbre.

"Twenty men and one woman," said Nadine, apparently enjoying both her meal and the revelation of her unusual knowledge. "Cole, are you dating anyone?"

"What?" asked Cole.

"Dating. Anyone."

"No. Good Lord, Nadine. Could we stay on the subject? This hidden library or repository or whatever. Do those documents help us in any way?"

No response followed, which prompted Cole to raise his beer at the waiter and signal for another one. The sheriff had clearly become frustrated, Francois surmised, by the lack of direct answers. He exhibited a lawman's drive for irrefutable facts, typical of such men.

"And so, Mademoiselle," said Francois after a moment. "I must ask." He felt it time to better understand this woman. The Ignota Libris! How could she know of its existence?

"Yes, Francois, I do," said Nadine.

"May I ask in what form?" She had leapt ahead in the conversation, somehow anticipating or predicting his question. What an amazing woman!

"Alright, someone give me a clue," said Cole. "What the hell are you two talking about?"

Nadine mopped her plate with a corn tortilla. "Whether I believe in God. And I'll get to that in a while."

They continued to eat. Thoughtful silence again ensued until Francois burped and fished for a smoke. The waiter brought an ashtray along with dessert menus. As he adjusted himself in the chair and smoked, Francois took time to gather his thoughts. *This Nadine—I have not taken her seriously enough. I shall not make that mistake again.*

"They knew God, the Hebrews. And their knowledge was passed on—the Old Testament, yes?" said Francois.

"I'm sensing lecture time, Francois," said Nadine. "No offense. Please just make it a good one."

He continued as if he had not heard her. "Knowledge of evil beings—not human—was also passed on. This, of course, was not so widely distributed. Why? Who can say?" He paused to smoke. "But the reality is well documented. And, my knowledge in this realm is quite extensive."

Francois leaned back, lips pursed, and moved his attention back and forth between the other two. It was time to let them absorb the information he had imparted. Cole stared at the table. Nadine's crossed leg began to tap the suspended flip-flop against her heel. One, two, three—an apparent metronome for her thought process.

"What you ask me to believe, and correct me if I'm wrong, is that there are actual physical beings among us who are not human," said Nadine. "This is a biggie, Francois." She paused to take a drink of beer. "You want my analysis to focus on walking, talking, farting nonhuman creatures. That's a leap beyond faith. It's leaping the Grand Canyon."

He nodded in response. This remarkably bright woman had succinctly grasped his contention, although the passing of wind by such creatures had not, he was certain, entered into his presentation.

He flicked ashes off his cigarette and said, "I must add another aspect. It pains me to have less than a definitive answer. Yet the ancient manuscripts leave open the possibility that a living demon can transfer some form of possession to a human." He felt it best to reveal as many factors as he could, particularly with the Mademoiselle.

"So let's focus on Moloch," said Cole. "Is he a demon? At least a kind of demon as differentiated from the invisible demons that possess people?"

"Such is my belief," said Francois. The sheriff's question showed a cultural affectation he'd experienced in past trips to the States. The Americans referred to it as "staying on the same page." One must adjust to local mores. "It is difficult. This I know. Their nature would appear to be the same. In classical theology, demons do not have bodies as we know them. And yet, and yet, it would seem that some do."

Nadine leaned forward and took another smoke from Francois's pack, then looked to ask "okay?" Francois brushed his hand through the air as an "of course."

Nadine lit the smoke and said, "Alright. This is a good time to answer your earlier question. I believe in a God. If you can call it that. Energy that moves through the cosmos. But I've never seen a tangible reflection of this on earth. Nor have I seen any of Satan's minions. I'm a product of my experiences, Francois. And I never experienced either your version of evil or the power of God on this little ball in space called earth. No boogeyman. No miracles."

Francois confronted such attitudes his whole life, including within the church. Unless this woman insisted on a more esoteric conversational path, he knew it best to keep things focused on the matter at hand.

"I understand," he said. "It is difficult to grasp. It is a different reality. You have asked. I have attempted to reply. Let us not get distracted. How, may I ask, will you find this Moloch?"

Nadine's flip-flop stopped its rhythmic slap. "Facial recognition. I doubt he'll use the same identification now. Could be wrong. I'll trace that as well. But cameras capture everyone at US airports. Most other countries do the same. He entered the US as Moloch. Unless he is disguised, he can be tracked."

"Excellent," said Francois.

"Once I've identified him, I'll find out about his past. Movements, activities, associations. Unless, of course, he appeared out of thin air."

Francois ignored this poke at his assertions, and Nadine continued.

"So let's say I pinpoint this guy. Find him. What are you going to do when you confront him? Challenge him to a duel?" She took a puff without inhaling and blew a stream of smoke at the ceiling.

"He must be confronted. This I know," said Francois with a definitive air.

"Bad answer," said Nadine.

They sat at an impasse across a table littered with small bits of corn chips and depleted stone salsa bowls. Francois smoked in silence. The triple slap of Nadine's flip-flop started again.

"Back to Nadine's point. Let's assume you catch him. Whatever he is. You corner him. Confront him. What then? How have you handled this in the past?" asked Cole.

"It remains to be seen," said Francois.

"You mean it's circumstantial. Every situation is different," said Nadine.

"I mean to say that I do not know," said Francois.

"Then what is the standard approach? Church protocol?" asked Cole.

Francois gazed at the ceiling fan, not feeling the answer of great importance. "This will be my first attempt. My first quest."

Cole exhaled and sat back.

"Cool!" said Nadine. "A blank sheet of paper. An unsolved puzzle. We can do that. Cole, do you want dessert?"

Nadine insisted and picked up the check. On the way back to her apartment, at a stop sign in her quiet neighborhood, she waited for a woman with a stroller to cross in front of her. Just past their vehicle, the woman stopped, left the stroller in the street, and approached the open windows of their car. No other traffic moved on the street.

Cicadas buzzed in the summer evening from the old river oaks lining the streets. The heat had dissipated, replaced with a desultory humidity.

The woman stopped a few feet away from Nadine's window, leaned over, and said, "You'll all die. You cannot defeat him."

The woman turned and walked back to her baby, grasped the stroller and continued to cross the street. She cast a look back at the three and delivered a big, toothy smile. Her eyes blazed.

"What the hell was that?" asked Nadine, as she continued to watch the woman move away.

"Exactement, mon ami. Exactement."

Chapter 14

Price Jones slid his knife back and forth over the sharpening stone with a steady rasping rhythm. Off to work soon, at that bloody blind school, but plenty of time to hone a prized possession. The Welsh Fusiliers trench knife, a World War I relic with an eighteen-inch double-edged leaf-shaped blade, had belonged to some toady prick prior to Jones's burglary. Unlike the previous owner, he deserved it—so much so that a tattoo of it adorned the left side of his neck with the blade sticking up above his shirt collars.

Jones lived in a seedier section of old Cardiff, but it worked well enough. Dole from the government and odd jobs would do, usually cleaning tables or washing dishes for the dinner crowd or, like now, a nasty temporary janitorial job. The tiny apartment did not represent home as much as online with his mates did. Fantasy war games and chat forums made for a comforting environment. Some of the forums linked to dark places, and while mates on those sites expressed plenty of adulation for murky forces, they never tossed negative judgments back when he expressed personal thoughts and feelings. Many people felt, and lived, as he did.

He flipped the blade over, one run on the stone per edge. Last night had been another bloody disaster, except for that old codger.

Bloody tarts. Women too stupid to grasp his qualities—good looking, fit, and smart. Anyone with half a brain could see that. He'd stopped at a pub on his way home from work. He stood at the bar, ordered a pint, and looked around. Two young women stood next to him, laughing about something stupid and lingering over the last of their beers. The woman next to him in a red sweater had her back to him, so he looked past her to her friend, a tall blonde.

"Sounds bloody interesting," he said.

"What?" asked the blonde.

The girl in the sweater turned around to see who her friend had talked to. She wasn't a bad looker and the blonde definitely wasn't dog food either.

"Whatever it is. You are both laughing at something. Must be bloody interesting." He made sure to sneer slightly when he smiled; it gave him a hot bad boy image.

"Not really," said the blonde. The girl in the sweater rolled her eyes and turned her back again. He pointed his chin at the other.

"You chat online?" Jones asked the blonde.

"What's that?"

"Forums. Chat rooms. You know, online."

The girl in the sweater swallowed the last of her pint. Her friend said to Jones, "I don't fancy those things. A bit of Facebook, but that's all. The rest makes no sense." She too finished her beer.

Stupid, stupid tarts, thought Jones. Sweater girl wouldn't even talk to him. But they were somewhat hot and you never knew. That leggy one was a nice bit of blonde. Online mates often told of conquests that started with more humble beginnings, and he had to look better than most of them. He finished his beer and followed them out to the dark street. The air hung with a light coastal mist, creating a sheen on the cobblestones.

"So where would you be off to?" he asked. The question clearly surprised both young women. They must not have heard him follow them out of the pub.

"Home," the girl in the sweater replied. "Alone."

The other one was better looking anyway, so Jones shifted his attention to her.

"And you? Up for a bit of late night fun?"

"Sod off!" said the young woman. "What makes you think I'd have anything to do with you?"

The two women linked arms and walked away. "That one's a beauty!" he heard one of them comment. The other laughed.

Jones stood seething in the dark mist and watched them disappear.

"They are stupid girls." It came low, accented, and empathic, from the street alley next to the pub.

"Who's that?" asked Jones, squinting into the darkness of the alley.

"Stupid, stupid girls," came back the voice, followed by the appearance—as he moved into the light from the pub window—of a tall, bald man. Hard to tell his age, but he had a tight smile and his hands were open and faced Jones, in a gesture of greeting.

Jones did a quick assessment. Some old codger, probably harmless. But to the old guy's credit, he'd seen what had happened and understood it.

"Frustrating, isn't it," said the stranger. "You have a lot to offer. More than most men. They couldn't see that."

"I could have shown them a good time. Their bloody loss, because I'm capable of a lot." Jones caught a final glimpse of the girls under a distant streetlight, the deep mist enveloping them as they continued.

The stranger moved closer.

"Yes. I'm very sure you are."

Now he returned the oiled blade to its sheath and stood to go to work. Later he would meet for a drink with the old git he'd met outside the bar last night. It struck him as weird that the stranger wanted to have a drink with him, not from some sexual vibe the guy gave off, but because of the way the stranger was able to know him. Empathize with him. But the old man said he'd buy the drinks. Jones could put up with him long enough to down several whiskies.

That evening, Jones slid into a booth at the Lion's Paw pub and waved off the waitress. He'd wait for the stranger, and the stranger's cash, before he ordered a drink. The lousy workday was over, spent wiping down hallways and cleaning toilets for a bunch of blind people. The Cardiff School for the Blind was arsehole central. They had a lot of inside jokes only blind people could understand. He suspected many of these inside comments, followed by general laughter, had to do with him. *Screw them*, he thought. *Stupid blind people. Ingrates.*

After-work patrons crowded the Lion's Paw, and Jones snapped his head up when the stranger slid into the booth opposite him. He had not seen the stranger enter.

"Right. So what's your name?" asked Jones. "And you said you'd buy."

The stranger put his large hands flat on the table, pushed himself back, and cocked a head toward Jones. "My friends call me Adal. Would that work for you?"

Those large hands, bristling with black hair on the backs of the fingers, highlighted how peculiar this old codger appeared.

"Fine. Whatever. Adal. Are we going to drink? I'm a bit hungry as well. Fancy a bite?" He might as well soak the stranger for whatever he could.

The server arrived to take their orders. "My friend hungers and thirsts. I will have whatever he is drinking. I will pay," said the stranger, never taking his eyes off Jones.

Jones ordered, satisfied that food and drink were not his concern this night.

"So tell me," said the stranger. "Tell me all about yourself. You strike me as a very capable young man. Very capable indeed."

This stranger understood. This old man could see. No one else did.

Chapter 15

They returned to Nadine's apartment and sat in their original seats. Mule, still on the couch, cast a jaundiced eye toward Francois. The priest returned the favor.

"Okay. I admit, that was unnerving," said Nadine. "Probably a psychotic. Let's not leap to the conclusion that demonic badasses pushing baby strollers are walking around my neighborhood."

She found the whole thing disconcerting as hell. It had come out of the blue and coincided with their discussion on demons and Moloch. Rack it up to happenstance, albeit long odds for such a coincidence. Still, that weird vignette had taken a little of the shine off this new adventure. The priest had painted an interesting reality—almost like a parlor game—but that crazy woman walking up to the car and making those statements made the whole thing darker. It felt good to be back in the apartment.

Cole retrieved the bottle of Maker's Mark from the freezer, poured a stiff shot, and held the bottle in Francois's direction. The priest nodded. Cole offered the same to her. She waved off the offer, focused on the moment. Cole kept the bottle on the small table next to his chair.

"You're drinking too much," she said to Cole. She meant no moral judgment. "This is new. What's different? Pain? Uncertainty?"

"I'm fine. Thanks for the concern," said Cole. "I mean it. But let's address the issues at hand. Starting with that woman with the stroller."

Watching their exchange Francois lit another smoke. "The issue at hand is most definitely related to that woman," he said. "She is a fiber—an associate—of that which we seek."

Nadine watched Cole down his drink in one swallow, and hoped he wasn't cracking at the seams. He'd passed through the grinder with the Rockport massacre, and the weirdness around Moloch and now stroller-woman only layered icing on the cake. Her skills in the body and soul repair business were lacking. While that was a bother, she could at least pick up on the connected dots, and a large set of those dots orbited around the arrival of the priest and his world of demons. Its effects on Cole, she would bet, looped back to his pounding down liquor. Plus the priest seemed so damn sure of himself and that in and of itself was irritating. Assuredness had a certain appeal in the real world, but anchoring arguments in fantasyland, as the priest did, hardly lent itself to supporting a guy like Cole, who'd been through an awful lot the last few days. Cole needed an ally in this whole mess. She would fill that role.

"Do you fear, Francois?" asked Nadine, turning to the priest.

"I have confronted such evil many times before." He blew smoke at the ceiling and paused. "No. Perhaps not entirely true. I have confronted spiritual evil. Possessions. And once, perhaps, the physical form. But not in a manner that allowed me to gain a great deal of insight."

"Care to elaborate?" asked Nadine.

"I have trained myself to deal with demons as I best understand them. My assistance with exorcisms brings, it should be noted, both resolve and battle scars," said Francois. He paused to take a sip. "Some of the victims moved most definitely against nature's laws—levitations, inordinate strength, and knowledge of things impossible to know. These experiences form a foundation for our current situation. Comprenez vous?"

Nadine turned to her keyboard and entered a few strokes. Search parameters needed refinement, one of the great allures of her work. The human/machine interface was everything. She sniffed a trail and Moloch couldn't hide. Run, certainly, but not hide. Several of the computer screens began quick, flickering search patterns. She sat back and returned her gaze to Francois.

"And the answer you wait for regarding fear," Francois said. "One cannot view it as a one-dimensional emotion. Within the components of my quest, then of course some elements of fear exist. Fear of failure. Fear of weakness."

"Are you afraid of Moloch?" asked Nadine.

This Frenchman was meandering around the core question, and enough was enough. She wanted Cole to hear that uncertainty and fear were okay emotions.

"I do not know him," said Francois.

"Then let me review," said Nadine. Her flip-flop began a new triple beat. "Walking evil that can leverage free will and commit physical acts. Worst of both worlds. I'm not saying I buy into it, but if I did, the actuality would damn sure scare me."

Francois's gaze moved from Nadine to Cole. He took a sip of whiskey and said, "One must accept Mademoiselle's irritation as a matter of emotional attachment. She most certainly feels a need to protect you, Sheriff. I fully understand this as a matter of the heart. And I, in her estimation, have presented you discomfort and perhaps spiritual pain. Such has not been my intention."

The flip-flop increased tempo. "Thanks for the Oprah moment, Padre. Now, about that fear. Topic of the moment."

"Then, yes. I have some level of concern. Of fear," said Francois.

She took in Cole as he absorbed Francois's admission. The slight relaxation of his body position indicated some level of newfound comfort. There was no point in her bringing it up, but the priest was no pushover. If that guy felt fear, with all his knowledge and experiences, then she hoped Cole could see that he had a kindred spirit, someone else who felt what he probably did.

Nadine turned back to her computers, input data, and refined criteria. Francois took the opportunity to address Cole.

"Are you well, mon ami?"

"Yeah, I'm fine," he said, and tilted the bottle to refill his glass.

She knew he wasn't. Anyone could see that. This whole construct had thrown him a curve ball, and he sat there doing his strong, silent thing. Couldn't he see that she cared deeply for him? She could help him through this tough situation if he wasn't too hard-headed or too drunk to open the door and let it happen.

"Any person would get rattled by this, Cole. Any person. Just because he"—she paused to raise a taut arm and point at Francois—"thinks he has the tools and techniques to deal with the unexplainable doesn't mean he has any better grip on this than you do."

Francois responded by lighting another cigarette.

"Alright," said Cole. He held up both hands, palms facing Nadine. "I'm fine. Really. And it's not Francois's fault that all this has happened. He's helpful. A little weird in some respects, but helpful. I'm just tired and need to digest all this. Shall we call it a night?"

Francois's eyes grew wide at the "a little weird" comment, but he remained silent.

"No," said Nadine. "Not yet. What's the plan? Do either of you have the foggiest notion of a plan?"

"I plan to go get some sleep," said Cole. "I want to get to the hotel and crash."

"Oui," said Francois. "A good night's sleep. We shall reconvene in the morning. Let us allow the computers to do their work, whatever that might mean. Searching. Finding our Monsieur Moloch. Identifying his location.

Then, of course, I shall have great gratitude toward you both for your most excellent assistance and I shall depart. I shall assume an acceptable breakfast exists nearby?"

Nadine had other plans. This endeavor held intrigue like no other in her career. Something different was going on, something she hadn't dealt with before. Cole seemed to vacillate between the whole demon thing and the hard facts sought by a lawman, and that mental ping-pong game was understandable. But in previous pursuits of justice she had seen in him absolute doggedness—a man hard, focused, and keen. Now he appeared to hesitate. This priest, on the other hand, was resolute, smart, committed, and surely a bit of a pain in the ass. But Cole would come around. She had faith in him. She could help him regain his justice-seeking ferocity as long as it didn't wash away his gentle side, which would be less likely if she could hang with him as leavening to the mix. It might stretch her social skills, but she had an advantage given the relatively pure simplicity of the man she would be helping. Simplicity in a good way—she knew Cole wasn't stupid.

"I have a better plan," said Nadine. "I'll pinpoint this creep. Then the three of us go after him."

Spur of the moment wasn't her usual approach, but this instance called for the injection of new options. The situational stasis needed a kick in the butt and she was the one to deliver it. Besides, her whole living in a box thing had become more and more an issue in her life. If this holing-up and playing super-sleuth behind closed doors constituted the entire future, well then, she figured, screw that and carpe diem.

"In a sense, I would agree," said Francois. "You possess very capable skills. I would most greatly appreciate your help when the time comes, but your help delivered from this location for the purposes of providing information, if such a thing is required."

She had seen that coming a mile away. She was to play the role of the priest's little helper, cranking out salient information at his bidding and accommodating his timelines, just like others who had tried the same tack many times before. It irritated her to no end. When others relegated her to an informational spigot, they overlooked her ability to solve things, piece things together, and get things done.

"Not going to happen," said Nadine. She turned and headed into the kitchen to put on some coffee, pausing long enough to address Cole. "We all need to go after this guy, right?"

He looked up with a wry smile and stretched. "Credit where credit is due, Nadine. You've pointed out the obvious, which I somehow shoved to the side." He popped his neck, some element of fire back in his eyes. His body language indicated returning resolve. He turned to Francois and nodded. She knew that was a man signal of some kind, so it was time to nip that crap in the bud, because it inevitably led to her being left out.

"I'm not a mind reader, cowboy," she said. "What's the obvious thing?"

"I need to stop fiddle-farting around and chase this sumbitch, whatever he is. I'm the Sheriff of by-God Aransas County. This is what I do. You've been pointing that out while I sat here a bit dazed and confused. So, thanks, Nadine."

"What does that translate to, exactly?" she asked. Big smile from Cole, which was good to see because it contained life and fire and determination.

"It translates to demon or not, Moloch's fixin' to find out I'm on his ass."

"Good. Now you might remember from about seventeen seconds ago that I said the three of us. Please don't parrot the 'little lady can sit here and do her thing' that Francois just tossed on the table."

"Well, he has a point," said Cole. "You could help a lot doing what you do right here. I'm sure the Vatican would pay for your services, right, Francois?"

She snorted and proceeded to the kitchen. Kitchen cabinets opened and slammed shut.

"Let's get back to my plan," she said, in the general direction of the two men. "It is sound. I carry a laptop and can perform what I do best anywhere. Plus, I can input my visual perspective as a set of added data points."

Silence answered her. Nadine plowed ahead.

"So, I'll find him. I always do, and then off we go. Easy, peasy."

"I cannot allow this," said Francois, loud enough to carry into the kitchen. "Danger exists at every turn. I cannot allow harm to come to you. The sheriff, one must assume, has faced such dangers before. If he is committed, then it shall be."

Conversation halted. Coffee cups clanged and Nadine strolled back in with three steaming mugs.

"Not up to you to allow, Francois," she said. "Three black coffees. I remember you liked stevia, Cole, but I don't have any. I need to try that stuff. Comes from a South American plant." She placed a mug in front of the two men, kept hers, and reached down to take a smoke from the pack Francois had left on the table. She did not ask if she could.

"Keys to the kingdom, compadres. That's what I've got," she said and waved her hand at the computer equipment. "Keys. To. The. Kingdom. So here's the deal. I'll find him. Then Cole and I join in the chase. Sabe?" She plopped down in her chair with satisfaction.

Francois emitted a low groan as he leaned forward to collect his coffee. Mule's tail flicked. Cole kept his eyes on Nadine, smiled, and said, "You are one piece of work, Nadine."

"Athos, Aramis, and Porthos," said Nadine, her smile wide and attitude smug.

She could bet Cole and Francois got the *Three Musketeers* reference, although neither acknowledged it.

Francois took a loud sip of coffee. "Mademoiselle. Please. I beg you. Your plan. Layered with danger."

Cole poured some of the liquor in his coffee, apparently bemused at the outcome. "She's fixed on it, Francois. Ain't much point arguing. I speak from experience."

His sanguine appearance gave her hope they would hunt together. She assumed Cole would take the lead when it came time to confront Moloch, which was okay since neither she nor the priest had that type of experience. But the whole pursuit thing was smack dab in the middle of her bailiwick … or at least the locating and tracking part was, and sometimes it simply felt good to be the critical element of a team.

Francois closed his eyes, apparently in prayer. He then took a loud swallow of coffee, slapped his knees, and rose quickly to his feet, startling Mule. "Bon. So it shall be. It is perhaps part of God's plan for me. And you, Mademoiselle, give definition to formidable. This said, I of course will lead."

Cole clearly opted not to argue the point at this time, while Nadine did not care, since leadership tended to be fluid and situational.

Nadine said, "All good, Cole. Life is a cavalcade."

Cole returned a quizzical look.

"Or maybe it's a carousel. Either way, see you in the morning bright and early. You, too, Francois."

***

Headed down the creaky outside stairs as Nadine stood in the open doorway, the two men paused.

"A most serious endeavor," said Francois.

Cole took in the damp night air. The temperature had dropped to the mid-eighties. A thunder buster moved from the Gulf toward Houston, and sheet lightning filled the eastern sky. Low rumbles of thunder followed.

"Yep. It is. That woman with the stroller," said Cole. "You reckon Moloch had his hand in that?"

"Oui."

The fresh smell of approaching rain filled the air. Cole lifted his head and inhaled deeply. "So, you're planning to rely on God when we find this guy?"

Francois gave a serious nod in response.

"And what if God doesn't feel like kicking ass at that moment. What then?"

Francois cast his gaze toward the sky's lightshow as the storm gathered. "This I do not know, mon ami. This I do not know."

Chapter 16

The call came at six in the morning. Cole rolled over and checked the caller ID and saw the name Nadine.

"Off to Wales, cowboy," she said, with far too much cheer.

Cole gathered himself. "You found Moloch?"

"Ye of little faith. He arrived in Cardiff. Grab the priest and come over. I'll do more digging on Moloch's background. So far, it's sparse. He may be using an alias."

"Okay. Fine. Good work as always," said Cole. "We'll hustle over there in an hour."

"I can't tell you how much I'm looking forward to this," said Nadine, hanging up.

Why couldn't the sumbitch have landed in Albuquerque or Memphis? The overseas pursuit thing added complexity and time. Plus, there were a couple of phone calls he would have to make about that, but all-in-all he began to feel better. Nadine had delivered something concrete. The lawman in him began to rise.

Francois received Cole's door knock attired in a silk robe.

"Let's get to Nadine's," said Cole. "She's ID'd Moloch. He's in Wales. Cardiff."

Francois showed a fire in his eyes, nodded, and turned to pack. Cole did the same. Wales became a destination. In hindsight it made sense that the bastard would leave the US. Moloch traveled on a foreign passport, so exiting the US and its large law enforcement network was a rational move. Why the SOB picked Wales to run to, or what his plans were, mattered less than the fact Cole would have the opportunity to confront him. He began to give serious thought to how the team would operate together, and how the other two might assist in the confrontation.

They hurried to Nadine's. She met them at the door to her apartment with the admonition, "We have to eat in a hurry. The plane leaves in three hours." She had just returned from a nearby breakfast restaurant with takeout dishes of scrambled eggs, biscuits, gravy, sausage, and fruit.

They talked about Moloch's whereabouts and the lack of any deeper information on him.

"Slim pickings," said Nadine. "But he's traveling on a Syrian passport. I know someone over there. He may help."

This was something he'd have to get used to. Nadine knew folks all over the world from her work projects. He'd never worked with spies or that clandestine world, but her contacts could come in mighty handy now that the chase pointed overseas.

"So you bought the tickets already?" asked Cole. "You need to know there's a budget available from the governor's office."

"And from the Vatican," said Francois, serving himself food and apparently contemplating the rationale behind the gravy.

"Not a problem. I'll invoice both. First one to pay gets a discount on my labor bill," said Nadine.

"The audit division in Austin will love that," said Cole, exhibiting for Francois the use of gravy as something poured over biscuits. Francois watched, having waved a hand at the minor issue of money and budgets.

"What about the cat?" asked Cole. He liked animals, especially dogs, but cats had their place, and Nadine was openly affectionate toward the gnarly critter she kept in her apartment.

"The name is Mule. Mule the cat. MTC. Got a friend to take care of him," said Nadine. "Plus, he's a guard cat. He'll protect the place."

Cole didn't think that too far-fetched, given the Francois-Mule stare downs.

Nadine had purchased first class tickets, one way. The flight traveled from Houston to Amsterdam, followed by a straight shot to Cardiff. They would arrive the next morning, Greenwich Mean Time. She explained the logic of one-way tickets, given their trip may well include other stops as evidenced by her past tracking of field agents.

"Man, I feel so alive," she said. "The whole idea of field operations after all these years of solving criminal puzzles from a distance gives me a high. Life is good."

Cole had never seen her so buzzed; she almost danced around the room.

On the way to the airport, Cole made several phone calls. The first to R.L., his best deputy, and an explanation he would be gone for a few days. He made clear R.L.'s job consisted of holding down the fort until he got back. A conversation with Mayor Remmy followed.

"Adele, it's not a big deal. R.L. is quite capable," said Cole.

"That's all fine. I'm glad you're taking some time off, albeit mighty close to the wrap-up of our disaster."

She had a point, and he acknowledged it. But Adele was sympathetic and, as Cole well knew, very competent. Given the abilities of R.L. and Adele he wouldn't be leaving Rockport in a tight spot.

The last call would be a bugger. Jeeter Johnson required some handling and the overseas component would raise hackles. He sat in the backseat of Nadine's car, feeling the heat of Houston blow over him. The windows, as usual, remained rolled down.

"Sir, Sheriff Garza," said Cole.

"Son, you sound like you're in a hurricane."

"Sorry. Hold on just a second," said Cole. Cupping the cell phone against his chest, he said to the front seat occupants, "Windows, folks. Can't hear a thing on the phone."

"Fine," said Nadine, using one hand to raise her and Francois's windows and the other to fiddle with the AC controls. Cole didn't think it wise for her to steer with her knees as Houston traffic sped alongside, but he remained silent on the subject. Francois shook his head and tossed his lit cigarette out the window just prior to it closing.

"Better?" asked Cole, speaking into the cell phone.

"Much better. What's going on among the world of high-level diplomacy? You don't mind if I keep you on speaker phone, do you?" asked Johnson.

Johnson had a lighthearted tone. He explained he had the phone on speaker so he could continue perusing the file he had open on a case in Hudspeth County. It had long been a favorite locale for smugglers crossing from Mexico. Combined with desert, mountains, and thorny plants, it made for a hard land and hard people. "Different turf than the saltwater territory you live in."

"I'm sure it is, sir. On this end, all is going fine. The three of us are traveling."

Johnson chewed on this for a moment. "You, the priest, and Nadine May?"

"Yessir. We're heading to Wales. The possible suspect has been identified as recently landing there."

"Wales? As in the UK?"

"Yessir."

The speakerphone shut down and Johnson talked into the hand receiver. "It's Nadine, ain't it? She's got you on a wild goose chase. At the expense of the citizens of Texas."

"Would you like to talk to her?" asked Cole. "She's here in the car."

"Hell, no. Now listen. If this is legitimate, why travel with the priest? If it's a desperado you're after, why drag him along?"

Cole had wrestled with the response to this inevitable question, and had formulated a reply hours earlier. "Well, sir, the Vatican representative feels we should travel together." This stretched things a bit, but the pact among them last night had solidified that morning and surely Francois now "felt" they should travel together. At Cole's statement to Johnson, Francois turned in his seat and lifted an eyebrow. Cole gave his best shrug back.

He'd shown a potent hole card—the Vatican—and Johnson would have to accept it, although not without commentary, apparently. "You're straddling the boundary of our obligation. You know it. Tossin' Nadine on the pile ain't helpful, either."

"I agree, sir. It's unusual. If it helps, the Vatican has a budget as well."

At this, Francois wafted a dismissive hand from the front seat.

Johnson sighed into the phone. Cole knew that Johnson couldn't prevent them from going, but it did now put the head Ranger in a tight spot. This legendary lawman deserved some ass-covering, and the right thing to do was provide it. "Odds are this will turn into a dead-end trip, and there's no way this tracks back to the Rangers, the governor, or, God forbid, the State Department. Just the three of us helping out the Vatican. You have my word," said Cole. A man giving his word wasn't something to be taken lightly. The phone fell silent for a moment.

The Rangers pursued bad guys to the ends of the earth and, well, if this fellow proved bad, he knew Jeeter would support him. Johnson shifted gears. "This suspect y'all are chasing, is he dangerous?" Johnson asked. A lawman, he now wanted particulars.

Cole considered the best approach to this question. It could open a new can of worms.

"Yessir. Something bad wrong with this guy. My gut tells me he's a nasty piece of work."

Johnson clearly went with Cole's gut.

"So this is real, son?" asked Johnson. "This whole thing. Just tell me that."

"I can't bet the farm, sir. But it's clear something's going on. Something bad." Cole hesitated before continuing. He trusted Johnson, which made it time to open the kimono. "I wish I could be more specific. This guy reeks of evil. That's about all I can point to right now."

Cole's hunch seemed to satisfy Johnson. Every lawman in the state knew Johnson's past as a field Ranger had frequently touched on the horrors inflicted by fellow humans. The drug trade, in particular, contained indescribably violent people.

"Keep it tight," said Johnson. "I'm backing you, but keep it tight. I do not want my ass in a wringer over this."

Relief flooded over Cole at Johnson's comment. This meant some third party support, if for no other reason than to justify this path. When the head Ranger said he'd back him, he would.

"Yessir. I appreciate it."

"Why's Nadine May with you and the priest?" asked Johnson.

"Leaving her behind wasn't an option, sir. You know Nadine," said Cole, eliciting a glance from Nadine in the rearview mirror.

"Boy howdy, do I know her. Alright. You armed?"

"No. I plan on working with the local authorities."

Johnson explained that he felt torn on this one. On one hand, Cole not armed would keep this mission out of the press if it got ugly. Let the local law handle it and keep the governor off his rear end. On the other hand, if this guy proved dangerous a sidearm provided good insurance. It was blunt talk from Johnson, covering media, politics, and safety for this little foreign fandango.

"Are they armed?" asked Johnson, indicating his suspicion the UK did not allow their police to pack firearms. "Because if they aren't—and I would bet that's the case—you'll need to keep more distance than usual from this suspect. So keep your distance."

"Will do, sir. Again, I appreciate the support."

Again, silence on the phone. "Comanche moon tonight. Good hunting, but watch your topknot, son."

They signed off.

***

They sat three across in first class, Nadine taking the middle seat. By design, any conversations between Cole and Francois would have to pass through her. They flew KLM, the Dutch national airline. All three commented on the extra seat room. Francois read an esoteric book about God and the nature of man. Cole ordered a double scotch and chatted with Nadine. They talked of past cases, criminals, and dealing with bureaucracies. Eventually the talk got around to Moloch.

"So I assume we'll utilize the local police to help pinpoint this guy. If they can't, I can. Don't ask how. So let's assume we locate him. Then what?" she asked. So far, the answers to this point had done nothing to satisfy her. Moloch wasn't charged with any crime. They had no hard evidence to connect him with the Rockport murders, other than him being seen at the nursing home by Cole. This wasn't all bad news in her view. It made the puzzle more of a challenge.

"Let's pretend he is the ultimate boogeyman," she continued. That statement caused Francois to lower his book and clear his throat. "And he decides to lay the bad mojo on us. Do we leave our response to Francois?"

The priest turned to face the other two. "Oui." He returned to his book.

"I want to talk with him," said Cole. "Question him as best I can without a formal arrest. He should tell us something, even inadvertently. I just don't know yet how I'm going to pull it off."

Nadine waved off the flight attendant checking drink orders. Francois, without averting his eyes from the book, raised an empty wine glass. Cole ordered another whiskey. These two evidently didn't care about keeping a clear head while discussing what anyone could see were gaping holes in what little strategy they had, one in which "muddling through" would not be a viable option. Her past work with field agents pointed to well-thought-out plans, backup plans, and alternatives, as well as what they called shit-hits-the-fan scenarios. Wine and whiskey were not ideal components of these strategy sessions.

"Fine. We confront him, talk with him," said Nadine. "And what's next? Hang around Cardiff and see what develops? Not your style, Cole, and it's not mine either."

Cole acknowledged that she had a solid point and explained that he, too, chafed under a weak plan, but it was all they had. They could make the case to the Cardiff cops that Moloch had fled the scene of a major crime, but there was no formal warrant, no Interpol lookout. They carried photos of Moloch from airport security cameras—which Francois had stared at for a long time—and could ask the local authorities to find and bring him in, but Cole seemed to think it unlikely.

"We follow him," said Cole. "Track him. Be ready. Engage if needed. It's the best I can come up with at the moment."

That felt better to her. At least it had a proactive tack. Francois shook his head and continued to read.

Nadine knew this was the time to flesh out their strategy. In her experience with field operations, events got moving fast and everyone on the team needed to be on the same page. If Francois chose not to participate in this important discussion, then so be it, because she and Cole could both formulate plans and execute them. The Frenchman's whole dismissive Buddha-of-the-inscrutable posturing was becoming a pain in the ass.

"So let's extrapolate a scenario," she said. "We catch him doing something nefarious. Call it evil if you will, to satisfy the ecumenical member of this troika. You aren't armed, so do we wrestle him to the ground? Kick his ass?" The time for particulars had arrived.

Nadine turned to Francois when he cleared his throat, shook his head, and closed his book, making quite the production of it. It wasn't a challenge for her to see he was amply demonstrating that this would be the price he would have to pay and the burden he would have to bear for his travels with her and Cole. Francois shifted to address both of them and said, "Guns and physical force will not defeat this one. Such talk is a waste of time." He rearranged his khakis and navy sports coat after the bodily shift, checked his fuchsia pocket-handkerchief, and smoothed back his hair. Nadine took in Francois's dismissive assertion with a single raised eyebrow.

"The boogeyman doesn't bleed?" she asked.

"Lighten up a little, Nadine," said Cole. "This isn't the Spanish Inquisition."

Francois waved him off and stared at Nadine for an uncomfortable amount of time. She stared back, yielding nothing.

"He will be defeated through the power of God," said Francois. He used a tone that implied great impatience. "You, Mademoiselle, do not believe such a thing. Fine. And yet I tell you the truth. This creature is not of this world. It is only through the power of God that this creature will be defeated. With this defeat, does he run? Disappear? Or, to satisfy your American sensibilities, explode into a fireball of body parts? Je ne sais pas. I do not know. But do not doubt the truth."

Nadine could see that Francois's vehemence could well have been hiding private fears and uncertainties. That was okay, since they all had some measure of the same, and admitting it wasn't the end of the world. It was a very human thing to do, and she wished Cole would demonstrate more of his inner feelings. Francois turned to face forward, adjusted position, and used both hands to confirm his hair still behaved. She turned to Cole with both eyebrows raised high, waiting for his response to Francois's statements.

"I just don't know," said Cole. "That's the best answer I can give you. Would a pistol shot to the head bring him down? Probably. Let's leave it for the time being."

Like Francois, few things intimidated Nadine May, and she possessed her own unique doggedness. "No one talked about pistol shots to the head. Drop the Lone Ranger stuff, would you? Neither I nor Francois look forward to playing Tonto." She turned to focus on Francois, then reversed course back to Cole. "Sorry. You're right. I need to lighten up. I know you're not like that. I'm just digging for answers."

"Yeah, well, me too," said Cole, and took a stiff drink. "No hard feelings."

There sat a good man. He evidently did not take her minor—very minor—diatribes on a personal level. He apparently understood that she was missing a cog or two inside her social watch and that sometimes the hands flew around the clock face. Maybe sometimes it came across as endearing, sometimes not. Either way, he gave every sign of having already moved on.

"Okay, Francois. Let's talk about your answer," she said and turned toward the priest, satisfied she hadn't angered Cole. "Unless you are too pissed at me to have a civil conversation. A conversation with someone who doubts, someone who questions. Because right now, what you've described sounds closer to a Disney movie. Wave a hand and the dishes get done. Say a prayer and a wooden doll comes to life."

Francois waved both hands. "It is a question of belief. Belief and faith. You and I may well have this conversation for hours, but unless we have a common foundation of belief and faith, my answers will never appear rational to you. Comprenez-vous?"

"Yeah, I get it," she said. "But let's tackle some variables. Suppose God, for whatever reason, decides not to get engaged. Doesn't act on your—on our—behalf. Then what? If this man, this creature, cannot be taken by conventional means, what do we do? And I can't believe I just asked that."

Francois shrugged and, without looking at Nadine, said, "It remains to be seen."

Cole leaned over to participate. "If it helps, Moloch can show fear. The sumbitch dismissed me at the nursing home with a snarl. After, he showed fear. Real fear."

She whipped around in her seat to face Cole, who drained his glass and addressed his companions. "I've told Francois a bit of this. There was another man. Old. At least his face, although he showed no old-man resignation. And he dang sure wasn't old in his movements or intent. Moloch disappeared when this guy showed in the alley next to the nursing home. Old, with a long gray ponytail. Moved like lightning. Plain shirt and pants from an old black-and-white movie. Fifties style. He hunted. He hunted Moloch. I'm convinced of it now. And Moloch was aware of him. Might have seen him. And Moloch showed fear. Gut wrenching fear and hatred."

They both stared hard while Cole wiped his mouth and looked down the plane's aisle. This was new information for Nadine and triggered strong irritation deep inside her. Why in the world would he withhold this from her until now? They were supposed to be on the same team and this type of information could be critical for their endeavors. What did Cole think he would gain by keeping this jewel of a data point inside when they were all struggling with tactical approaches to their quarry? Moloch could be intimidated. That was a big deal.

"When did you plan to spring this little revelation?" asked Nadine. "Now? On the plane? This is data I had not figured on. Thanks, bud. Oh, and by the way, might there be any other little pearls of insight you'd like to drop on me?" What in the world was wrong with people when all she wanted was to have data dumps? People could tell her everything they knew, and she would sort through it. She never understood why people did what Cole had just done.

"This element of fear, this is of course new to me as well," said Francois. "Although it is not a great surprise. This creature is not all-powerful. Non. Evil has weaknesses."

Francois leaned back to ruminate on this. Nadine looked from one man to the other and remembered to close her mouth. This was unbelievable to her. End of discussion, no further digging, and no exploration of how to leverage this new information. What was wrong with these two?

Their in-flight dinner arrived and they remained silent while a flight attendant took drink orders. After several bites, she dove back in.

"So this other man. He knew some vulnerability of Moloch's," she said, looking back and forth at both men. "We need to exploit this vulnerability."

Francois chewed his food with eyes closed and held his fork upright, forefinger extended the length of the handle and the tines pointed toward him. "And so. It is true," he said.

"Any ideas on how best to do that?" she asked him.

"Do what?" replied Francois, taking another bite.

Nadine wiped her mouth, crossed her arms, and addressed Francois. "You're talking about food, aren't you?"

Francois finished chewing. "Oui. A rumor exists the Dutch hired French culinary experts for their airline. Clearly true."

Nadine crossed her legs, the suspended foot tapping in threes against the forward seat.

Francois pointed the fork at her foot and said, "You perhaps send a message in the Morse code to the unfortunate person seated in front of you?"

Nadine uncrossed her legs, straightened herself, and looked at Cole. He responded by focusing on the plate of food and acting as if he'd never heard a word of the immediate conversation. She did not relent and lowered her head in gradations until she was eventually looking upward at Cole eating, forcing him to smile.

Cole wiped his mouth and reached over to give her a quick squeeze on the knee. "Okay, the bottom line. I had little to give you on the other man. One of my deputies also saw him for a moment during that hellish scene. That's it. No one else has any recollection of him." Cole explained that he had continued to ask witnesses at the nursing home if they had seen someone fitting the old man, long ponytail descriptive. To a person, they'd all shaken their heads.

"Fine," said Nadine. "What are the possible motives for his pursuit of Moloch? A relative, father, grandfather of another crime Moloch was involved with?" This ponytailed stranger added several new pieces to her puzzle. She relished the as-yet-unknown aspects of this new player and his relationship to Moloch.

"I've got nada," repeated Cole. "It happened so fast. A body lying on the parking lot next to the back door, the building on fire, and I had to enter to see what I could do. The whole timeframe after I saw Moloch leave and the other stranger looking for him lasted only a second or two."

"Tell me more about his appearance. I got the clothing, the old man face, the ponytail. What else?" she asked.

Cole stared at the floor and gave her a stream of consciousness. "Sorta like he was old, but wasn't. He moved with such force. Such intensity. He hunted. His quarry had disappeared. He had no fear. Almost ... almost illuminated. He stood in the deep shade of the alley, but I could see him well. His body language was aggressive. But an aura of something good, something righteous, had come from him. He paid me no mind. None whatsoever."

Nadine digested this, and took the opportunity to pat Cole on the back of the hand as a combined gesture of "thanks" and "sorry about my outburst." Her mind tumbled with possibilities. Could he have been some other law enforcement personnel? FBI? CIA? Secret Service from another country? Interesting. Moloch fled. Very interesting.

Francois had finished dinner, and placed his coffee and cognac order with the flight attendant. He cast a comment to the other two. "A force for good."

"Alright, Francois. I suppose so," said Cole. "It doesn't help a heckuva lot. Sometimes I think I'm a force for good. Batman is a force for good. This guy dang sure wasn't a county sheriff or a superhero."

Francois shrugged, peering down the aisle for his cognac.

"Francois is thinking more along the lines of the supernatural," said Nadine. "A man—a being—with some extra and inexplicable whup ass in his arsenal. A cosmic badass. An avenging angel." Turning to Francois, she asked, "Would you get me one of those? A cognac. Please."

"Just remember, this creature we pursue is not all-powerful," said Francois to no one in particular, as their drinks arrived. After inserting his nose into the snifter of cognac and taking a loud inhale, he said, "Only God is so. All-powerful. Much of the pleasure of this glorious French liquid is to relish it with the senses." He turned to Nadine and tapped the side of his nose, emphasizing the point.

"Alright," said Nadine, as she cupped the snifter and inhaled deep, made a face, and turned to Cole. Francois's statement about a force for good provided nothing new and Cole's stream of consciousness seemed to have emptied him of pertinent data. "Let's talk about us," she said to Cole.

"Us?"

"You and me. Why aren't you dating anyone?" Nadine had now turned her whole body toward Cole, both knees tucked and both feet on the seat. Francois may as well have been sitting on another airplane, and that suited her just fine.

"Mercy's sakes, Nadine."

This constituted thin-ice territory for her, but Cole was seat-belted in and a captive audience. By treading carefully she thought this might just work. Past conversations she'd had with Cole painted a picture of Martha as serene, quiet, and gentle. Martha had clearly infatuated Cole with her calm and loving approach to life and their relationship. Nadine couldn't make claim to calm and quiet. Then again, maybe he was at a place in life where change presented itself as a good thing, although too much change tended to scare people. Then again, dating her wouldn't be boring, and you could ask anyone for confirmation of that. His kids were out among the world, creating few demands on his time, parenting-wise, and his role as Aransas County Sheriff couldn't be too time-consuming. She knew the round peg, square hole challenge existed if they were to date, although that was supposed to be the spice of life or some such thing.

"Do you consider us friends?" she asked.

"Of course."

"Don't friends talk about these things? You're good-looking, gainfully employed, and a good and fine man. A catch. Why aren't you dating?" This approach resided in her comfort zone—straightforward, but not too abrasive.

"It's hard, I guess," said Cole. "You're married a long time, you get set in your ways." He paused to take a drink. "Suddenly she's gone. And you settle into life without her and focus on raising kids. It's different phases. Now the kids have scooted off on their own. I suppose it's another phase in life and I just haven't come to grips with it."

She appreciated his honesty. It registered a little one-dimensional and offered nothing of great depth, but it showed progress having him divulge personal thoughts.

"Don't you get horny?"

"Nadine." Cole shook his head and looked at the ceiling of the aircraft.

"I mean, the plumbing down there still works, doesn't it?"

"Nadine!" said Cole.

Francois took this opportunity to lean forward and look past Nadine at Cole, raising an eyebrow. Cole looked at the priest and unbuckled the seatbelt.

"I've got to go to the bathroom," Cole said, departing.

Dammit, she thought. *Dammit. Spooked him. A duck on a pond and I got too close. Took off quacking about the bathroom.*

She turned to look at Francois, jaw tight. "Were you going to contribute to the conversation, Mr. Celibacy?"

Francois gestured "such is life," apparently not offended by her question. "No. But one may want to consider the sheriff's longer perspective. The years ahead. And not, perhaps, the immediacy of the plumbing."

Francois was right. She'd remember this strategy for future reference. Start at the end game and work back. Reverse chronology. She acknowledged as much, saying, "Yep. You're right." She slumped back. "I'm not very good at social stuff. Never have been."

Francois took her hand. "Mon ami, there is always help. Guidance. You simply must ask for it."

"The higher power thing?"

"Oui."

"How is God on making me easier to get along with?"

Francois smiled. "More than adequate, I assure you. And we will need him, of this I am certain. The three of us—Athos, Aramis, and Porthos as you say—should all be asking for help."

Chapter 17

Assistant Chief Constable Jenni Thomas left work earlier than usual. Her daughter was staying with a friend for a birthday party, so she traveled to the edge of town to see her niece Anwen, who worked at the Cardiff School for the Blind. She'd arranged to take her niece for dinner as a treat. Anwen filled a place dear to Jenni, and no special occasion was needed to prompt the offer. Anwen loved chatting with her, particularly about men. Jenni expressed her lack of expertise within the men department, but her niece remained convinced she knew a great deal on the subject.

She arrived late afternoon and parked near the large, old stone building that had been converted from a shipping warehouse built several centuries before. Jenni considered it dark inside, but her niece explained the students were after all blind, and lighting was not a major issue. The school had seventy-three students and a staff of eighteen. As Jenni entered, the ancient hallways filled with the usual sounds of young people laughing, talking, and making their way to the final class of the day. They brought a sense of light to the stone structure, more than compensating for the lack of electrical lighting.

Jenni headed along a hallway to her niece's office, knowing enough to offer a cheery "hello" as she walked, to let the students know of her presence. A janitor far down the hall stood with mop and bucket, leaning against a wall as he waited for classes to start and things to settle.

"Where to?" asked Anwen, as she put desktop items away for the day. Jenni leaned against the doorframe.

"Your choice," said Jenni. "Chinese? Pizza? Whatever strikes your fancy. I'm foregoing my diet in your honor. How's that for an excuse? And how's life as an administrator these days?"

They chatted about budgets and government funding while Anwen finished her duties.

"Well now," came an unexpected voice behind Jenni. "Aren't you something to look at?"

Jenni snapped around to see the young janitor a few feet away. Her radar switched to high alert. Something wasn't right about this fellow.

"Pardon me?" she asked, assessing the young man. Arms crossed and a smirking smile conveyed a weird, unsettling assuredness. The young man apparently took her response as a positive.

"You're looking good, all I'm saying," said Jones. "What's your name?"

"Assistant Chief Constable Thomas. What's yours?"

She thought her police status would throw him off and change the dynamic. She also wanted his name. The guy, however, continued to give off a disconcerting vibe. The young man must have thought it positive progress when she'd asked his name. He edged closer, invading her personal space.

"Jones. Price," he said. "Although my friends call me a lot of things, including stud." His smirk widened, with one lip raised more at the corner, giving the effect of a toothy sneer. He moved even closer.

"Well, stud, if I do a quick records search, what little surprises am I liable to find about you?"

She returned no smile and posed with the constable stare, hands on hips and full of official business.

This seemed to throw Jones. He held both hands in a "whoa" position and cocked his head, the smile becoming a display of teeth, with no sign of humor or social grace. "I'm just being friendly, ACC Thomas. You looked tasty, so I'm just being friendly."

"Be friendly somewhere else," said Jenni.

Jones kept his hands elevated as he stepped back and turned, his smile gone, replaced with contorted anger and burning eyes. She remained with hands on hips as he strode back down the hall casting a look back of unhinged resentment.

Anwen moved to the door to see who her aunt was talking to. "What in the world just happened?" she asked.

"Stay away from him," said Jenni. "I don't like his approach, or attitude, or demeanor. Do you know him?"

Anwen replied he was a new janitor and that she had seen him only recently. They had never spoken.

Before they left the parking lot, Jenni fetched her laptop and did a search for Price Jones. "Several arrests for bar fights, once for vandalism, a sexual assault charge later dropped, and a suspect in a burglary we couldn't nail down," she said, scrolling the screen. "I'm going to file a formal notice with the school about this guy. Stay away from him, Anwen. Bad news."

***

Jones grabbed the mop bucket and left for the cellar where the school kept the cleaning supplies. It took strength—great strength—to hide the quivering anger. The basement had two small lockers for the janitorial staff and he began to change the work coveralls for street clothes. "Enough," he said to no one. "*Enough*. Screw her. She's not that f'ing hot. Screw all of them."

"She should have accepted you as her lover. How much more do you plan to take?" came a voice emanating from a dark corner.

Jones banged against the open locker door as he spun around and squinted into the far reaches of the room. The tall stranger he had eaten with last night came out of the shadows.

"What?" asked Jones. "What are you doing here? You scared the hell out of me."

"Not likely," said his new friend. "But to the point, how much are you going to take? When will you make people notice you?"

Still shaken by the sudden appearance of the man, Jones said, "I asked you what you're doing here, mate. It's weird."

"I rent a place nearby. You told me you worked here," said the tall, pale man.

"Oh yeah? Well, I'm off work now," said Jones. "And I want to go home." Enough of this day and its realities—it was time to get online with his cyber-mates.

"Do you believe in God?"

No telling where the old man was going with this, but once he peeled off these work clothes and got back into jeans, this whole blind school could kiss his arse. His new friend was a little creepy and some sort of God question fit the guy's style, but Jones enjoyed talking with him. The conversation last night at dinner ranked as the best conversation he'd had in years. The man—Adal—made a great listener.

"Yeah. When I'm Kanamel the Crusher. It's a great online game. I'm level thirty-seven. Crushing enemies, causing devastation. Whacking off heads." Jones slid into his shoes. "I use a two-handed sword—a Scottish claymore. Seizing women, who always yield to me. They want me to take them. Then I'm God. Then I'm respected. And feared. A god."

Moloch gave his tight smile. "Yes. Yes, you can be God here, too. Among these stupid people."

"Oh yeah?" asked Jones, tucking his shirt. The inside of the locker door held a small mirror. Jones checked himself, smoothing back his hair, and caught Moloch motioning a hairy hand in the reflection. The mirror image changed. Now stood Kanamel the Crusher looking back at him, armored and wielding a sword. He looked strong, handsome, and feared.

"Do you know how to hate?" asked Adal. "Really, truly hate?"

"Oh yes," said Kanamel, still looking in the mirror. "Yes. With a passion. Hate is power."

Chapter 18

The team arrived in Cardiff. They cleared customs, assembled, and argued about the next immediate steps. Cole wanted first to go to the local police and introduce their effort. Nadine wanted to go to the hotel and establish a base of operations. Francois agreed both these endeavors were important and could take place after he stopped at a shop or two so he could dress in an appropriate manner. They went to the hotel.

Nadine had booked three adjoining rooms and they agreed to meet at the bar/coffee shop off the lobby. She unpacked, recharged her tablet, calibrated her two laptops, and connected through the hotel's Wi-Fi with her security encryptions. No new information on Moloch showed, but she expected those results. He couldn't hide from her and once she found him, they would tail him. She hummed a Gillian Welch tune as she worked. This whole field agent thing beat the pants off being cooped up in the apartment providing information to others. Plus, this case had a religious and spiritual dimension which was completely new and a little weird.

Completing her work, she considered the act of prayer. *It wouldn't be weird to do that,* she thought. *This whole thing has such a metaphysical component.*

She had associated her consciousness with a higher being before, but not applied in a structured manner. So she forced herself to do something she'd never done before—have a dialogue, a formal prayer. She stood still, tilted her head, and looked at the ceiling.

Okay, I believe in you. That's the biggie, right? So let's get over that. It's the whole bearded looks-like-grandpa thing. I'm sorry, but I don't buy that. Maybe that's not a deal-breaker. I know you are out there. But how active are you? Hand of God and all that stuff.

Eyes closed, her breath came deep and slow.

I've read the Bible. Digested it. I guess you'd know that. I don't get you in the Old Testament. Sorry. I just don't get all the death, destruction, and revenge. Particularly when the New Testament is all about love. I sure wish that segue was a little better defined.

Here she smiled and rolled her shoulders, keeping her eyes closed. *Okay, this probably isn't the time to provide literary criticism of that book. Your book. Sorry.*

She moved to sit on the edge of the bed, clasped her hands, and bowed her head. Maybe the whole physical prayer bit with hands and head and who-knows-what-else was important, although a playbook or flow diagram would make things a lot easier. But she sensed the physical posture was worth a shot in case some physiological channeling took place in this position.

Okay, let's go to the current situation. This whole thing with Cole and Francois—it's got me messed up metaphysically. Evil as a walking, talking thing.

She shook her head and began to stand, sat back and crossed her hands, and closed her eyes again.

So, a little clarity on that would be good. And thank you for everything. I suppose I'm blessed. My life's pretty good. So thanks. Whatever you have done in my life, thanks.

She stood, still unquenched. She looked around the room at the laptops and tablet and cell phone. She opened her arms and held her palms upward in supplication.

Let's give this position a try. Now, I know you've got a lot on your plate, but I want to ask for one more thing from you. It seems selfish. Put all those starving kids and people living in horror and despair ahead of me in line. That's more important.

She paused.

Okay, maybe assuming you have a queue shows the limits of my thinking. I'm not telling you what to do. I do that a lot, but not now. Not with you. So here's the problem. Help me understand love. There's a hole in me. I try, God, I really do. My wiring just doesn't let me interact and understand. I need your help on that. It would mean a lot. And again, thanks for all you have done for me. Please just toss in that one thing. That one request. Thanks for your time. Amen.

***

Cole met Nadine at the elevator. Off the lobby, they found Francois in a clothing shop trying to decide on a woolen scarf. He chose the teal color, draping it around his neck.

"We need to get you a coat, Cole," said Nadine as they waited for Francois to make the purchase. "This isn't summer in Texas."

He smiled back. "Later. I'll survive. Let's get some coffee and get to the local cops. I've called them to let them know we needed to talk. Let's find Moloch. Let's get some answers." A fresh trail started here and the hunt was on. The chaotic horrors surrounding that day in Rockport still came hard and sure. The smells, the cries, the death—justice called and now was the time for answers.

The one distracting element—a burr-under-the-saddle realization for Cole—was the lateness of his call to the Cardiff police. The team introductions and information on Moloch should have been passed on prior to their departure from Texas. It was unprofessional to appear at their doorsteps without a prior briefing. Moloch was dangerous. Cole owed it to the local cops to let them know of the man's arrival on their turf. He would expect the same courtesy. The phone call that morning to the Cardiff police was routed to a low-level clerk who told Cole to "drop by." An earlier warning would have connected him to someone higher up the Cardiff police food chain. He'd screwed up, and it rankled him.

The three of them strode into the empty pub and headed for a table in a remote corner. Nadine and Francois led the way. Cole froze. The hair on the back of his neck stood on end, his nostrils flared, and his jaw clamped while he instinctively slapped his right hip, reaching for a nonexistent .40 caliber pistol. He scanned the room.

In the opposite far corner sat Moloch. Surrounded by empty tables, near a door leading to the outdoor porch, he perched upright and observant. Before him sat three cups of coffee, untouched and steaming. He gave a slight nod and signaled with one long, hairy finger. Come.

Cole's chest contracted and fear coursed through him. *Move*, he thought. *Move. You are Cole by-God Garza. Go right at that sumbitch.*

Resolve shoved aside fear. He strode toward Moloch's table.

He took the chair opposite, their eyes locked. "Let's talk," he said, spinning the chair around prior to sitting, in case events required sudden action.

The glass door behind Moloch lay ajar. The sound of birds chirping combined with the clink of glasses behind the coffee bar. Cole's senses, flooded by adrenaline, caught everything.

Moloch chuckled, speaking with mirth. "Oh, yes. Let's do. Tell me. How is Martha? Or should I tell you?"

Cole jerked back, recovered, and coiled to spring across the table to take Moloch by the neck. From across the room Francois barked, "L'ennemi!" and Cole risked a quick glance over his shoulder to see the priest flinging one tail of the scarf around his neck, girded for battle. Francois's face had become florid, his blood on fire. He drove toward Moloch's table, leaning forward and aggressive—a knight charging. Nadine lagged behind.

Cole turned back to Moloch, but the enemy's tight-smiling gaze had left Cole and now focused on Francois's approach. His face changed to anger and disdain. Cole remained coiled, hearing the tromping of Francois's advance on the wooden floor.

Moloch emitted a deep, sibilant, growling hiss—a sound Cole never imagined a human could produce. Every hair on his body stood at attention.

Francois had clearly not considered sitting. He stood at the edge of the table, leaned far forward and placed two curled fists on the tabletop. "Through the power of Jesus Christ!" he spat at Moloch. Francois leaned toward Moloch's face, eyes boring holes.

"Tell your priest friend to be quiet," said Moloch, turning to Cole. "You and I have things to discuss." The table began to shake. Cole smelled something putrid, something long dead.

"Through the authority and power of Jesus Christ!" repeated Francois, hard and commanding. His body vibrated with righteousness, face scarlet.

"Make him be silent, or I will silence him," growled Moloch to Cole. "You have questions and I have answers. We cannot talk of such things while the priest babbles."

The table shook with more violence. All three coffee cups spilled over into their saucers.

"I rebuke you. Through the power of Jesus Christ, I rebuke you!" commanded Francois, fists clenched like a boxer's, and fire in his voice. He leaned closer to Moloch, spitting at his face. "You have no dominion here. By great God almighty and his son Jesus Christ, I command you to depart!"

Cole focused on Moloch's face, now contorted as a cloth sack full of writhing creatures. Cole's heart pounded as he gathered his resources, still intent on physically confronting Moloch. The strength of Francois washed over him as the remnants of fear left, replaced by power and conviction.

Moloch's rage spilled over. The table flew toward Cole and Francois as Moloch stood and pointed a long, hairy finger at Nadine, standing several feet away.

"Too late!" howled Moloch. "Too late for the little chat you just had! Your god won't listen!"

Cole and Francois turned to Nadine, seeing her stand statue-still, horror painted on her face. The patio door behind Moloch's chair opened further, and when Cole and Francois whipped back around, Moloch was gone.

Cole rushed to Nadine's side and grabbed her upper arms. She broke his grip and hugged him hard, repeating, "No, no, no." Francois bowled through the patio door, searching.

Francois came back and approached them, shaking. "He has fled. A coward, a liar. He has fled."

Nadine took one arm from around Cole and wrapped it around Francois's neck, dragging him close and tight. The three of them stood as one.

They released each other as the sole wait staff approached to straighten things. Cole and Francois helped to upright the table. Both saw the claw marks etched in the tabletop where Moloch had sat. They looked at each other, neither saying a word.

Chapter 19

They walked, silent, to another pub that was quiet and mostly empty at this early hour. None of them wanted to remain at the hotel. Francois led the way. Cole held Nadine's hand.

They went to a waist-high table wrapped around a wooden support column. All three stood, leaned on the tabletop and used the barstools placed around it for footrests. Francois ordered three cognacs and coffee, lit a cigarette, and cast glances back and forth at his friends. He held suspended a shaking hand, the Gauloises pinched between thumb and forefinger, and pointed to it with the other.

"Not fear," he said. "Consequences. The aftermath." He had battled evil, one on one. The enemy had fled, to be sure, and as such some measure of victory may be claimed. The encounter provided insight and knowledge if one might reflect. The creature had the ability to foresee their movement. The encounter clearly had been planned. The creature feared—not him, perhaps—but feared the power he brought. Such a thing was to be expected. The creature moved with an inhuman rapidity. The outside porch was large, yet no sign of the creature remained once it had fled. And it *had* fled, of this he could be sure. The question of conflict and possible outcomes had it remained and fought still loomed unanswered.

"I know it's not fear, Francois," said Cole. "I've met some tough hombres in my time. You're one of them. Fearless." He shook his head and scanned the room, jaw tight.

"He will not reappear among us," said Francois. The sheriff stood on high alert, but Francois knew such a response was unnecessary at this point. "He has other business here. Business that he does not believe will include us. And so, that is our next task."

Nadine tossed back the cognac with a grimace. "I could use some help. I rarely say it. But I mean it now. I'm shaking, and it damn sure is fear." Cole squeezed her upper arm. Francois lit her a smoke. She took the cigarette, hand trembling. "And don't either of you mentally place this moment in your personal 'well, she's a woman' box. You will mightily piss me off if you do."

"I don't think that," said Cole. "You're a hard biscuit. This was traumatic as hell. It's understandable. You should have seen me coming out of the nursing home after all the carnage. I was a mess."

Cole's confession appeared to help. Nadine nodded, still attempting to take deep breaths.

"What was all that? For a singular moment, we existed inside a different dimension. A different reality," she said, as she took a puff and blew smoke at the ceiling.

Francois did not respond, lips pursed, staring into personal space. Cole let go of her arm and signaled to the barkeep for another round.

"What did he mean, Nadine?" asked Cole. "Too late for that chat. What was that all about?"

"Not yet. No," said Nadine. "Who is he? Did you smell him when Francois got in his face? I've never … I mean never ever. What is he? Those three cups of coffee? Do you have another kind of smoke, Francois? These don't taste good. He was *expecting* us."

"And yet you do not inhale, mon ami, so one must question why it matters."

"I don't poke myself in the eye with forks, either, so what the hell does inhaling have to do with anything? What was he?"

They were on perilous ground at this fragile moment and yet Francois was certain such a reality must be reinforced. This woman held, it was true, keys to the secular kingdom with regard to tracking the creature and providing details on background and potential movements. She must accept the spiritual ramifications if her contributions were to be fully realized.

"Evil. A creature. Do not be alarmed, but do not doubt, mon ami."

She leaned back and asked Cole, "Am I going crazy? Did I really see all that? His face—contorting. It's not so much what I saw. It's what I felt. The power. It stank. Actually smelled."

The other two nodded.

"And your power, Francois," she continued. "I felt it. Stronger. Clean. A surge of unseen power. Except it shone. Somehow, unseen, it shone."

They leaned silently for a while, their heads close together above the high table. The pub's lone staff cleaned glasses behind the bar. A slight salt tang filled the air from two open windows.

"He mentioned Martha," said Cole. "Dead these five years. I want the bastard. I want to throttle some answers out of him."

"Such a thing will not be possible," said Francois.

Cole snapped his head toward the priest. "Why not?"

"I have learned," said Francois. He went on to explain this encounter, his first true effort, had taught him some things. He had acquired a sense the creature would not succumb to coercion or direction. At this point, he could only force Moloch to leave, to run. He still had no clear idea how they would defeat this enemy. Then he gently explained that Cole would not find answers from this creature—only pain.

They all spoke in short, hushed sentences, digesting the encounter. Each snippet of conversation showed him that Cole and Nadine had internalized the scene in some way that made sense to them. Francois recognized this form of rationalization, and would not allow it.

"It is not terribly complicated," he said. "He is evil. A creature of evil. Do not use the mind to rationalize. These encounters do not have to take place in the middle of night, in an old house, or on a mountaintop. No. They walk among us. It is not complicated. Do not let it be so."

"I'm with Francois," said Cole. "He's right. It's taken a while, but Moloch is what he is." The sheriff squinted into Francois's face. "But I'll bet the sumbitch can be taken down."

Francois sighed and turned to Nadine. "Please tell us, mon ami. What is too late? This chat the creature spoke of."

Nadine placed her palms flat on the table, stared at the space between them, and told them of her prayer, her first true talk with God.

"Yes! Of course," said Francois. "I felt it within you. A subtle change. Now this I shall tell you is of the greatest importance. Please look at me."

Nadine lifted her head, lost.

"It is *never* too late," barked Francois. "*Never*! You have begun on a path. Walk it. Persister! Continue. God listens. God loves you. Do not listen to the deceiver!"

"I agree, Nadine," said Cole. "Believe. Just believe. But don't expect immediate answers. Those can be a might hard to come by."

"You perceive that as helpful?" Francois asked Cole, removing his glasses and waving them toward Nadine. "To cast restrictions?" It was unbelievable to him that the sheriff would add such a personal comment at this point in time.

"It's personal," said Cole.

"Mon Dieu! But of course it is personal. That would, in fact, be the entire point!" He turned to Nadine. "No. Continue your path. Answers will be revealed. Perhaps not with the speed and clarity expected by our sheriff, but revealed nonetheless."

They finished their drinks and formulated a plan. The first step entailed calling on the local police, an activity Francois understood to be integral to the tracking of Moloch. Cole confessed to both of them that he should have done more to prepare the Cardiff authorities for their arrival and, more importantly, the arrival of their quarry. Francois accepted this as a matter of police protocol, but remained focused on the upcoming battle. He knew, beyond a shadow of a doubt, that Moloch would perpetrate evil in Cardiff.

As they gathered to leave, Cole grabbed Francois by the arm. "Thank you. Merci beaucoup. From the bottom of my heart. If I had tangled with Moloch, I don't know if I could have handled him without you."

He patted Cole on the side. "Please forget all of this tangling business. It cannot come to physical violence. But be assured, we are not through, my friend. We are not finished with this thing."

Chapter 20

Price Jones slid the Welch Fusiliers trench knife into his backpack and went to work, the large leaf-shaped blade honed to a razor's edge. The time had come. They would see. Someone walked with him—someone inside his head. Kanamel the Crusher emanated hatred, plucking slights and wrongs against him from both recent and long-ago memory. So many wrongs heaped and piled on in the past, delivered by those too stupid to know. Now they would pay. Kanamel held no fear. Kanamel stood strong, righteous, and absolute.

Last night, he'd walked with the tall friend back into Cardiff's city center. His friend Adal wasn't a stranger anymore. Adal understood him and all his frustrations. More importantly, he implied he knew how to do something about it.

"Take the bus?" Price had asked last night.

"No. Let us walk. We can discuss plans," said Adal Moloch.

Jones didn't know what plans he referred to, but a walk with his friend beat a bus ride. A fine mist moved from the sea, and streetlights few and far between shone this far from the city center. The rejection by that bitch, the constable, still left him seething. She wasn't that fucking hot. Certainly not so hot that she could reject him as if he were garbage. What a stupid bitch. To compound the shame, several of those pathetic blind students—with their damn acute hearing—had overheard the conversation. They'd talked and laughed about it when he strode along the hall to retrieve the mop and bucket. They rejected him. They laughed at him. Stupid ingrate blind kids.

The darkness enveloped them as they walked. The tang of salt air lay on Jones's face, and his blood pressure was still sky high.

"What it is, is disrespect. For a bloody fact," said Jones. "Disrespect from a bunch of damn blind people. And that damn constable, Miss thinks-she's-so-hot. They can't treat me that way!" He spat the words. "I deserve better. I demand better." He used his jacket sleeve to wipe flecks of spittle that formed at the corners of his mouth.

"I know you hate them," said Moloch. "But you won't change it, will you? You won't show them. Show them your power. Your capabilities."

They approached a lone streetlight. Moloch flicked a finger and the light sputtered off. That was cool. This codger—no, this friend—had capabilities, too. Righteous capabilities. The darkness continued, their wet footfalls the sole sound.

"How?" asked Jones. "They are too stupid to understand if I did show them. Stupid. Goddamn stupid people."

An arm took his shoulder and the back of two long fingers touched his neck. Bristly hair rubbed, comforting. They stopped and stood still.

Adal's voice came loud and clear but no words were spoken. "Hate them all. Show them. Be proud of what you can do. Become powerful. Thrive on the hate you feel. Thrive, grow strong, Kanamel. Show them."

A new power surged. His power, the power of the Crusher, given by a force inside him. Oh, it felt so good. He could see, now. It was clear what had to be done. What must be done. Now, yes, Kanamel the Crusher lived.

Chapter 21

Rattled to the core, Nadine began to recover. Something inside had changed. On the drive to the police station both Cole and Francois insisted she sit in the front passenger seat. She sensed this was their way of ensuring she wouldn't feel isolated, and her comments during the short drive were met with affirmations and support. She began to develop, for the first time in her life, a feeling of something bigger than herself—the love of her companions and calm from another source. It was all good, and clean, and too new to completely digest. She thought it best to ride it like a wave and absorb the process. Then there were the bookends—Cole and Francois. Both displayed remarkable courage, undaunted. The whole scene with Moloch had rocked the foundation of her belief system, but those two buttressed it and, most importantly, provided her an empathetic environment to sort things out. All those years as ostensibly a member of numerous teams, she had never felt a real part of any of them. Those past endeavors had relegated her to the geeky sort-the-data and find-the-answers role. But not now. Nope, this was a team, together, and teammates supported each other.

They walked into the South Wales Police office, manned at the entrance by a desk sergeant.

"Hi. My name's Cole Garza. I'm the Sheriff of Aransas County, Texas. I called earlier today." Cole presented his badge and ID.

The desk sergeant took a glance and nodded.

"These are my companions, Francois Domaine and Nadine May. We'd like to talk with someone in authority."

"And now what would that discussion with someone in authority be pertaining to?" asked the desk sergeant, continuing to look at his computer monitor while he worked.

Nadine's blood rose. She stepped forward and said, "Pertaining to matters of international security. May I assume you're willing to be held personally responsible for obstructing the information we wish to convey?" Her right hand tapped a triplet beat on the sergeant's desktop.

She then turned to Cole and Francois. Cole cast glances at the ceiling and Francois shrugged. She turned again to glare at the desk sergeant, who deigned to use the phone and make a call, clearly attempting to rid himself of this crazy American woman.

"ACC Thomas. Sergeant Mills here," said the desk sergeant. "I have a law officer—an American—here with some associates who would appreciate seeing you. Yes. Yes. Thank you, ACC Thomas. I'll send them up."

The desk sergeant pointed to the elevators. "Fifth floor. Assistant Chief Constable Thomas."

Cole thanked him, Francois gave a short bow of appreciation and rearranged his teal scarf, and Nadine scowled. Jenni Thomas met them on the fifth floor, introductions were made, and they moved into a small conference room.

"What can the South Wales Police Department do for you, Sheriff?" asked Jenni.

Cole explained the Rockport murders—Jenni let them know she had read about them through the world news outlets—and the pursuit of a possible suspect who had appeared in Cardiff and had encountered them just two hours ago.

"I should have contacted you folks about this suspect the moment I knew he'd landed in your jurisdiction," said Cole. "My screw-up. I believe this guy is dangerous. This isn't the right way to do this, showing up out of the blue, and I apologize."

Nadine knew that was a hard thing for Cole to do, since it painted them in an amateurish light. But the apology would help in her area of expertise—the coordination of information flow.

Jenni apparently decided this was legitimate business and called ACC Gavin Morris, asking him to join them, and explaining that protocol dictated the head of the street cops for Cardiff should become involved.

"And you, Ms. May. Your involvement?" asked Jenni.

"Data. Information. Search criteria, etcetera. Finding answers, primarily," replied Nadine. "Do you use AHT here?"

She had invented The Advanced Heuristic Toolset. Leveraged by the NSA, CIA, Homeland Security, FBI, and shared around the globe with other law enforcement entities, AHT had become an investigative standard. It allowed discovery through data mining and algorithmic assumptions under less than optimal input ranges. Within the often-murky world of crime, it comprised a valued tool.

Jenni's surprise showed. Outside law enforcement and intelligence communities, the AHT remained unknown. "We may," Jenni said. "Why do you ask?"

"I created it."

"Did you now? Well, yes," said Jenni. "In fact we do utilize it." Her body language indicated that she found this extremely cool. "You and I have a lot to talk about, Ms. May. I've some ideas about the application I'd love to discuss with you, if you wouldn't mind."

Nadine relaxed. Jenni was one of her "people"—a computer savvy cop who bridged theory with practical application. "Love to," said Nadine. "But first, this thing the three of us are chasing. We could use some help."

"Thing?" asked Jenni just as the door opened and ACC Morris entered, followed by introductions.

"Right," said Morris. "What's this all about?"

Cole repeated the tale to Morris. Jenni piped in with Nadine's credentials, although Morris snorted at the AHT reference.

"Alright. What about you?" asked Morris, pointing at Francois. "Father Domaine, was it? What's your association with this case? Spiritual advisor?" Morris gave a chuckle as he finished.

"I am here to do battle," said Francois.

That landed with a thump, so Morris turned his attention back to Cole. "Sheriff. A Texas sheriff."

"Yessir," replied Cole.

"Is there some sort of arrangement with our governments regarding this case?" asked Morris.

"Not exactly," said Cole. "Although the Vatican supports our efforts."

Morris and Jenni looked at each other across the table.

"The Vatican?" asked Morris.

"Oui," said Francois.

"Yessir," said Cole.

That's a pretty nice hole card, thought Nadine. *Support of the pope and all. Well played, Cole.* Catholic or not, few could remain immune to the gravitas the head of the church carried.

Jenni became more animated. "This is proving a great interruption in what had turned out a boring day. The AHT creator, a Texas sheriff, and the Vatican. Goodness."

"So on whose authority do you request assistance?" asked Morris.

"God's," said Francois with finality. "It is possible to smoke here?"

"No," said Morris. Francois's exasperation showed.

"Would any of you like something to drink?" asked Jenni. "This may develop into a longer discussion than anticipated."

"Coffee, if you have it," said Cole. "All around."

Jenni pushed an intercom button and asked for three coffees. The sterile white room was cool, and Francois rearranged his scarf.

Nadine saw that Cole had clearly tried to avoid the "on whose authority" question, instead leveraging universal cooperation among all legitimate law enforcement organizations. But now Francois had stated his case and brought the issue to the forefront. This would require some sidestepping from her and Cole, which was fine except that Francois would undoubtedly keep coming back to his anchor point. Any spiritual component in a case, she knew from past experience, drove law people nuts.

"God's authority," said Morris as he cast a glance at Jenni. "That's quite potent. Anyone else? Someone of a more secular position?"

"Well, sir, in the non-spiritual realm, I suppose the authority of the folks who elected me in Aransas County," said Cole.

Eyes hooded, Morris did not react. Nadine eyeballed this Morris person as her foot began a triple rhythm on the floor. The whole bona fides thing had become tedious. She had worked with law enforcement types like Morris many times. They were good cops, but in her opinion they got too bogged down in dotting the i's and crossing the t's.

"Have him call Jeeter," said Nadine. "Let's get going on this."

"Who?" asked Jenni.

"Captain Johnson," said Cole. "Head of the Texas Rangers. Although at this point I don't think it's necessary to contact him." He gave Nadine a look. She smiled back.

This got the attention of both Jenni Thomas and Gavin Morris. Nadine understood that when you toss out the head of the Texas Rangers as a contact point—especially outside Texas and more so outside the US—the response would invariably be heightened curiosity. But Cole didn't need to give her that "Why in the hell did you bring up Jeeter Johnson" look. After all, he'd played his hole card about the Vatican and the whole point of the entire silly exercise was to get cooperation from these folks.

A soft tap on the door, followed by the appearance of a young assistant carrying a tray with three cups of coffee, allowed for a small break in the conversation. Nadine could read Cole's body language, indicating he would try and formulate some action to avoid the phone call. That made no sense to her, since Jeeter could provide a kick-off point.

"It's still early in Texas," she said, pointing to the table's speakerphone.

Jenni moved the phone closer, hit the speaker button, and asked Cole for the number. She dialed and three rings later Jeeter Johnson answered. Cole shifted uncomfortably. Francois sniffed at then sipped the coffee. Nadine was looking forward to the exchange.

"Captain Johnson," said Jenni. "ACC Thomas here, along with ACC Morris of the South Wales Police Department."

"Are my people alright?" asked Johnson. "Any problems?"

Francois looked at his companions, apparently unaware he had become one of the head Ranger's "people."

"No sir, no problems, and everyone's fine," said Jenni. "We're just trying to get an understanding of the lines of authority. Sheriff Garza, Ms. May, and Father Domaine are here with us on the speakerphone."

"Cole, you okay?" asked Johnson.

"Yessir, fine. This call wasn't my idea. It's at the insistence of ACC Thomas and Morris."

A short pause followed before Johnson asked, "Y'all keep tossing that out, so what the hell is an ACC?"

Gavin Morris began to interject, but Jenni raised her hand, stopping him. "Assistant Chief Constable, Captain," said Jenni. "Again, no issues other than some clarification. We are here to help."

"Nadine, you there?" asked Johnson.

"How you, Jeeter?" Nadine replied. She had worked with him multiple times and liked both him and the professionalism of the Rangers, although she didn't buy into the whole Lone Star ethos and the added baggage that mindset carried. She also knew she scared them for some reason. That made for interesting dynamics and awfully short conversations, so Jeeter wouldn't chat with her beyond the minimum, which was okay.

"I'm fine. Father Domaine? We haven't met. I hope things are going well."

Nadine had dug up enough background on this case to understand that Jeeter likely intended to keep the Vatican happy, and keep the governor off his butt. If this blew up, the governor would insist Jeeter deal with what he'd call "the morons" at the State Department. She'd snooped and read communiqués on that history and "hot pursuit" simply pissed off the Harvard School of government bureaucrats at State.

"The honor is mine, Capitaine," said Francois. "The sheriff speaks highly of you, and the church is most appreciative of your assistance. Oui, things are moving. How they will culminate, one does not know at this point."

"Alright, we've got the verbal arm-squeezin' out of the way, so what's the issue?" asked Johnson.

Morris took this opportunity to interject. "Again, Captain, no particular issue. We just want context. We can assume this is, in fact, an official visit by the sheriff and his cohorts?"

The five waited through another pause on the speakerphone, this one longer than the last. "Official in the sense it's part of an ongoing investigation. That's about it," said Johnson.

Morris and Jenni looked at each other, nodding with satisfaction.

Johnson continued. "Cole, are y'all convinced this hombre is dangerous?"

"Yessir," said Cole. "Pretty much guarantee it."

A third pause, this one the longest yet. Nadine knew guns would surely be the next topic. Regardless of Jeeter's sometimes annoying outlook, he had exhibited time and again that when he backed a team he took that with the utmost seriousness, and would now consider the three of them his responsibility. He never left someone on his team hung out, exposed, and would do his best to make sure they were protected by what he considered the answer to pretty much any situation—firepower. And the more the better. You couldn't fault the guy, since he was a product of his environment and all that, but this would fly like a lead balloon with the Welsh police.

"Thomas, Morris, do you people carry?"

"What?" asked Morris. Jenni's body language indicated she knew what Jeeter meant.

"Arms. Weapons. Guns," said Johnson.

"Absolutely not," said Morris. "This isn't the wild west where we shoot criminals on sight. A bit of a thumping, perhaps, then off to jail."

There it was, a cultural disconnect as wide as the Atlantic Ocean. Nadine's gut told her that Jeeter likely had come to expect such gross oversimplification of his world and had certainly heard it more than a few times in his own country and, knowing him, would get all prickly, which wouldn't be helpful.

"Y'all might consider just shooting them. Saves on court costs," said Johnson.

Silence ensued on both ends of the line for several seconds. Johnson continued, "What's the chance of making an exception for the sheriff? Not a hog leg, just something that can inflict lead poisoning if needed."

Neither Jenni nor Morris understood "hog leg," but they evidently grasped the reference to lead poisoning. "Sir," said Jenni. "We are in no position to fulfill such a request. We will offer whatever assistance we can within the laws of Wales and the United Kingdom. And we're happy to, now that we have had the opportunity to talk with you."

"Well, I had to ask," said Johnson. "Anyway, Cole, you keep your head down. And tight, remember? Damn tight."

"Will do, sir," said Cole.

The five sat around the speakerphone and looked at each other, all but one ready to end the conversation.

"One final thing, Captain," said Morris. "I assume Sheriff Garza is in charge of your contingent?"

"Right out of the chute, I'd say yes," said Johnson. "But anytime you toss Nadine in the mix, 'who's in charge' sorta goes out the window."

She took this as a vast compliment, and smiled. She had received more backup, more support. Jenni smiled as well, apparently enjoying the assertion that this woman from Texas was a force unto herself.

"Actually, sir," said Cole, "Father Domaine in many ways leads this effort. At least when needed. All in all, we're working as a team."

"Alright, Cole," said Johnson. "This doesn't sound like I need to make any phone calls myself. Communicate, son. And keep it tight."

The phone call ended. Morris looked hard at Cole and added, "No wild west, Sheriff. We do not do such things. Understood?"

Jenni jumped in to keep the conversation civil. "I'm sure the sheriff understands. Now, let's get to the details. Who is this suspect?"

Nadine handed her a thumb drive with Moloch's picture taken from several angles.

Cole described their encounter with him a few hours ago, opting not to include the parts inexplicable in earthly terms, including the part where Moloch had been expecting them. "He fled when we questioned him," said Cole. "He's up to something. And it's liable to be a very bad something."

At that moment, a policeman flung open the door and blurted out, "School for the Blind. Five separate emergency calls. Killings. A lot of them."

Chapter 22

Kanamel the Crusher emerged from his basement locker space, wearing street clothes and wielding the sword-like trench knife. The time had come. They would know him now. Oh, the power, the power and the righteousness—shining bright and true and strong.

He ascended the first flight of stairs and stood near a classroom with ten students and an instructor. The door stood open and he entered.

"Yes? Can I help—?" said the instructor. He saw the knife and yelled, "Get out! Get out now!"

Jones swung a backhand blow. The instructor hung on the blade, gurgling, as blood flew from his carotid artery. Jones held him suspended on the blade, and looked over his shoulder at the room of students, smiling. Several of them already fingered their cell phones, frantically dialing. Their acute hearing caught the death rattle from the instructor. Jones snatched the blade from the instructor's throat, let him drop, and screamed, "Put down the phones! Now!"

Vicious slashes rained on sightless students. "Silence!" said Kanamel the Crusher. "You will be silent! You will pay attention to me!"

Spoken prayers from several of the students mixed with the moans of the wounded. Cell phones lay on the floor, lines still open to the Cardiff Police emergency center.

"Listen to me, you stupid people!" said Kanamel. "*I'm* your Lord! *This* is your heaven. I'll decide who lives and dies. Listen to me!"

The uninjured students shivered and wept, listening as he paced the wooden floor among them. This was too easy for Kanamel. The situation presented no challenge for a man of his capabilities. He moved to the door, wooden floor creaking under his footsteps. Outside the door, a female administrator shook as she whispered urgently on her cell phone. She raised her head and saw the magnificent figure standing before her, speckled with blotches of the enemy's blood. The knife thrust in below her sternum and he lifted her off the ground.

"I decide," he said. "I wield. Kanamel the Crusher. Know who I am." He let her body fall, her weight pulling her off the blade. He moved down the hall to enter another room.

***

Jenni and Gavin Morris leapt from the conference table at Police Headquarters and rushed from the room where they joined dozens of officers taking the stairs. No one waited for the elevator.

Francois broke the spell among the three of them. "We must go there as well! Aller!"

"Damn right," said Cole, on Francois's heels. He turned and saw Nadine hesitate, an element of fear back in her eyes.

"We can do this, Nadine," said Cole. "We can all cowboy up together, and do this."

She snapped out of it, fire returning. "Okay. The team. Yeah, we can do this," she said, nodding to him and accelerating out of the room.

The elevator doors stood open. On the ride down, Cole took Nadine's hand and squeezed. Francois saw the gesture and took Cole and Nadine's free hands, making a circle. "The power of God through his son, Jesus Christ," said Francois.

"The power of God," said Cole.

"We could use a can of whup ass, God," said Nadine as the elevator doors opened.

"Suffisant," said Francois to Nadine as they rushed to the parked car.

Cole drove their rental car at breakneck speed to the school, surrounded by cop cars and sirens and flashing lights. None of the officers paid them any heed.

He wheeled around the parking lot, took a small gravel drive to the back of the school, slid to a stop, and flung open his door, exclaiming, "Stay together!"

They approached one of several back doors and heard screams from the window of a corner room. The three burst into the hallway and dashed toward the sounds of terror, Francois leading. Cole slowed long enough to confirm Nadine followed. With Moloch on the loose, he wanted her to stay close.

Cole saw Jenni Price enter a door at the front of the building, adjacent to where cries of horror emanated, having a slight lead on the three of them. She did not hesitate, and entered the room.

"My date!" a voice screamed, echoing down the hallway. "She's arrived! Let's consummate this arrangement, Assistant Chief Constable!"

Sounds of a struggle followed. Francois moved as a fired cannonball, showing amazing agility and speed. He accelerated and entered the room at full speed, Cole on his heels. They entered the hellish scene of dead young people, a floor flooded with blood, and a nightmare sitting on the floor, legs spread, with a knife blade against Jenni Thomas's neck. His other hand jerked her hair back to give his blade more exposure. Both Cole and Francois knew the look on the madman's face, one having seen it twice before and the other many, many times.

"She fought!" the nightmare screamed. "She tried! But Kanamel conquers!"

"Exorcizo te, omnis spiritus immunde, in nomine Dei Patris omnipotentis, et in noimine Jesu Christi Filii ejus," blurted Francois as rapidly as he could.

"No! In *my* name, priest," interrupted the madman. "In *my* name!"

This monster would kill Jenni and the only shot they had was to go right at him. That one thought flashed as Cole burst toward the two on the floor, making four accelerating sprint strides across the large room before losing his footing and sliding on the thick blood pooled around him. He crashed through several desks as he headed for the two, feet first.

The killer released Jenni, rolled to one side, and rose to his knees to meet Cole's slide. He prepared to arc the blade into Cole's belly. Cole focused on the man's actions and lifted his knees to his chest. There was no stopping his momentum on the gore-drenched floor. The killer raised the blade, lips curled in triumph as he slid closer. At the final moment, Cole kicked both feet forward with every fiber, the effort so extreme his back left the floor. The kick delivered to the man's chest knocked him off his knees and sent him skidding against the back wall. Pools of blood waked in front of his slide.

Jenni rolled away and stood, prepared to reengage. Cole scrambled to his feet. It wasn't over. The apparition pulled himself up the back wall, smiling and verbally mocking in Latin.

A strange lull descended, ending when the madman threw back his head, howled with laughter, and drove the blade into his belly, ripping upward as he continued to howl. He slid back down the wall, sneering at Francois until his eyes ceased to show life.

Chapter 23

The police rushed toward the dead killer and the living students, some who now breathed their last breath. No one approached Cole while he took it all in. Cardiff police bumped Nadine aside at the entrance to the schoolroom-turned-abattoir as she absorbed the carnage, the groans, and the sickly-sweet smell. She retched and held back vomit. Francois took the opportunity to leave the room.

Nadine recovered enough to walk over to Jenni and hug her. Jenni hugged back and they stood alone in the moment.

Cole left the room, weaving through the throng of cops and emergency personnel, and saw the priest hesitate at a hallway intersection. He jogged to catch him.

"I don't know if he's here," said Cole as he pulled alongside Francois.

"I do not feel him," said Francois. "I fear he has fled. But let us look together."

They worked the halls and glanced inside the rooms, some littered with slaughtered students. They went to the basement, out a cellar door, and emerged to the waning overcast Cardiff day.

Francois stood and smelled the air, opening and closing his hands into fists. Tears of frustration and anger streamed down his face.

"The fault is mine," he said, turning to Cole. "I must learn; I must anticipate. This thing can be defeated. It is a coward, a liar, a deceiver. I do not fear it."

Cole had nothing to add that could help his friend. The man had shown bravery beyond measure, and Cole gained comfort standing next to him— a comfort from being with someone who would cover your back in the most extreme circumstances.

"Nadine," said Cole. "Let's get her."

"Oui, of course," said Francois. "Allow me to wait here. A warrior of God should not be seen weeping. S'il vous plait."

He squeezed Francois's shoulder and turned back into the building. Gavin Morris met him at the entrance to the room where the killer lay. Police continued to swarm the entire space.

"I want some answers, boyo," said Morris, jabbing his finger into Cole's chest. Gore still covered Cole's entire back, some of it dripping onto the floor. "And you're going to give them to me."

He looked past Morris at Nadine and Jenni still huddled, speaking softly to each other. Clearly Jenni had gone through hell during the encounter with the madman. Cole moved to join them.

"We'll come by later tonight. Your headquarters," said Cole, brushing past Morris. His black Comanche eyes conveyed the unmistakable message of "now is not the time." Morris let him pass.

As Cole approached the two, Nadine saw him and shook her head, leaving Cole to stand an awkward two paces away. When Jenni recognized him standing there, she pulled away from Nadine and gave him a look of "why?"

"Let's get out of here," said Cole, taking both of them by the arm. "Come on. Outside."

The three walked out the back door. Francois stood like a round rock, nose in the wind, fists clenching and unclenching. Hearing their footfalls, he turned and approached with concern.

"Mademoiselle Thomas, what bravery, what resolve," he said to Jenni. "A lion. Undaunted." He took one of her hands. With the other he started to reach for Nadine's hand, but she brushed by the gesture and embraced him, towering over him by several inches and burying her face in his hair.

"Francois, Francois," she said, eyes closed.

"It was me. I failed," said Jenni, biting her lip and looking to the distance. "I had him. I slipped. Then he had me. My daughter. All I could think of with the knife at my throat was my daughter." She fought back a sob, and straightened up, releasing Francois's hand.

"Sheriff," she said, turning to Cole. "You saved me. You. Undaunted, indeed."

"I slipped, too," said Cole. "Fell on my butt. Did what I had to do at the moment."

Nadine released Francois and walked over to him, taking his face with both hands. "You took that monster on, Cole. I saw it. I stood at the doorway when you kicked him."

They hugged, slowly rotating. "What happened to Moloch? This ... this horror. It was him, wasn't it?" she asked, pulling away.

"Oui," came the voice behind her. "Do not doubt it."

Emergency vehicles continued to pour into the front and back parking areas. Officers took Jenni and put her into an ambulance. Her niece, Anwen, joined her to provide support. No one paid the three Americans much mind, although an officer wrapped a blanket around both Nadine and Cole, helping cover the blood. They drifted back to their car.

"Shower, change, then back to the police station," said Cole.

"Is that necessary?" asked Francois. "They will focus on earthly matters. We must focus on other things."

"And I'll find where the sonofabitch went," said Nadine.

They drove in silence to the hotel, then entered the private sanctuary of their rooms and prepared for whatever lay ahead. Cole had never imagined such a sight of blood, death, and despair—Satan's slaughterhouse.

***

A sparse crowd occupied the airport at Cardiff when Moloch checked in for his flight. He addressed the staff member of Syrian Air and confirmed the direct flight to Damascus. He strode down the boarding tunnel, remaining inconspicuous for one of such peculiar appearance. The doors to the Airbus closed, and he sat back as the plane left UK airspace.

It had been years—decades—since anyone had pursued him. Science had taken over this world's approach to life. It made things so much easier now. And yet, there was resolve in the sheriff and fearlessness in the priest. The woman appeared tenacious and showed signs of finding the path. But they were scum, a mere diversion. It was time to return to his current base of operations, a place ancient and filled with the screams of scum centuries past and days current.

Chapter 24

Nadine showered, put on fresh clothes, and did not rest until she'd found him. It took her less than an hour. She uploaded Moloch's photo, added a descriptive, and sent it to an old friend. She knocked on Cole's door and pushed through when he opened it.

"Syria," she said. "We missed him. He lands in Damascus early tomorrow."

Cole closed the door behind her and she let him digest this information. Everything now existed in a much more complex environment. All the slaughter, chaos, and now the prospect of Syria had begun to get too large to grapple with. Her apartment was a long way away, and she began to yearn for the slower rhythms of her previous life. The whole affair—the whole quest—stood at a crossroads. The scenes and images from today were forever etched in her memory and made her skin crawl, made her question the worth of humankind. If that was what was in store down the road, she thought it perhaps best to chuck the whole thing. But that meant chucking this growing relationship with Cole, and while Francois took some time to warm up to, she would sorely miss him as well. She struggled to find the right way, the appropriate direction.

Cole evidently had similar feelings. "I just don't know, Nadine," he said, walking over to the small table where a bottle of scotch stood, delivered by room service on a tray with two glasses. "Syria. This thing is big. Maybe too big for me—for us."

Nadine sat at the table, stripped the plastic off a hotel glass, and poured a drink. So many thoughts were pinballing through her belief system; the horror of the school—the gore and blood, the dead bodies, the senseless evil—would affect the rest of her life. *I need an anchor point,* she thought. Her entire being, approach to life, and understanding of the world were in flux. While hard, definitive data of the physical realm always provided comfort, where the heck was the comfort in classifying Moloch in a new reality checkbox which included demons, evil spirits, and their interface with the human race? Cole appeared to have fewer burdens with that part of the puzzle, and she envied his conviction. She didn't share his consternation over whatever part he'd played in the lack of early coordination with the Cardiff police, which he exhibited with "should have" and "could have" comments. She swallowed the drink and poured another one.

"I'm so sorry," said Cole. "Sorry you had to see all that today. The worst of the human condition. Ugly, nasty stuff. You okay?"

"Not really," she said. "Not really okay at all."

Cole opened the window and traffic noise drifted in, along with a light rain. The cool salt air felt so good on her skin.

"We never did buy you a jacket," she said, making an attempt to converse about something real, something moored to her world.

They both stared out the window, lost in thought. "We could end it here," said Cole. "We tried. Go back to our normal lives."

"Mine is never going back to normal," she said. "At least not what's been normal until today. All the savagery. Mindless savagery. How do you cope with it? I mean, you've witnessed this before. What do you tell yourself? What do you key in on?"

"The little things," said Cole, turning to her. "I focus on the little things, the small miracles, the good things. The beauty of a wildflower, the laughter of a young child, a purple-hazed sunset. All the little wonders. I don't find answers among these, Nadine. I just find solace. Some measure of peace."

Nadine understood. Not to the extent Cole did, but she understood the context, the feeling. "And the big picture?" she asked. "What about that."

"Workin' on it," said Cole. He turned back to gaze through the window, swallowing the last of his drink.

They sat in silence. The smell of whisky mingled with the salty night air. A couple walked below their window, chatting.

"Do we end it?" she asked.

"I don't know," said Cole. "Workin' on that, too. Let's get with Francois in the morning. We've got to go by the police station. Should have gone today, but I don't think any of us needed that on top of everything else. Let's have a sit-down with Francois. We'll see."

Nadine stood and moved to the door, Cole following. She hesitated, hand on the doorknob, and turned to Cole. "So brave. Almost reckless. I knew you'd be like that in a tight spot. I froze."

"I slipped," said Cole. "Don't paint my taking on that lunatic as an act of bravery. And don't beat yourself up. There wasn't anything for you to do right then. Remember, Jenni Thomas and Francois had already arrived."

Nadine felt closer to Cole than ever before. She took a small step toward him, hoping he'd fill the small physical separation.

He did. Taking her in his arms, they kissed. Not with lust, passion, or intensity, but with a soft tenderness they both needed. Then it was over and they pulled apart, both a little embarrassed.

"Good night, Nadine," said Cole.

"Good night. I ... I just feel adrift. Right now, you're my rock to hold onto."

At dawn the next morning Nadine checked her inbox and noted the reply from her old friend. He said it would take a while to find what she looked for.

***

The three met for breakfast. Francois poked and took sniffs of the laverbread while he discussed it with the waitress.

"And so. It consists of what?" he asked.

The waitress seemed good-natured, apparently used to questions from tourists. "It's a seaweed puree mixed with oatmeal and then fried. Quite nice."

He remained unimpressed and lifted a corner of the laverbread with his fingers to check the underside. The saving grace consisted of a small side order of fresh cockles, which he ate with relish. Cole and Nadine ate little, neither with an appetite, although Cole commented that he found the Welsh seaweed concoction tasty. This was just another burden of traveling with his sheriff friend, although a relatively minor one. One could not expect the man to possess a great deal of appreciation toward cuisine, as evidenced by Cole's American tendency to pour salt and pepper and, disgustingly, ketchup on anything and everything placed before him.

"He's in Syria, Francois," said Nadine. "Damascus. I have a friend there who is trying to find the trail."

This left their next steps up in the air, and Francois digested the news in silence.

"Nadine and I wondered if it's over," said Cole, addressing the elephant on the table. "It's not just Syria, which is bad enough, but we have to ask ourselves to what avail. Can we do anything? I'll admit my tank's running on empty."

Francois raised a hand while he chewed and said, "Let us wait for a short moment. A park is nearby. It is a beautiful day. We shall talk there. You are both recovered?"

Cole and Nadine murmured affirmations and Cole tried to pay the breakfast check, a gesture Francois adamantly refused. "The church. Allow me. And I could not in good conscience have you pay for the seaweed substance. Perhaps ketchup may have helped."

The team walked in the park for a short while and paused to let Cole investigate the old roses. He explained the appeal of this variety known as ramblers, known for their toughness and fragrance. Francois politely feigned interest.

They settled at a park table. Cardiff's morning commute had just begun, the traffic noise muted. Francois lit a smoke and gave another to Nadine.

"We should discuss our situation," said Francois. "I shall begin. However, I shall first note how much the two of you have assisted me. Both of you. Of enormous help."

"It's been a team effort," said Cole. "But where do we go from here? Syria is a whole different ball game."

He again ignored the American tendency to address immediate actions without first exploring the periphery. "We must all learn," he said. "I have learned from yesterday. I now grasp more of the nature of this particular enemy." Francois better understood this creature's modus operandi. He comprehended some of the challenges. He remained unsure of resolution, but was more determined than ever to find out.

"Let us begin by calling this creature what it is," continued Francois. "Our Monsieur Moloch is a demon. We must all recognize that, understand that, and prepare for that. Comprenez vous?"

"What does 'a demon' mean, Francois?" asked Nadine. "I need to understand. What defines the attributes, the taxonomy, of a demon? I don't doubt you, I'm just trying to comprehend."

"Oui. This is normal," he said, pausing to take a long drag of the Gauloises. "It is a minion of Satan."

"Hmmm," said Nadine. "Okay, let's start instead with specific attributes. I'm not ready to internalize Satan, fallen angels, armies of darkness, and heavenly entities other than God."

Francois used both hands to slap the park tabletop, startling both of them. He rose from the plank seat. "You must *get* ready! Yesterday's events did not consist of a single madman! Those slaughtered young people represent Satan's work! Etre prepare! Be ready!"

He sat back down. Swans congregated along the riverbank moved into the slow current away from his strident human voice.

"Moloch is a demon. Under the direction of Satan," continued Francois. "This is what we deal with. Powerful, oui. But not without limits. He has taken an airplane. He cannot fly. He cannot personally inflict the atrocities we saw yesterday, although he caused them. Created them. With the help of someone who chose a path of evil. If we could arrange to see the past, with certainty we would view Moloch and this killer spending time together. N'est-ce pas?"

"I've become a helluva lot more matter-of-fact on the subject since last night. The evidence has piled up. So I believe you," said Cole. "Although I'm not convinced high-speed lead wouldn't work as well as an invocation. And Nadine, I understand the confusion. The skepticism. It has taken me awhile to get here, but I'm dang sure there now."

They both looked at Nadine. A flock of teal whistled overhead, turned, splash-landed on the river near them, and called to each other with feeding chortles. Nadine watched the ducks and spoke, barely audible.

"My world has changed beyond either of yours. Gimme a break on this. You've had years—a lifetime—Francois. And you've had a week, Cole. I know that's not a lot of time, but you began with a Christian foundation. And you've dealt with it twice. You've seen things before yesterday I hadn't. My timeline consists of twenty-four hours, and I have to tell you both it's unfair. I'm beginning to understand and my head has begun to filter stuff, but this is too quick. I'm asking you both, as dear friends, to cut me some slack." Her voice trailed off, her eyes pleading.

Given the twenty-four hours, the savagery, the other plane of consciousness to immediately accept, and their deep affection toward her, both men backed off.

Francois squeezed her hand. "Je comprends. I understand. Then allow us to talk of the more outward effects. The attributes, if you will."

Francois spoke at length of what he knew—of what people since time immemorial knew. He spoke of the ancient manuscripts, the encounters and descriptives. The crumbling documents buried deep within the Vatican. He explained how Ancient Hebrew was a primitive language, which made interpretation difficult. They had not discovered vowels, their vocabulary was quite small, and punctuation was not part of their writing. It had become a dead language by the time of Christ. Yet these documents, as well as those of the Babylonians, Egyptians, and other ancient cultures, shared common threads regarding Satan and his acolytes.

Nadine probed, looking for associations and causation to paint a more complete picture. Cole asked at length about conflict, about how to address this enemy and how to defeat it.

"This creature deceives. He implants. He can perform tricks, but nothing more. He has but one purpose," said Francois. "Inflicting evil as his master demands."

They all absorbed this bedrock notion. "What was the Latin you spoke when you entered the room? I heard you using a loud voice, just before I ran and skidded on my butt," asked Cole.

"The Rite of Exorcism," said Francois. "The young man was possessed. I have seen it many times. In this particular form or purpose, perhaps not. But the look is the same. This demon planted himself, or a part of himself, or planted another demon, in that person. Believe this. It does not mean all evil is so implanted. We have sufficient free will to carry evil on our own. But with this case, oui. He was possessed."

"I've seen it, too. Three times. Martha's killer. Burt Hall in Rockport. And that evil bastard yesterday," said Cole. "What about the Latin he spoke?"

"Mocking God," said Francois. "Ancient words of the deceiver."

Two fat harlequin ducks waddled to their table, quacking, looking for a handout. With no food forthcoming, they plopped on the grass nearby, grooming themselves.

At the mention of Cole's murdered wife, Nadine leaned forward and looked deep into Cole's eyes. "You've carried this all these years? And the last week you've seen it twice again?"

Cole nodded. Francois responded to him, "Then, perhaps, mon ami, some answers become clear to you."

Cole stood and moved a few feet away from the park table. The two ducks kept an eye on him and continued to groom. The sun peeked from clouds and traffic increased. Cardiff's day had begun.

"Answers. I don't know. Maybe to the 'how.' Not the 'why,'" said Cole. "I've gained no more clarity on the reason for it all. Let's get to the police station. They're waiting."

And so the conversation ended. Francois stood and said, "Oui. We shall continue this later. There remains much to absorb. To digest. Oui. Let us walk. I do not believe it a great distance."

***

They walked, each absorbed in thought. As they entered the police headquarters and made their way through the swarm of media, the desk sergeant picked up the phone and called upstairs, then signaled them to a hallway entrance. He took them away from the cameras and microphones and along a labyrinth of hallways until they came to another set of elevators. "Fifth floor. They expect you," he said, and returned to what must have been his own personal hell of reporters yelling questions at him.

ACC Gavin Morris met them when the elevator doors opened. "What happened to coming by last night?" he asked Cole.

"Sorry. We weren't in any shape to grind through the events," said Cole. He committed to cut Morris some slack. After all, this horror happened on the guy's home turf, and Cole had firsthand knowledge of what that felt like. "Hope you understand. But we're here now."

Jenni Thomas saw them and waved them toward her and the situation room, where a variety of cops worked phones, huddled around small tables, and pinned photographs and documents to a large corkboard.

Jenni hugged all three of them and made sure they got something to drink. Nadine and Cole asked for coffee. Francois opted for tea, asking first what type it might be.

"Oolong," said Jenni.

"Bon. S'il vous plaît."

Jenni began the conversation by explaining the doctors had not wanted her to work today, and they would have said the same thing to all of them.

"We're okay, really," said Nadine. "Horribly brutal stuff, but we have each other to lean on. How about you?"

Jenni explained she'd spent the night holding her daughter, reliving the day's events. It was cathartic as she enveloped the thing she loved most, knowing all could change with the blink of an eye.

Most of the cops treated them with great deference, these foreigners who managed to arrive in the midst of the crisis. The round, determined French priest, unafraid to dash into the situation. The Texas Sheriff who'd delivered a debilitating blow to the fiend holding their Jenni Thomas at knifepoint. The rangy woman who'd joined them and comforted Jenni during the aftermath.

"Some kick, mate. Texas-sized, I'd say," said one of the cops to Cole.

"I slipped."

"The mule kick to that lunatic wasn't a bloody slip," said another cop.

"He was fixin' to gut me," said Cole. "Didn't have a lot of choice."

They all seemed to view him as a man being modest. He viewed his actions as damn lucky.

Jenni displayed a photo of Moloch she'd printed from Nadine's thumb drive. "Is he associated with yesterday?" she asked.

This was Cole's world and it was time for him to tread with care. He gave Francois and Nadine a "let me handle this" look. "He's the guy we trailed from Texas. He flew to Syria yesterday."

"Syria?" asked ACC Morris as he joined them at the table. "How do you know?"

Cole pointed at Nadine, a more than sufficient answer.

"Right," said Jenni. "So even if there was some connection, he's in a place we can't touch."

Morris turned his attention to Cole. "Do you find it strange that your appearance coincides with this horror?" asked Morris.

"Look. Let's baseline a couple of things," said Cole. "I've been in your boots, Morris. It sucks. My town had a similar massacre take place. And I wish to hell I'd given you folks more of a heads-up on Moloch. But you and I want the same thing. Justice."

Jenni interrupted and took over the conversational thread. She clearly saw these three as allies—lifesavers—but as a good cop she, too, appeared to want some clarity. "So, could you please explain what prompted you to join the fray? To rush to the school?" she asked.

"Him," said Cole, tapping the photo of Moloch. "We thought he'd connect with it. We thought we'd find him there. We were wrong."

Jenni nodded and made notes. She and Morris would sense a hole in the answer if they had any salt as cops. Cole knew the presence of the same man in two towns an ocean apart during two separate mass murders would not pass muster.

"Was he in the middle of the mess-up in Texas?" asked Morris.

"On the periphery," said Cole. "A suspect with some connection to it. I can't put my finger on what that connection is, just like I can't figure it out here. The sumbitch doesn't seem to get his hands dirty."

"Can any of you tell us anything about Price Jones? The killer?" asked Jenni.

The three shook their heads.

"Father Domaine, you began speaking Latin," said Jenni. "When Jones had me on the floor, knife to my throat. What was that all about?"

Jenni's aplomb impressed him. "Knife to my throat" did not make for a casual reference. *She's a tough cop*, thought Cole.

Francois cleared his throat and said, "The ritual of exorcism. I only had time for the first few words."

"Why?" asked Jenni. "And why did it elicit such a response from him?"

Francois looked to Cole. Cole nodded back. It was best to get this on the table now, and then move through the facts.

"I believed him possessed," said Francois. "His response was quite normal for someone possessed."

"Possessed," said Gavin Morris.

"Oui."

Cole had seen Jenni's silver cross, worn as a necklace, the first time they met. She would most likely believe evil an active force among us. But he knew the cop in her would gravitate toward the work of a single madman.

"Well, we'll never know," said Jenni, steering the conversation. "Sheriff Garza, I want you to know I called your Captain Johnson this morning and left a voice mail. I know it's three in the morning in Texas, but I wanted to alert him to his team's heroism and great help as soon as he got to work." Jenni cracked a smile. "I would suppose Captain Johnson might become quite … excited when he hears of yesterday's events. Consider it a preemptive maneuver."

"Thank you," said Cole. "But I imagine 'excited' an understatement when he and I talk later today. Although I do appreciate the effort. By the way, are any of us—myself, Nadine, or Francois—associated with the crime? I mean the media. Have our activities leaked?"

Being positioned smack dab in the middle of yesterday's events would cause sufficient grief with Johnson, but logarithmically worse if they appeared as part of the story with the media.

Cole breathed an audible sigh of relief when Jenni confirmed she and her fellow officers were the only people engaged, as far as anyone outside the situation room knew. She explained she planned to keep it so, unless Cole wished to inject himself into the public narrative.

"Lord, no," said Cole. "Please, no. Keep a lid on it. A tight lid. What about these folks?" Cole asked, using a hand to indicate the room of busy cops.

"They'll keep it, as Captain Johnson would say, tight," Jenni said. "You have my word. We may sing about you in the distant future over a pint or two, but for the time being it's locked down."

Jenni and Morris walked through the timeline of the terror, making notes. Jenni remained polite; Morris acted professional at this juncture. They returned to Moloch and the link between two barbaric events thousands of miles apart.

"So no connection to this Moloch person?" asked Morris one last time.

"Not that we can pinpoint," said Cole. "I wish to hell we could."

ACC Thomas and Morris continued to pick. All evidence pointed to a madman, acting alone. Correlation did not mean causation. Still, it clearly felt discordant to the Welsh police. They circled back to Moloch several times, always with the same results. After half an hour, they both lowered their pens. Cole relaxed.

"So, what's next for you three?" asked Jenni. "Texas? Syria? Parts unknown?"

"Another and different conversation," said Francois. "May we be permitted to leave so such a conversation might take place? It is rather important."

They exchanged goodbyes and hugs all around. The Welsh cops in the situation room surrounded them and tears were shed. They left through a back entrance.

***

"Let us dine," said Francois, clear of the building. "Perhaps a French restaurant? Would such a thing be possible?"

Nadine searched her Android. "There's an Italian place with great ratings just a couple of blocks away. Would that do, Francois?"

"If such a place is nearby and the food reasonably edible, then oui, it shall do."

"Do they have a bar?" asked Cole.

She locked arms with Cole and Francois and pulled them in the right direction. It was weird to feel so much improved. Yesterday still loomed large and those mental images would never leave her, but today held a new promise. The sun shone, the sea air refreshed, and relief flooded at being alive to enjoy it. A tinge of guilt at feeling this way stayed stuck on her corkboard, and maybe it would forever, but her gut said it was critical to push ahead. To stroll with bookends and security and, man, who could not help but love these two? Opposites in some ways yet similar in others. Plus, Cole's kiss last night lingered and that was all more than okay.

"Do we need to shop, Francois?" she asked, slowing her pace as they passed small shops. "Cole needs a jacket. You will certainly need an article or two. I may get a Welsh woolen product. Que pensez-vous?"

Apparently taken aback by her French, Francois dragged the lock-armed trio to a stop then added, "One must never underestimate you, cher." He glanced at several storefronts. "Oui. We shall peruse the local offerings. It will stimulate the appetite. Our sheriff, an unwilling participant, shall protest, but such is the nature of those less cultivated. Is this not so?"

Cole grunted a response and she guided them to a nearby clothing shop. Again that guilt at participating in such a triviality as shopping gave her some discomfort, but it would allow them all to gain their sea legs during this storm. It was harmless, stable, and human. The close proximity to each other continued to foster her newfound support mechanism and allowed the element of love that had grown over the last week to do its job.

Chapter 25

Thirty years as a field agent had hardened Andrew Wilczek body, mind, and soul. The CIA tried to pull him back when he hit fifty, providing him with a desk job in Langley. The assignment lasted three months. Both the agency and Wilczek agreed the field made for a much better fit.

He spoke most Central Asian and Middle Eastern languages, managed to get shot twice—only one of which needed to be reported—and survived over a dozen assassination attempts. It was best to give better than you got, and it didn't matter one damn bit that peers and bosses saw him as irreverent or tough as nails as long as they stayed out of the way so he could fight the bad guys. He went by "Check," an American abbreviation of his last name. His parents emigrated from Poland after the war, escaped through England, and landed in Chicago. A good student, he joined the CIA and exhibited a natural ability to learn languages. The agency settled him in the Middle East. With the exception of the three months at Langley, there he stayed. Never married, his family consisted of fellow operatives and support personnel. He only trusted Americans, and not too many of them. A jaundiced view of his fellow humans kept a man alive.

The email from Nadine came as a pleasant surprise. It had been a couple of years since he'd worked with her as she got drawn tighter into domestic terrorism prevention. But her tendrils reached far and wide, and the spy community held her in high regard. He held her a lot higher than that. She found answers. She drilled for the truth—or as close to the truth as the shadow world could provide.

He knew of this Moloch she asked about. Wilczek based his operations inside Turkey, but made regular surreptitious forays into Syria, Iraq, Jordan, and Lebanon. He maintained a vast network of informers whose loyalty he gained and kept with US dollars and fear of retribution. He knew the Arab mindset. Life worked as a zero-sum game. Every transaction, interaction, and relationship had a winner and a loser. Win-win did not exist. He used this to his advantage and allowed everyone in his network to occasionally lie to him and continue to get paid so they would see themselves as winning and the gruff American as losing. What dumbasses.

Wilczek lied to Nadine when he replied he didn't know of Moloch but would find what he could. This allowed him the opportunity to find a backstory thread before he showed his cards. So far, he'd discovered little.

Nadine was traveling with a priest and a sheriff as a field team. It was pure amateur hour, but their endeavors existed for a reason. He just couldn't pry it from the available information.

He did not offer information without a quid pro quo, but on rare occasions would provide intel to someone such as Nadine. With her, he could call in favors. World-class at her craft, Nadine enjoyed her work and on occasion helped friends and allies with salient information. Having her at his disposal for judicious use provided a powerful lure, so he didn't mind dumping a little information her way.

Moloch nested in the Dead Cities of Syria, but he left to go who-knows-where with regularity. Wilczek knew little about him and had nothing on his history. Everyone had a trail, a tale. This guy—nothing. That smelled of an operative, a plant from the outside. Russians, maybe. Iranians, possibly. Fifteen years ago he showed up and assembled a gang of cutthroats and killers called al Garal. These guys made girl scouts of al Qaeda, Hamas, ISIS, al Shabaab and all the rest. Al Garal lived to kill anyone and everyone. A bizarre desire to wipe the earth clean drove them, with little religious conviction. Small in number, they had kept their terror confined to Syria, Lebanon, and Iraq. Other Middle Eastern terrorist groups despised them for their pure chaos and lack of order. Wilczek kept what little eye he could on them, but since they didn't pose an immediate threat to the US, the powers-that-be showed little interest in them.

Wilczek operated from the small Turkish city of Iskenderun on the Mediterranean coast. It had all the amenities of any larger city with the added benefit of sitting forty miles from the Syrian border. He could come and go into Syria with relative impunity. He crossed the border illegally, never stayed longer than necessary to buttress his network and pay bribes and gather information, all the while avoiding capture, torture, and eventual painful death. He loved his job.

Nadine would call after the email string and he'd do what he could to help her, as long as it didn't interfere with his work and afforded her the opportunity to provide him with future information. He'd never known her to leave the States, so this smelled like a strange lark—amateurs on the road. As long as the road didn't lead in his direction he would participate. This part of the world—rife with intrigue, war, conflict, murder, and mayhem—was no place for an amateur, much less three of them.

He slipped into swim shorts, grabbed a towel, and headed for the beach. There, armed with some dog-eared pulp fiction, he would take a lounge chair, wear the darkest of sunglasses, and wave off all the beach vendors except the ones on his payroll. He allowed the informants to squat in the sand next to him, as if selling their wares, while they told him what they could. Much of it involved Turkish politics; some involved rumors from across the border. He truly loved his job.

Chapter 26

They spent an hour together, shopping. They orbited each other, always in close proximity, and dropped little reminders of yesterday. In Cole's experience, it was best to talk it out. Death had to be acknowledged, and then you moved on ... or at least tried to. It was pretty clear they would all carry the scars from the experience for the rest of their lives, but the small community of three took solace in each other, and through that association and that love began to look forward and not dwell on the past. They all admitted feeling some guilt in doing so. They all admitted the key was to focus on life, on the living. It gratified Cole to see Nadine back on her feet. He expected Francois to rely on a priest's deep belief system, but even the Frenchman displayed a rattle or two. The fact that he didn't display more showed a deep conviction in the muddy trail they now followed.

They made their way to the Italian restaurant and gravitated toward a corner table. Nadine and Francois carried several shopping bags. Cole offered to carry Nadine's but she smiled and told him to "bugger off." She and Francois had apparently satiated their wool fix, at least for the time being. Nadine insisted on buying him a lightweight wool jacket. He protested, without adding it looked pretty dang good on his frame.

They ordered drinks, Francois visibly pleased to find Pernod available. Their corner of the restaurant sat quiet.

"Folks, let me start off with some tactical considerations," said Cole. He thought it best to avoid the initial conversation devolving into spiritual definitions and arguments between Nadine and Francois. Cole had very real concerns about geography. Syria created a different and gnarly dimension.

"He's in Syria," Cole continued. "Before we talk about him and the options for addressing him, let's focus on his location."

Francois and Nadine nodded in agreement. Francois lit a smoke and crossed his legs. Muffled kitchen sounds floated across the room as their drinks arrived. The fresh herb-laced smells of an Italian cucina filled the place.

"Now, Nadine, you can expand on this with more detail, but from what I know, Syria is messed up beyond imagination. It's about as dangerous as it gets for hardened operatives, which we aren't," said Cole, pausing to take a sip. "So just as a reality check, what will we be able to do down there? As far as moving around without getting killed." He stopped at this point, wanting to talk through the first stumbling block to their progress.

"Syria is a horrible mess," said Nadine. "Constant civil war. Tribe against tribe, clan against clan, religious sect against religious sect. Now it's spread into other countries. This ISIS group wants to establish a caliphate in the region. There isn't a more dangerous place on the earth."

They remained silent while the appetizers of various antipasti arrived. Francois then had his say on the subject. "We may wish to consider it a test. A test of our resolve. Our commitment."

"Okay, let's put a pin in Syria for the moment and talk about commitment," said Nadine. "What exactly do we commit to? Moloch's physical makeup aside, what do we hope to accomplish. Let's pretend Moloch lands in downtown Houston. So what? What's the end game?"

"Ah," said Francois. He smiled, eyes closed, chewing on a mouthful of tapenade. The man clearly enjoyed his food. "Again so quickly to the heart of the matter. I must become more comfortable with this from Americans. Perhaps there is no end. Perhaps each time should be viewed as an experience to build upon. And from these experiences we can develop a way to destroy such evil when encountered."

That had no end game, for damn sure. Cole shook his head, saying, "Yesterday was a pretty big experience. I don't want any more of those."

"It is quite personal," said Francois. "Each of us has reasons to pursue or go home. For myself, I must continue. It is my path. Is this creature the only one? Of course not. But this creature is the one I know. Can I defeat him? This, I still do not know. But I do not fear him. I do know Moloch fears God. I do know he cannot stand against the power of God." Francois paused to wipe his mouth, took a deep drag and stubbed out his smoke, and finished with a sip of Pernod. "We all stand at a point, a crossroads, where each of us must decide. If I may suggest, look in your heart."

Cole appreciated this approach. It would help to talk it out.

"And what does your heart tell you, Francois?" asked Nadine.

Cole was impressed. Her tone and expression had changed. Gone was her usual sardonic approach toward the Frenchman, replaced by a respectful and sincere enquiry.

Francois cleared his throat, nodded with a grave expression, and addressed Nadine. "My heart now has a sense of validation. My purpose ... my belief, is no longer shadowed by doubt."

Cole had seen dang little of that doubt, and appreciated the priest's admission of its existence.

"How about your perspective on how to take on Moloch?" asked Nadine. "Has that changed?"

More patrons entered the small restaurant and waiters moved about, taking orders. The background noise increased, filled with good-natured chatter from the people sitting down to lunch.

Francois gazed at the tabletop, apparently considering the question. "I now have a sense of power. Of righteousness. And yet, it does not originate from me. It is not of my doing." He lifted his head and locked eyes with Cole. "I accept this, of course. But do understand, I have only chased him away. My capabilities to channel such power to destroy him raise a new doubt. A new concern."

Cole tilted back on his chair, holding the position with a hand on the table. He gave Francois a nod of acknowledgement. "Hell, we all have concerns, Francois. At least your conviction hasn't wavered. And I appreciate you fessing up to any doubts and concerns you might have."

Nadine reached across the table and squeezed Francois's arm. "Concerns aren't fear. You're about as fearless as they come. Concerns we can manage."

Francois returned a sad smile. "I have yet to reveal my fear, cher." He placed a hand over hers still resting on his arm. "I fear for you both in traveling with me to Syria. It will prove to be a very dangerous place, of this I am sure."

And I fear for Nadine, thought Cole. *You and I are dang near expendable, pard. She isn't. She's special.*

"Thank you, Francois," said Nadine. "Good stuff. Now it's my turn." She released Francois's arm and dug in one of the shopping bags, pulled out a sweater, and draped it around her shoulders. One of the waiters had propped open the front door and the cool salt breeze drifted in. She started with something about God and a power curve inside a probabilistic formula, then looked to Cole and Francois for affirmation. Cole didn't have the foggiest notion of what she was talking about, but nodded seriously as if he did.

"So as for Moloch," she said. "He scares the bejeesus out of me. Is that a cuss word?" Francois shrugged in response. "Anyway, I have the same fear as Francois. You two guys are over your head down there."

"I don't doubt that one little bit," said Cole. "But that isn't the point."

Nadine held up a flat hand, palm toward Cole in a universal "stop" sign. "So let me finish by going straight to the point," she said. Focusing on Francois, she stated, "You might be a tough little round guy but going it alone in Syria is nuts, especially if you think dressing like one of the Village People is going to pass muster. You need help down there. Professional help."

Apparently the priest got the Village People reference, indicated by a roll of the eyes and waft of the hand.

She then grabbed Cole's hand and pulled it toward her. "I've fallen for you, big time. I need to process my way through that. But I can tell you right now that I won't have you getting killed in Syria. Sabe?"

Cole felt his face flush red and was greatly relieved when she released his hand. She must have seen or sensed his discomfort, and rolled her eyes prior to addressing both of them.

"Neither of you has enough situational awareness to navigate in such a dangerous place. Plus, I love both of you and simply won't tolerate either of you dying on this little foray into hell."

Cole extended a hand to order a Coke, buying time. The other two stared at him, both extending identical arched eyebrows. "Tag, you're it, Cole," said Nadine. "So what's in your heart?"

"Okay. First, why can't I just shoot the sumbitch and be done with it?" asked Cole. "You're a badass, Francois. I'll be the first to admit it. But if we go down there, why not try the sure and quick way?"

Nadine rocked her drink glass side to side, pausing after each count of three. "That's your idea of opening up? Of telling us what's in your heart? Just shoot him?" Her volume had risen well above that of her earlier heartfelt statements.

"I'm just being practical. And thinking safety and risk. Right, Francois?"

The priest would not deign to look at him, having shifted position to gaze toward the kitchen and light a smoke. Nadine's glass continued to rock from side to side, tapping triplets.

Silence ensued for a few uncomfortable seconds. "Alright. This isn't easy, so cut me some slack." He put a hand on Nadine's glass to prevent it from rocking back and forth. "If I head back to Rockport, it would feel like a half-assed mission accomplished. Besides, the kids are grown. While I don't have a death wish, if I get whacked in Syria both kids would get by without me."

"Please shitcan the getting whacked talk," said Nadine. She conceded her drink glass to Cole, crossed her legs, and began moving a suspended foot in sets-of-three air taps. "The goal is to not get whacked. What else you got, cowboy?"

He knew Nadine had a point on the whole open-your-heart thing and was prepared to go that route, thinking it was like pulling a mesquite thorn out of your finger: don't fiddle-fart around, just do it. "So here's the deal. There's some connectivity to Martha in all this that I don't get. Moloch isn't likely going to provide any answers in that regard, even though it might be worth a try. But I guess the main thing is justice. I'm certain Moloch drove the mass murders. I want justice. Plain and simple."

Nadine's look had softened a bit, but not enough to put him at ease. Clearly something was still stuck in her craw. Francois continued to smoke and look toward the kitchen, insouciant as ever. Mercy, he could be irritating at times.

"And?" asked Nadine.

Fine, he thought. *The whole nine yards*. "Francois is an easy target down there. You are even more so, Nadine. I have dark skin and could potentially blend in. Both of you are going to stand out like diamonds in a goat's ass. I probably have the best shot at pulling this off."

He knew it was true. If Moloch could be taken out with a bullet, he was the guy to carry it out. "And, yes, I have a deep affection for both of you, and special feelings toward you, Nadine, but any kind of romance will have to wait. This isn't the time to wrap my head around that."

Nadine stopped her foot tapping and Francois looked over a dismissive shoulder to give him pursed lips. Cole had no clue what that meant.

As if on cue, food began to arrive.

"Bon, bon, bon," said Francois, clapping his hands once and investigating the dishes. The Italian food smelled delicious. They began to scoop food on each other's plates, while Nadine responded positively to the waiter's question of wine.

"Something French," she told the waiter.

They ate in silence, except for an occasional grunt of satisfaction from Francois, until Nadine broke the ice. "So, at the crossroads. Everyone has expressed their feelings. Which way is everyone heading?"

Francois chewed, breathed heavily through his nose, nodded, and washed it down with a drink of Burgundy. "I shall continue to Syria. This of course you would already know."

"Yep. Me, too," said Cole. Over the course of the day, quitting the chase had fallen off the option table for him. Besides, Francois would sure as hell be toast down there without him to help. The decision to pursue and get answers had a comfortable finality.

Francois quickly said, "Bon. I shall relish the opportunity to hunt with you, mon ami." He raised his wineglass in a brief salute to Cole, saying, "It is a formidable team. And I must say, Nadine, mon amour, your assistance has been invaluable. We shall both miss you most terribly."

"Amen," said Cole. "You've been great, as always."

She sat ramrod straight and looked back and forth at the two men, clearly locked and loaded. "I will join you," she said in a level, matter-of-fact tone. "You two are hosed without me. I have physical contact on the ground there. An old friend. I'm the only one who can backdoor the intelligence streams there. I'm the only one who can ascertain and utilize both hard and soft assets there. I'm going with you. Let's not ruin this lovely meal by making me upset. Pass the wine, Francois. Have I left any gray areas for either of you?"

Cole fought the urge to argue. He had a real and realistic concern for her safety. Yes, she could be of immense help, but this would entail travel to a nasty, dangerous place. He would never forgive himself if something happened to her. On the other hand, he knew Nadine had made up her mind, and there was nothing—absolutely nothing—he and Francois could do to change it.

"I would ask that you reconsider," said Francois, leaning across the table to make his point. "Perhaps pray on such a perilous decision. Converse with the Almighty."

"I did. And I asked God if it was wrong to tell you both to kiss my butt if y'all tried to leave me behind. He said it was perfectly okay. Pass the bread, please."

Francois threw both hands in the air. Cole took it to mean some sort of universal frustration with such hard-headedness. Nadine apparently tired of waiting for the bread to be passed, and reached across Francois's plate to retrieve a slice.

Francois then displayed his amazing ability to move on. He pulled himself straight and raised his wineglass again. "And so. Perhaps it is God's will. Our team becomes even more formidable. De notre succès. To our success." He extended his glass to a now smiling Nadine and they clinked glasses. Both turned to Cole, who had yet to raise his glass.

"I wish you wouldn't," he said to Nadine. "I really do."

"It will be alright, Cole," said Nadine. "Everything will be fine."

With resignation and a touch of sadness he picked up his wineglass. "I doubt it, but I know I'm not going to make you change your mind," he said, touching their glasses with his. "Alright then, compadres. Let's saddle up."

Chapter 27

The Dead Cities lay scattered across the limestone massif of northwest Syria, built between the first and seventh centuries. Many of them had been Christian communities. Abandoned by the tenth century, only the remnants of stone buildings, churches, pagan temples, and houses remained. Lost to history, there exist no definitive reasons for their construction, although some suspect ancient trade routes drove their development. Strife both religious and geopolitical led to their decline and abandonment, a common theme in that part of the world, and carried on to this day. Few of the Dead Cities have any archaeological activity and all stand ignored by the villages nearby, except when they herd their goats through the stone remnants.

The ruins of the Church of St. Ageranus rest in one of these abandoned settlements, surrounded by the crumbled stone remains of houses and granaries. Here, Moloch established a base of operations for al Garal.

Moloch took succor and nourishment from the location. An elaborate tent on the grounds of the ancient church made for a fine personal residence. Al Garal soldiers camped among the other white stone ruins. For a radius of seventy miles, factions in the Syrian civil war attacked, murdered, raped, beheaded, burned, and summarily executed any perceived enemy. Horrific chaos ruled, and Moloch relished it. It created his personal version of heaven.

He had fifty al Garal fighters, a small contingent compared to many of the other insurgent armies, but of a size that fit the needs of the time. They moved with speed, remained easy to maintain, and would strike without mercy when told to do so. For scum, they lived a malleably vicious existence and killed anyone and everyone once directed.

"We have the four from yesterday, Sayyid," said one of the fighters. "What is your will?"

The al Garal fighters addressed him as Sayyid, or Master. He represented an example of purity to them. Muslim, Christian, Jew—it did not matter to Sayyid. They all fouled his land as apostates. They would be cleansed.

Moloch spoke Arabic, albeit an ancient dialect with hints of Aramaic. There still existed one town in the entire world, a hundred miles south of them, where Aramaic—the language of Christ—could still be heard. His fighters assumed he came from that region.

The four apostates captured the day before had attempted to establish a clinic at a nearby village. They comprised a party of one of the numerous nongovernmental organizations who tried and failed to deliver humanitarian relief to this war-torn part of the world. Their NGO focused on the relief of pain and suffering for those wounded during the constant battles across northern Syria. The four consisted of a Syrian guide, a Lebanese doctor, and two French male nurses.

"Bring them," said Moloch, adjusting his position in a chair constructed of wood and human skin leather. He lifted his head into the breeze and smelled for scent. Numerous crows cawed among the ruins.

The four were dragged before him, hands and feet bound, and made to kneel in his presence. The Syrian begged for release, the Lebanese doctor bowed his head, and the two French nurses looked about with wild eyes. They spoke French at a frantic pace and explained their mission to help others. A dozen al Garal fighters surrounded them. The fighters laughed and delivered occasional kicks to the ribs of the four. This activity produced small clouds of flour-like sand, which rose and drifted off.

"Add them to the collection," said Moloch. "The Syrian dog first."

Hundreds of severed heads placed on the tops of the ancient walls of these ruins made up the collection. The heads perched in various states of decay, some no more than skulls, picked clean by crows and insects, some still fresh and baked by the sun.

The Syrian guide cried for a pardon, a release. Laughter met his cries. One of the fighters grabbed his hair and wielded a twelve-inch blade. Death did not come quickly as the executioner sawed through the man's throat. With the severed head held high, cries of exultation erupted from the al Garal members.

Other fighters jerked back the heads of the three that remained bound and kneeling, and began their bloody work, accompanied by the screams of the victims and victorious yells of the killers. Moloch smiled with benevolence, his head rested on one hand.

Moloch instructed them to remove the bodies and place the heads. He signaled one of his key lieutenants to approach him.

"Yes, Sayyid?"

"We have a mission soon. A nest of transgressors, apostates. There will be many heads."

"Most excellent, Sayyid. As you wish."

Moloch dismissed him and exalted at the sight of the old church's walls around his large tent. The executed victims' blood pooled on the dusty sand, congealed, and with finality was absorbed to join blood from centuries past. Ruined churches, the spilled blood of scum, minions that did his bidding—his own master would be pleased.

Chapter 28

Nadine's name flashed on Wilczek's encrypted cell phone. He answered after two rings.

"Check, it's me."

"You got in the middle of the blind school murders," he said as way of greeting. The usual pleasantries had long ago left his repertoire.

"Yes. And I don't want to talk about it," she said. "Moloch had involvement, too."

Wilczek emitted a low whistle and shook his head. She had no business being associated with ground work in Wales. He'd run a trapline behind the scenes to find any knowledge of her involvement. The traps returned a mention in the Welsh secret internal police report of her and her two companions. He told her of this, and made a suggestion she do some cleaning.

"Thanks, Check," she said. "I forgot to dig there. It's been, well, crazy. But I'll go wipe the reference clean before we leave."

"Back to Texas?" he asked.

"Nope. Headed your way," she said.

The pause extended so long Nadine offered a "hello" to confirm they remained connected.

"Vacation?" asked Wilczek. "Because if it's anything other than a vacation, don't do it. You'll get your ass killed."

Wilczek bear-walked to the apartment's bar and poured a stiff drink. He kept the sliding doors open to the Mediterranean breeze, the ceiling fan on high, and the AC on. This resulted in a constant background noise of wind and mechanical hums. He also had the place swept for bugs every week by one of his geeks.

"We don't have a good plan, I admit," she said. "But we're all hell-bent on going to Damascus. I'm just looking for some informational help, Check. Drinking the DP on ice now?"

Nadine had evidently discerned the clink of ice in his glass. She was referring to his Diet Dr. Pepper addiction, served warm. Wilczek held the cold glass to his forehead, rolled it back and forth, and let the icy condensation collect in his furrowed brow.

"No. I prefer my whiskey cold," said Wilczek. "Okay. Informational help. Make sure your will is in order. How's that?"

Nadine remained silent, clearly deciding to let the storm play out.

"Syria isn't amateur hour," he continued. "Well, at least not your type of amateur. Lots of amateur armies, amateur killers, and amateur genocidal maniacs. Which isn't much of a recommendation for three supersleuths such as yourselves."

He let that sink in for a moment. She needed to understand the seriousness of the situation. "So let's review. A systems hotshot who just left her bits and bytes world, some redneck sheriff, and a French priest. Shithouse mouse, Nadine. It doesn't get more amateur. What the hell are you people thinking?"

There was another pause with a Nadine-interjected "hold on," followed by, "I'm thinking I need new nail polish. I used to balance better than this. I'm pulling up a foot for inspection in a weird kind of yoga pose and keeping the phone hitched in my neck. There. I know it's nuts, Check. No argument here. What do Western women wear in Damascus this time of year?"

He had worked with her enough to recognize the conversational tone she now delivered, a tone renowned among the intelligence community. This presented a fait accompli, a la Nadine May. He could talk until he was blue in the face, but it wouldn't change her chosen course of action. That didn't mean an ass-chewing wasn't due.

"This is a helluva lot different than you figuring how to connect data tendrils in multiple rabbit holes. This is field ops. It's different. Do you get that?"

"Should I get sunscreen?" she asked.

He stared out the open sliding glass door. The Mediterranean reflected azure blue from the late day sun. "I've heard of and dealt with a lot of dumbass things in my time. This sits near the top. Dumb. Ass. Could you run it through one of your software programs so we—you and I—can identify what type of person would do such a dumbass thing?"

Wilczek paused to take a large gulp of the liquor. Nadine remained silent, probably lifting her other bare foot for a nail inspection.

"Oh, wait. Never mind. I just figured it out. Dumbasses do such dumbass things. Yeah, that's it! Which means you and the other two bozos you're with must swallow dumbass pills by the handful."

"Any hotel suggestions in Damascus?" she asked. "TripAdvisor suggests I haul butt to some other destination. Which tells me I'm liable to get some pretty steep discounts on rooms."

"Really? I can't imagine why, you dumbass," said Wilczek.

"The weather looks hot according to AccuWeather. Kinda like Texas. Should I get a special shot of some kind? Tetanus? Influenza?"

He had to accept the inevitable, knowing she owned some unique place in the world where mental wiring looked like a rat's nest. He sat on the couch, put his sandaled feet on the coffee table, and leaned back to stare at the ceiling fan.

"Shithouse mouse, Nadine. Shithouse mouse."

"Yeah, I know, Check," she said in a voice not entirely unsympathetic.

If it was a done deal for her to come to this neck of the woods he'd do what he could, keeping any assistance buried deep. Langley would go ballistic if they got wind of it. But Langley, by and large, left him alone because he got results. He had a great deal of free reign and could pull from a variety of tools and assets with few if any questions. These included the usual informants, operatives, and paid killers. Counterparts from Russia, China, Iran, Israel, and all the rest had the same. None of them, however, had the special assets that flew, unmanned, over much of Syria 24-7.

"Come to Turkey," he said.

"Really? That doesn't appear a direct route to Damascus," said Nadine. The intelligence-gathering dance had begun.

"Your guy operates in northern Syria. I'm in Turkey. Not far from the border. Don't go to Damascus," said Wilczek.

"Okeydokey," she said. "And you have him somewhat pinpointed in northern Syria?"

Wilczek far exceeded Nadine at the interpersonal intel game. "It depends. It's a large area and makes the Wild West look like *Sesame Street*. It would help if I knew a bit more about your Mr. Moloch."

"Well, he's different, Check. In oh so many ways."

"Such as?"

Nadine stalled, and he appreciated the maneuver from a professional perspective. He would probe on the phone, but since the door had been opened to come to Turkey she'd push for a face-to-face, all the while positioning herself, and the two bozos with her, as close to this Moloch guy as possible. Then she'd get captured or killed, but prior to that he could get in front of her and assess the situation, and maybe provide some assistance that would increase her odds of survival. The "why" of chasing that guy remained a wide-open door and direct interaction with this group of amateurs would be the only way to get those answers.

"Can we talk about it in person?" asked Nadine. "We'll come to your city. In Turkey. If that's okay. I know it's your turf, Check. It's an imposition and I get it. I'll owe you, big time. But at least let us get within spitting distance of the border, and we'll take it from there. It's a big favor, I know. So I'm asking a big please. And you have my word there is a quid pro quo attached."

He noticed that Nadine kept geography discussions at the fifty-thousand-foot level. Of course she knew where he lived, including his apartment location. It was a nice gambit for an amateur, and again, a hat tip to Nadine for keeping that information in the hole.

He weighed the options. Nadine had dangled an appealing asset—her and her abilities. To have Nadine May as a personal intelligence concierge for a short time was value beyond measure. On the other hand, you could lay smart money on her getting killed before he could ever collect the debt. He also didn't appreciate these amateurs in his city, his base of operations, although any involvement could be kept deep among the shadows and if—or when—she got killed, no strings would tie him to her or her two companions.

The potential upside of Nadine nestled somewhere in Houston as she rooted behind electronic firewalls and encrypted security, for him and him alone, constituted the brass ring. "You'll land in Istanbul. You've got several options from there. If you don't want to do a lot of driving, catch a flight to a city called Iskenderun." Wilczek continued the game and spelled it for her. Responding to the game, she asked for a second or two to get a pen and paper. She was probably standing there digging in her ear or scratching her ass to let some time pass.

"Get a bus at the airport to the town of Kirikhan. It's a large town." He spelled it for her. His gut told him Kirikhan wasn't on her radar—yet. "Make reservations at the Parlak Hotel. Get a suite. Do not get three separate rooms. That's important. A suite. Brush up on your Turkish; no one will speak English except maybe the guy who takes reservations. Email me your itinerary. Got it?"

This kept the three stooges from polluting his base of operations and sequestered them in a nondescript town in the boonies of Turkey. The lone Kirikhan hotel had one suite, never rented unless he placed someone there. Wilczek kept it bugged with audio feeds. Its close proximity to the Syrian border made a good launch point.

"Got it. Thanks so much, Check. You know I'll return the favor," said Nadine, and ended the call.

She'd be online, immersed in her world, checking out Kirikhan in three, two, one …

***

Jeeter Johnson received the expected phone call from Cole. "I got a voice mail from those Welsh folks," said Johnson. "Said you were a tough hombre during the massacre at the blind school."

"Luck and circumstance. That's a fact. And there's no media about us, Captain. Not one of the three of us has any association as far as the public is concerned. I've kept it tight."

Johnson shook his head and looked through the window. The steaming Austin air draped over everyone as they went about their day, keeping their movement desultory. Folks didn't want to move too fast and risk the sheen of sweat turning into a torrent.

"Well, at least that's something," said Johnson. Having the Sheriff of Aransas County gallivanting around a foreign country under the tenuous auspices of the head Ranger was bad enough, but any association with the world-news event of a blind school slaughterhouse might cause a man to drink early in the day or, God forbid, take up golf. The shitstorm would come from all angles—the governor, the State Department, and perhaps the Vatican.

"Headin' home?" asked Johnson, with hope. Cole on a plane back to Texas made for the best possible outcome at this point. The priest could head back to Rome. Nadine, well, she would do whatever the hell she wanted.

"Soon," said Cole.

That wasn't a good answer. Johnson's radar went on high alert.

"Tell me," said Johnson. "Without the bullshit. Just tell me."

Cole explained the situation. He focused on Moloch's whereabouts and what had to be his involvement with the Cardiff murders. Tenuous ties, but ties nonetheless. Johnson didn't argue. The fact this suspect had appeared in Rockport and Cardiff just in time for two mass murders eliminated coincidence in his book. But Syria took the adventure to a whole new level.

"How dead set are you on going?" Johnson asked. If Cole and the priest had committed to such a hellhole of a place, they might as well put it on the table and chew on it.

"We're all going, sir," said Cole. "Including Nadine."

Johnson stretched his neck, heard vertebrae pop, and put boots on the desk. He'd sent men into danger before, but nothing similar to this. He'd been shot three different times during the course of his Ranger duties and understood dangerous situations. But this was far removed from his experiences. He knew enough about Syria since he worked a border state and had helped Homeland Security with possible terrorist suspects from that part of the world. He'd read the CIA briefs.

Johnson sank into the chair. It looked possible this would mark the last time he'd talk with the Sheriff of Aransas County. He could handle the fallout, if any occurred. But he didn't like the potential loss of a good lawman.

"Son, what can I do to talk you out of this?" he asked. "You'll be traipsing around an Arab shithole where everyone's killin' everyone. You, a French priest, and a good-looking gal. Y'all ain't exactly going to blend in."

"You think she's good-looking?"

Johnson dropped boots to the ground and dragged the phone over to the liquor cabinet. He poured himself two fingers of bourbon, which disappeared in one gulp. Cole waited for a response.

"Good-looking? Is that what you pulled from that statement? Good Lord, son. I might as well be talkin' to a mesquite stump."

He had a point, and Cole told him so. They talked further, Cole mentioned Nadine's "friend" in that part of the world, and the conversation wound down.

"Keep your ass low, son," said Johnson. "And get some firepower of the automatic kind. I mean it. I would bet you can pick up some damn potent weaponry at the corner grocery store over there."

"I'll do my best, Captain."

Mercy, this was it. Cole Garza would go into the abyss—directly into the current anus of the earth called Syria. "My friends call me Jeeter. I wish you would."

"Alright, sir. Jeeter. I'll let you know what's going on when I get the chance," said Cole.

"You do that, Cole. You do that. I'm afraid the Rangers can't saddle up and provide any help. I wish to hell we could, but you're on your own. Remember to keep your ass down. Utilize Nadine—she's going to be damn handy in this situation. Don't tell her I said that."

"I'll keep low, Jeeter. I fully intend to get back to Texas."

Johnson would have another drink as soon as he hung up with this dead man. "I'll say a prayer for you, son."

"You do that, sir. It could be big medicine right now."

Chapter 29

The flight to Istanbul and on to Iskenderun proved uneventful, although the last leg had no first-class seating, and the two men squeezed Nadine in the middle seat. Francois planted his elbow on the divider, apparently unaware—or maybe fully aware—that such an action cut her space considerably. Cole didn't want to chat with her at length and mentally holed-up. She empathized with his conversational reticence, given this whole thing had moved from adventure to very thin ice. Seat of the pants stuff, all this, and he clearly wasn't comfortable. Francois, on the other hand, remained sanguine. She sat, emotionally and physically, somewhere in the middle.

They waited around the open-air airport for their scheduled bus while they drank tea and snacked on börek, a savory rolled dough that wasn't bad, although it was made worse by Francois's smacking. The weather warmed her bones and she did what she could do to ease Cole's anxiety. He had explained that he knew Turkey was a safe, modern country with marvelous food and attractions, but it still represented a kissing cousin to the Middle East, and as such carried flavors and nuances signaling they had arrived on the border of the Western world.

Francois let it be known he took comfort from the permission to smoke everywhere and the possibilities of a vibrant and spice-driven cuisine. He also explained that Turkey encompassed Corinth, Tarsus, Ephesus, Smyrna, and many others—all integral to the New Testament. He told them he felt a spiritual connectivity.

Nadine relaxed, knowing they'd arrived in Check's domain. He was a pro's pro, and she had little doubt his people were watching them right now.

They chatted on mundane subjects and gained their sea legs in this foreign land. Nadine reviewed again, without too many details, their as-yet-to-be-established association with Wilczek and his well-established abilities in this part of the world. She crafted her portable office and moved between the two laptops, tablet, and smartphone. She read up on the northern Syrian conflicts and players and sent electronic sniffers to collect data and help verify assumptions. Francois spent time perusing the lone small shop at the airport. Cole paced.

The bus arrived for the forty-minute trip to Kirikhan. Francois and Nadine sat together at an open window and talked while they both smoked. Francois explained the importance of their current geography within a biblical context. Two-thirds of the books of the New Testament originated from the early Turkish churches. She loved to learn, and with Francois she had a knowledgeable and enlightened teacher.

At the Parlak Hotel, the desk clerk spoke no English, but Francois conversed with him in rudimentary French. Francois explained to the other two France's centuries-long influence in the area and how it had been codified after World War I when France acquired domain over Syria.

The two-bedroom suite had a large common area. At Cole's insistence, Nadine took one room and Francois the other. Cole explained he could sleep anywhere, a trait he'd developed in the Marine Corps. The couch would suit him just fine.

***

As they unpacked, Wilczek strode in. He assessed the two men with an up-and-down look, and grabbed Nadine in a big bear hug. They had never physically met before, although hours had passed on video calls, either one-on-one or within a team setting. He'd wink at her in those calls after he'd pissed off other participants and she'd laugh. It was hard for him not to like her.

"You're a lot prettier in person, dumbass. Are you sleeping with this guy?" he asked as he threw a thumb toward Cole.

"Oh mercy, he's wearing me out," she said. "The man is a sexual marvel."

Wilczek cast a quizzical look that said, "Really?" while Cole turned beet red.

Francois strode toward the man with the crew cut, hand extended. "Francois Domaine, at your service."

"Call me Check, Father Domaine."

"Francois, s'il vous plaît."

"Done and done," said Wilczek. He turned to Cole. "And you're the cowboy."

Cole extended a hand. "Cole Garza. Not much of a cowboy. Not a bad sheriff."

Wilczek shook his hand and set a canvas bag on the central large table. He rummaged a bit and removed a can of Diet Dr. Pepper. "Got a glass?" he asked.

Nadine grabbed one from the small kitchen. Cole asked him if he wanted ice.

"Nope. Like it warm," said Wilczek. "Always have."

Cole took a seat at the table and asked, "They have DP here?"

"Nope. Flown in. Warm Diet DP during the day, cold whiskey at night. About all I drink. Heart healthy. Now let's get to it," said Wilczek, as he pulled folded maps from his bag and opened them on the table.

Francois and Nadine scooted their chairs closer.

"I've already told Nadine what I think of all this, so I won't bother repeating it. I can't fix stupid. This mission of yours, or quest, or death wish, or whatever the hell you people call it, takes you smack into the middle of the most chaotic place on the planet. And it isn't organized marches or loud yelling that makes it chaotic. Real bullets, real bombs, real artillery, real poisonous gas, and most important, real lunatics."

Nadine, Francois, and Cole nodded. Wilczek went on to point out the locations and players.

"This is Aleppo," he said as he pointed on the map. "Largest city in Syria. Larger than Damascus. Heartland of the Syrian civil war. The Syrian Army fights insurgents day and night while bombing the shit out of their own people. Tens of thousands dead, almost all civilians."

He paused to sip some DP, following up with a loud belch. "The insurgents—a word used by the buttlicks at the State Department—consist of every shitheel jihadist from all over the Muslim world. Syrians, Iraqis, Saudis, Libyans, Chechens—even Frenchmen." He looked at Francois, who waved a dismissive hand in return.

"These people, when not killing Syrian Army regulars, kill each other or torture and kill whatever civilians happen to be handy. Our State Department, run by top men, help support them." Wilczek stopped to pour the rest of the Dr. Pepper and tossed the can toward a wastebasket.

"Assad isn't much better," he said, referring to the dictator who ran Syria. "Bombs and gasses his own people. A sweetheart. The same as his dear old dad."

Wilczek pulled a more detailed map and spread it.

"Idlib," he said as he pointed to the town on the map. "Thirty miles southwest of Aleppo. It's full of Syrian Army regulars and surrounded by jihadists as well, but it's near your guy Moloch."

Wilczek paused and looked at Nadine, waiting for some input with regard to Moloch. She shrugged back, so he continued.

"Idlib may be your best bet for this little cannonball run. Near Idlib sit clusters of ruins, the Dead Cities. I'd focus on these," he said, as he took a pencil and circled several areas five to ten miles north and west of Idlib. "So if you make it there, which I doubt, get a room on the outskirts of town with some villagers. Don't stay inside Idlib proper."

Wilczek tossed the pencil on the map, sat back, produced a toothpick, and rooted around a back molar.

Cole and Francois continued to study the detailed map. Francois used a finger to trace minor roads and tracks extending from Idlib. "And so," he muttered, stopping to retrieve the pencil. He circled a tiny dot on the map labeled St. Anthony Monastery.

Cole leaned closer and asked, "And so, what?"

Francois lit a smoke and sat back, legs crossed. Wilczek continued working the toothpick as he stared at the priest.

"And so," said Francois, "I have as well made several calls. The convent at St. Anthony is where we shall attend. They expect us. Do not underestimate the church's resources."

Cole and Nadine both looked at Francois with wry smiles. Nadine went so far as to give him a light punch on the shoulder and said, "Not bad for a chain-smoking French priest with questionable taste in clothes."

Francois pretended to take umbrage at her remark. Cole looked back at the map. "Good for you, Francois. A base of operations. That's a big deal."

Wilczek remained unimpressed. "They just sawed the head off one of the monks there," he said to Francois. "The monastery is now rubble. They made a video of the beheading. Wanna see it?"

"I am well aware, Monsieur, of this tragic situation," said Francois. "Yet the nearby convent remains open, with several sisters continuing God's work."

Francois turned to Cole and Nadine to explain the long history of the Syrian Church and of how ten to fifteen percent of the population remained Christian with their own villages and churches. He further detailed how the Assad regime, for all its terrible treatment of citizens, never persecuted Christians, unlike the current crop of jihadists who appeared intent on wiping them out. This area of the world now saw the church's presence, after century upon century, slip away.

The sheriff apparently connected a few dots and turned to Wilczek to ask, "So our State Department sends money and arms to the side slaughtering Christians?"

"Top. Men." Wilczek pulled out a fresh toothpick.

Nadine dug further with Francois on the logistics and security of staying at the convent. In the course of the discussion, she let it be known that it sounded solid, although the large matter of how to get to the convent from where they currently sat hadn't been resolved, nor had the question of how they'd move around the area searching for Moloch, but at least they had a base, if they could get there.

"I know you're waiting, so let me start on Moloch," said Nadine. "I'll give the secular version and that way you can mentally prep and not choke on your toothpick when you hear from Francois." She leaned back, crossed both legs under her, and moved an errant strand of hair away from her eyes. "Moloch showed in Texas. Cole saw him at the scene of those murders. I tracked him to Wales. We encountered him in a hotel bar there. He ran. Later in the day those blind kids got slaughtered. He wasn't physically involved, the same as Texas. He flew to Damascus the same day."

Wilczek fished in his bag on the floor and produced another warm DP and poured it. He waited for Nadine to continue. She'd cracked open her personal dossier on this case, probably sensing—rightfully—that he'd been waiting for this intel. The priest's perspective didn't matter. Hers did.

"So, it's weird, Check," she said. "Not just his physical location during these grotesque things, but I can't find anything on him. I didn't look inside your personal data stores—give me some credit—but e-worms inside all the usual places came back with nothing. Nada."

He looked at Cole and Francois for any further feedback. None came. "Okay. Well I don't have much on him either. A dozen years ago he showed on my radar in Syria. Came and went, but always returned. When the current shitstorm happened, he formed a group called al Garal. Murderous psychopaths. Just a few dozen of them, but it's enough in the boonies to cause chaos and foment a tipping point. They aren't religious jihadists. Nihilists more like it. Life has no value. Everyone and everything is offensive and corrupt. So better to just kill and start clean. I can't pinpoint his whereabouts any better than what I've given you. He sounds like a real piece of work."

Wilczek took another sip of warm, bubbling Dr. Pepper and turned to Francois. "So, since the Vatican seems to be in on all this, what might they have to say about our Mr. Moloch? Anything?"

"Oui. Quite a lot," responded Francois.

"I'm all ears, Padre," said Wilczek.

Francois took a deep drag of his smoke and exhaled across the table. "The hour is far too late to play games. He is not a man. He is a demon. A creature walking among us, driving evil. I, or rather we, have confronted him once. He ran. He ran from the power of God. I intend to confront Moloch again and, if it is God's will, destroy him."

Wilczek absorbed this for a moment. Nadine looked back and forth between the CIA operative and the priest.

"Alrighty then," said Wilczek. "How about you, Sheriff? Any insights on Moloch you might want to share?"

Cole shifted and cleared his throat. "Francois is right. I've got a reason to chase him. He's involved in mass murder in my jurisdiction. But Francois is right. He isn't human. At least as far as I can see. I'd appreciate the opportunity to put a bullet in the sumbitch to confirm the theory."

Cole halted and leaned toward Wilczek. "He came to my town. My people. He had something to do with the deaths of some of those fine people. In my damn town. I want answers. If those aren't forthcoming, I want to take him down. I know you think I'm sheriff of some Podunk county in Texas, and you're right. But the folks in my Podunk county elected me. They have for six straight elections. They trust me. They expect me to keep the peace and not be an asshole. They expect me, on the rare occasion it's necessary, to go right at the bad guys. That's why I'm here, Check. And I'm not going to apologize for it. I'm after a very, very bad guy. Whatever the hell he is."

An impressive response, particularly since he'd been prepared to dismiss this sheriff as a one-bullet wonder, elected as someone's son or nephew. But this guy showed moxie. He had an edge. This was no dime-store sheriff.

He nodded in respect toward Cole and turned to Nadine. "Well?"

She took the time to reach toward Francois, her first two fingers separated to show an empty space for a cigarette. Francois lit it for her and inserted it into her hand. She sat back and took a puff without inhaling before she looked at Wilczek.

"Cards on the table, Check. I just don't know. He's at a minimum capable of preternatural activity. He talked to me and knew things. Knew things no one knew. And he expected us. The three of us, in Wales. He's nothing I've ever encountered, tracked, or had a part in capturing. He's dangerous to an extent I've never seen."

Wilczek finished off his second DP, nodded at the three of them, reached into his pocket, pulled out car keys, and tossed them on the table.

It all sounded more than a little crazy, but he lived in a sociopathic crazy world. The priest had a personal mission and was sincere about it. Raised a Catholic, Wilczek didn't doubt the man's conviction about demons. He didn't buy into it, but it didn't matter. The sheriff showed commitment. Cole's mission had a solid purpose. It had a personal vendetta element, yeah, but he chased this guy across oceans and that for damn sure showed commitment. Nadine, on the other hand, came across as part of the team on some strange life quest, or deep-seated desire to participate in field ops, or both. He didn't buy into the Cole-as-lover story, but she had committed for whatever reason felt right to her. And he didn't want to lose her. He'd lost a twelve-year-old daughter. He'd raised her. Her mom, a Lebanese hooker, had handed the child to Wilczek at birth. "Take her," she'd said. He did. His daughter was murdered in the Lebanese civil war. No one knew of her within the CIA, which meant no one knew of her. He'd do what he could to keep Nadine safe.

"So pay attention. Everyone. Especially you, Nadine," he said. "Those keys go to a Land Cruiser parked outside. It's white. The letters AHF are all over the damn thing. Arab Humanitarian Fund. A nonexistent NGO. Everyone got that?"

"NGO?" asked Francois.

"Nongovernmental organization. Not affiliated with any government. Do-gooders. Relief efforts. Food, medicine, whatever. Prevent human suffering. Cure psoriasis. Whatever the hell you think will sell over there so you won't get pulled from the vehicle, tortured, and shot."

"Got it," said Cole. "Thanks, Check. Sincerely."

"Stand by, cowboy. I'm not finished." Wilczek pulled a wrist-sized GPS unit from his bag and tossed it on the table. "A route to Idlib is preprogrammed in there. It will take you on smuggler tracks across the border and back roads—all unpaved—to Idlib. Jerry can of extra gas in the back, two spare tires on the roof rack. You're on your own finding the convent. Everyone got it?"

Wilczek looked at each of them with intent until he got an affirmative nod. "Dress in jeans, long-sleeved shirt, and ball cap. All of you. From a distance, Nadine, you might pass as a man. Got it?" Again, nods all around, although Francois's nod was accompanied by a shrug. "Get your stories straight. Doctors, agricultural experts, yoga instructors. Doesn't matter, but get it straight between yourselves. Oh, and 'priest' is not a good cover. Got it?"

"But, Monsieur Check, this is what I am!" said Francois.

"Yeah. I get it. But claiming priesthood endangers your friends. Understand?"

Francois looked off in the distance as he contemplated for a moment. "Oui. Then perhaps a culinary expert. A nongovernment culinary expert."

"Yeah. They need those big-time in Syria right now. Nadine, I'm making you responsible for the cover. Get it straight," said Wilczek.

"Okay, Check," she said and touched a pouting Francois's arm. "We'll talk later, Francois."

Wilczek stood, left the maps, and grabbed his canvas bag. "Nadine, give my number to the cowboy just in case. Cowboy, if it involves Nadine, call me. Not much moon tomorrow night. Good time to roll. Any questions?"

They all stood as the men shook hands and thanked him. Nadine hugged him, kissed him on the cheek, and said, "I owe you."

"I'm counting on it," said Wilczek. "Oh, one last thing, cowboy. There is a compartment under the back seat. Get to it by lifting the seat forward. You will find an ArmaLite M-15. Full auto with select fire. Keep it on single shot until things get too hot. Five thirty-round clips. Show Nadine how to use it. A Mossberg 12-gauge pump, eight in the magazine. Thirty extra rounds. All number four buckshot. For up close and personal work. Show Nadine how to work that too. And a Kimber .45 pistol. One extra clip on the holster. Nadine already knows how to shoot the pistol."

Cole looked at Nadine, clearly not surprised. She responded with an imitation of a Francois shrug. Wilczek had heard her brag about her ability with a pistol during one of their conference videos. She belonged to a group of Houston ladies who would go shoot early on Saturdays before it got too hot, and then retire to a club swimming pool for bloody marys and a dip.

Wilczek pointed a finger at Nadine. "Call me. I can do things."

"Will do, Check," she said. "Thanks again."

Later in the day Wilczek played the recording of their comments. "Well, what did you think?" asked Nadine.

"Glad he's on our side," said Cole. "Damn glad."

"Exactement," said Francois.

Glad I'm on your side? You had better hope God is on your side, dumbasses, he thought.

Chapter 30

They left at midnight the next day. The time spent prior to departure consisted of rest, food, and at least for Francois, the acquisition of clothing. They discussed terrain and approach. They each prayed.

Nadine scribbled "this place is bugged" on the back of a map and showed it to Cole and Francois. Cole nodded. Francois did not understand, so she wrote a more detailed descriptive for him. Francois snorted and waved a hand with broad brushstrokes across the room—a gesture of pure disgust.

She and Cole agreed that archaeologists mapping and cataloging Arabic antiquities made a solid story. They purchased several shovels, rakes, and small bags to lend validity to the cover. Even Francois agreed.

She accompanied Cole to check the vehicle and its special compartment. He let her know how much he appreciated Wilczek's armory, stating that this wasn't Wales and the firepower stowed in the truck alleviated a major concern for him. She understood where he was coming from, and his act of running his hands over the hardware, she knew, was a guy thing. Nadine shook off the brief thought that it would sure be nice if that kind of touch were applied elsewhere. They drove to the rugged terrain on the outskirts of town and he showed her how to operate and shoot the automatic rifle and pump shotgun. It was a good exercise, but one she hoped wouldn't be put to use. François surely wouldn't participate if it came to gunfire. That left her as half the equation for the team's use of high-powered weaponry. She was okay with that. More importantly, a data map of wireless connectivity showed good coverage around Idlib. Real power lay there, not in guns.

She'd planned on jeans, shirt, and a ball cap, as did Cole, so dress did not present an issue. Francois purchased baggy white linen pants and several pastel shirts large enough to drape over his round frame and extend to mid-thigh, secured at his waist by the rattlesnake belt. Cole told him he looked like an Arab pirate. Nadine sang the chorus of "Y.M.C.A."

Francois took pleasure explaining to his companions about the straw hat he wore. It hailed from Montecristi, Ecuador, where they made the world's finest. Montecristi hats folded into a suitcase, and would pop back into shape with the snap of a wrist. Apparently a common ball cap would not do. Neither Cole nor Nadine burned any calories trying to talk Francois out of his chosen attire.

Cole insisted—over dinner the night of their departure—on a discussion about the specifics of the potential encounter with Moloch.

"We need to do it together, Francois," he said. "I'm doing this in part to find answers. If we corner him, I want to talk to him. I need you with me for that." Cole cleared his throat, adding, "Nadine, I'd like your insights from the exchange with Moloch, if we can pull it off."

She pushed Cole to further define his intent. She listened, asked a few questions, and focused on the context. Cole explained that any information gathered from Moloch might allow law enforcement to get in front of these type of killings in the future. She felt great personal satisfaction when Cole elaborated on his hope that she could glean sufficient data points from Moloch to do predictive modeling.

Francois ate, listened, and contributed little to the conversation. As the meal finished, he said, "The deceiver. The liar. Anything he says is a lie, meant to inflict more pain. Such questions as to context and selection and nature are beyond pointless." Francois signaled for more wine. "I shall do what I can to support such an enquiry during the brief time you and I engage with him, but I must destroy this creature. My goal has not changed."

The entire conversation revealed more of Cole's thought processes and deep beliefs—information she relished. Francois's assertion that he would bring the heavenly mojo gave her more than a little concern, although he'd certainly demonstrated sufficient ecumenical whup ass in the Cardiff encounter.

"Okay, let's say I get nothing from him. Nothing which helps me," said Cole. "He still caused the deaths of an awful lot of people. So let's talk justice." He paused to sip his bottled water. "Specifically, let's talk shooting the bastard."

"Then shoot him," said Francois as he selected a piece of the sweet cheese pastry called künefe. "Shoot him multiple times, mon ami. It will perhaps satisfy your American inclinations."

Coffee arrived. She and Cole exchanged incredulous looks. Nadine emitted a raucous laugh loud enough to draw the attention of fellow diners. "My, my," she said. "We've turned you into Clint Eastwood, instructing Cole to spit lead. Whatever would the pope say?"

Francois slurped some thick coffee to wash down the künefe and smacked his lips. "His Holiness would concur. It is a useless activity, all of this spitting of the lead. But I do comprehend you feel you must do so. So do it. It will have no effect."

They all drank coffee. Francois and Nadine smoked. Nadine experimented holding the cigarette between thumb and forefinger, butt toward the palm, in an affectation from a silent movie as she tapped the ash on the ashtray. One, two, three.

"So what happens when you need help?" she asked of Francois. "Let's say God isn't using you as a conduit that day. What then?"

"It's a matter of faith," said Cole, squeezing her hand. "Faith doesn't vacillate for some folks. Francois is one of those folks."

"You are growing, mon ami," said Francois.

She took a deep breath and added, "My faith is growing, but it's not enough right now. Not to face Moloch. Is yours, Cole?"

Cole released her hand, shifted, and took another sip of water. "I don't know," he said.

They remained silent until Nadine said, "I just want you both to know this is the most meaningful thing I've ever done. Bar none. That whole thing about living life to the fullest never made sense before, but it does now. And I owe you two for opening my eyes."

Neither of them responded, so she added, "I also want you both to know I love you." She left it on the table.

"Bon. You as well are growing," said Francois. "This love, which I share, is natural and God-given. It is what Jesus instructed us to do."

Cole remained silent, clearly uncomfortable with the conversational theme.

"And I've developed a special kind of love for you," said Nadine as she leaned toward Cole. "It wasn't on purpose. It just happened. I need you to know this before we take off on the midnight express."

Cole cleared his throat and nodded at the tabletop.

Nadine had sufficient social skills to recognize Cole's discomfort. She turned to Francois and asked, "Why do men get so uncomfortable with this type of discussion? It's from the heart. It's nothing to be embarrassed about."

Francois lit another smoke, signaled the waiter, and asked for another coffee as well as a cognac. "An excellent question. Many factors play a part in this. A man such as our friend Cole is, perhaps, fearful. Such a discussion could create an opening of the heart, not an endeavor a man takes lightly."

"But he should be comfortable with this setting. Good grief. We both love him. Does he think we will jab an ice pick in his heart if he opens it?"

"He fears the opening, not the situation once it becomes opened. This is one perspective. Perhaps he lacks emotional development. Another possibility."

Cole turned to look for the waiter and showed an empty brandy snifter. "You folks realize I'm sittin' right here, right?"

"Do you think he can only express matters of the heart physically? He gave me an incredible kiss in Cardiff. Deep and loving. Not lustful," she said to Francois.

"A possibility," said Francois. "A man finds more comfort in action. Action allows him to express through an emotional filter."

"Still sittin' right here," said Cole. "Not deaf. Wishing the damn subject would change."

"Am I obligated to pull emotion, particularly love, out of him all the time? It would exhaust me," said Nadine.

"Then perhaps it's a matter of training. Of awareness. He surely can be taught such things."

"One would think. But at the end of the day, I guess I don't know him all that well," said Nadine.

"This is great, folks," said Cole. "Why, let's keep this going for hours. A dinner dissection of ol' Cole. Good times, good times."

Nadine and Francois exchanged identical shrugs. She had developed an expertise at it.

"Here's your cognac," she said to Cole as the waiter placed a new snifter on the table. "Sorry if the conversation caused you any discomfort."

"Oui. My apologies, my Texas friend. Would it provide relief for you to shoot some people?"

Francois chuckled, Nadine's raucous laugh erupted, and Cole looked relieved. The subject changed.

After dark, they loaded the Land Cruiser and waited for midnight. On the couch, Cole shut his eyes and got a couple hours of sleep. Francois did the same in one of the bedrooms. Nadine spent the time on one of her laptops, too excited to sleep.

At midnight, they assembled at the vehicle and held hands, forming a circle and smiling at each other in the faint light of the hotel parking lot.

"And so," said Francois.

"Well?" asked Nadine.

They all squeezed hands tighter. Cole nodded at them both. "Let's ride."

Chapter 31

The smugglers' trail rose into the highlands, far from the paved roads ribboned across the flat desert near the border. They made slow progress. Deep ruts and the occasional small boulder lay across the trail. The stars shone bright, reflecting off the white rocks in a moonscape view that allowed Cole to turn off the headlights. Nadine rode shotgun and managed the small GPS and its backlit topographic map while giving Cole directions.

"We'll curve to the right in half a mile and dip into a ravine," she said.

"Got it."

Conversation was minimal. Nadine gave occasional instructions in a quiet voice, Cole acknowledged them while he focused on the dim trail, and Francois remained silent in the back seat. Twice they perceived campfires in the distance.

After three hours at slow speeds, Nadine checked the GPS and softly announced, "We're in Syria." Neither man responded.

The trail stayed on the edge of rises and utilized ravines. It never exposed its travelers to profiles against the night sky. Cool desert air covered the area. They rode with the windows down and listened to the tires crunch over shards and stone. A jackal watched them pass, its ears high and curious. Cole stared back as the vehicle passed within a few paces of the animal.

"Another two miles and we'll drop to the southeast and intersect an actual gravel road," said Nadine. "I've programmed in the location of the convent and we can get there on unpaved roads the entire way. We'll be a few miles from Idlib, so if we need supplies we might be able to shop there."

The city of Idlib lay six miles from the highlands they descended. When they made a final sharp turn out of a ravine, the Idlib plain stretched before them. In the predawn hours, Idlib was recognizable not by its city lights but by the vivid explosions of mortar and artillery shells and the small pinpoint lights of small arms firing. Cole stopped the vehicle and they all got out.

"Holy shit," said Nadine.

They stood and watched the fireworks as the low rumble of artillery echoed across the plain. Small blasts within Idlib marked artillery return fire. Some of the shells landed several miles to the east of where they stood.

"This is madness," said Francois. "Absolute madness."

"There goes the shopping trip," said Cole.

Nadine explained Assad's troops occupied the city, and various jihadist groups attacked them. Since the assorted attack groups also intended to kill any competing jihadists, random patterned crossfire also occurred.

"So they lob shells at the government troops in Idlib?" asked Cole.

"Yes," said Nadine.

"And the government troops lob shells back?"

"Yes."

"And the jihadist groups toss a mortar or artillery shell at each other for good measure while they shoot at the government troops?" asked Cole.

"Welcome to Syria," said Nadine.

Cole and Nadine huddled over the GPS unit and studied the tracks leading to the convent. The deep reverberation of explosions continued unabated, washing the Idlib plain with sound. Cole stared in the direction of the convent and commented to Nadine that the general area of the convent did not have much action. This observation gave him some small measure of relief. His arms ached from his death grip on the wheel the last several hours and he rolled his shoulders to loosen up.

The cracks of automatic gunfire came from their right, somewhere nearby.

"A little too close for comfort," he said. "We can either turn back or move forward, but I don't think staying right here is a good idea."

Nadine noted daylight would soon begin creeping over the mountains to the east. Francois returned to the backseat, pointed a hand forward, and said, "Aller!"

Cole looked at Nadine in the starlight and asked, "What did he say?"

"His version of 'Wagons Ho!'"

The next litany of sharp cracks from automatic weapons came much closer from behind them and to the right. Nadine ran around the front of the Land Cruiser and jumped into the passenger seat while Cole leapt in and fired the engine. He threw it into gear and glanced at the rearview mirror. Bright muzzle blasts came from all directions behind them. Several bullets gave their distinctive angry bee sound as they whizzed past the vehicle's windows.

"Get down!" Cole yelled as he slammed the accelerator to the floor and took off toward Idlib. Nadine complied and lowered her head to the area between the two front seats and looked through the back window. Cole's side mirror reflected the illuminated gun blasts of the fighters, several of whom appeared to run after them. He threw a quick glance over his shoulder at Francois. The priest sat stoically, looking straight ahead. "Dammit, Francois, get the hell down!" The extra jerry can of gasoline perched behind Francois became an instant concern. A stray bullet into that thing would not be good. Not good at all.

"Please get down, Francois!" said Nadine, clearly desperate to have him make less of a target. Another angry bee sound flew past her window.

Cole glanced back to see Francois respond with a repeat of the forward hand gesture and another "Aller!"

"Sweet Jesus!" said Cole.

"Exactement," said Francois with no excitement.

Cole continued to hammer the accelerator as he alternated between looking through the windshield and watching the side berm of the gravel road as a marker to confirm he still traveled on some semblance of road. Heart pounding, he focused on the immediacy of finding the convent. He kept the headlights off.

"You may want to notice we're heading straight toward Idlib," he said, speaking over the racing engine. "That ain't good, Nadine."

Nadine stared at the GPS, tracking their progress. "There's another dirt road, fifty yards ahead. Turn right," said Nadine.

He threw frantic glances to the right as the vehicle flew along, prepared to swerve hard once he spotted the other road.

"We missed it!" said Nadine, holding the GPS unit inches from her face.

Cole slammed on the brakes and skidded to a sideways stop. He threw the vehicle in reverse and turned to drape an arm over the back of the seat and look through the back window as he accelerated backward. The red glow of the taillights turned on once he began in reverse.

A mortar round landed thirty feet away, sending shrapnel in all directions.

"Are you shittin' me?" yelled Cole, using the taillights to try and find the missed intersecting road.

A second mortar round landed close enough to rock the vehicle as it still plowed in reverse.

That did it. He slammed on the brakes, threw it into first gear, swung the wheel to the right, and took off across the ruts of the road and onto the desert floor. He switched on the headlights as a third mortar round landed nearby.

"There!" said Nadine, pointing ahead.

A second later he recognized the road she pointed to and turned the headlights back off as the vehicle swerved onto the new gravel road and accelerated through the gears until wind and engine noise filled their space.

"Turn right in a mile and a half," said Nadine. She leaned toward Cole as she spoke, to ensure she could be heard. "And a half a mile on that road and we'll be there!"

The dirt road accommodated speed and he kept the accelerator floored. "I don't want to miss the next road, Nadine. Give me some warning."

"Then maybe you'd better slow down a little!" she said, trying to focus on the GPS and their progress on the tiny electronic map.

"To hell with that!" said Cole, loud and adamant. "Just give me enough warning."

Nadine counted the distance to the next intersection with hundred yard increments. When she gave the final hundred-yard warning, Cole took his foot off the gas and prepared to make a hard right. Those red backup lights weren't coming on again.

"There!" she said.

"Got it!"

This road, little more than a track, forced him to downshift and go much slower. The Land Cruiser bounced over ruts and rocks as it ascended a small rise. Half a mile later they could discern a large wall in the starlight. Cole pulled alongside it, kept the engine running, and could just make out the crumbled remains of the roof and three walls.

"Is this our convent?" he asked.

"No," said Francois. "This is what remains of the monastery. The convent surely will be nearby."

He turned off the vehicle. The distant sounds of artillery shells drifted through to combine with the light ticking of the Land Cruiser's stressed engine as it cooled. If they were close by the convent, they could wait until daylight. He explained this to the other two and added the vehicle itself made a target. They would hunker down among the monastery rubble until they could see and make their way to the convent. Nadine and Francois accepted without comment.

Once the three left the vehicle, Cole opened the back door and pulled the backseat forward to reveal Wilczek's special compartment. He grabbed the shotgun and handed it to Nadine.

"You remember how to use it?" he asked. He kept his voice low, hoping it wouldn't carry.

Nadine nodded, her action just visible to Cole in the dark.

He removed the M-15, chambered a round, and pocketed two extra clips. He shoved the .45 into the back of his pants.

"This, too, is madness," whispered Francois as he watched Cole and Nadine arm themselves.

Cole led the way into the stones and bricks that lay jumbled next to the lone standing wall. They managed to stumble their way into a protected area surrounded by stones. They sank to the ground, to wait for sunrise.

"We are on a hill, no?" whispered Francois.

"Yes," said Cole.

"And, shall we say, sufficiently surrounded by these stones?"

"Yeah, I suppose."

"Bon." Francois's lighter sparked into life and he lit a cigarette.

"Are you out of your freakin' mind?" asked Cole in a loud whisper. It didn't help when Nadine asked for one. Francois promptly lit hers and passed it through the dark predawn.

They all leaned back and struggled to find a resting spot for their backs among the sharp rock edges. Cole's adrenaline began to subside. What absolute madness had entered their lives. The three of them had just been shot at by rifles and mortars and now they sat among rubble on a Syrian hill hoping to take sanctuary at a convent sitting somewhere out there in the dark while civil war raged a few miles away. And all this after having flown to Wales and become immersed in mass murder, not to mention the involvement of a demon-like creature he'd talked to up close and personal. *Five days ago I was having breakfast at Shorty's and wondering where to go fishing this weekend,* he thought. *You damn sure can't say you're bored, son.*

The first signs of daylight began to emanate from over the eastern mountains. The Land Cruiser's engine continued to send cooling-off metallic ticks. With decent visibility for the first time, they inspected their surroundings. The monastery of St. Anthony had not covered a large area. Olive trees came to the edge of the fallen structure and the birds occupying them began their morning calls. The distant fighting had tapered off. It appeared the dark of night was the preferred time to wage battle.

He turned and told the other two to stay put while he made his way to the olive trees and gathered a view of the surrounding area. He carried the M-15, kept low, and moved with caution to avoid stumbling. At the edge of the olive grove, he squatted to wait for further daylight, the automatic rifle across his lap, finger on the trigger.

The sounds of war continued to diminish. A distant mosque began the call to prayer through loudspeakers. The gunfire stopped.

Cole jerked the weapon up when a voice close by yelled in Arabic. A tiny woman dressed in a white tunic and a black scarf, clearly upset, stood with hands on hips and yelled at him again. Cole lowered the weapon and stood, at which point she changed to French. The verbal assault did not diminish. He shook his head, which prompted her to change to English.

"Are there not enough guns?" she yelled. "Do you feel an obligation to add to the killing? Do you take joy doing this? Go to Idlib! There is a lot of killing there! Go!"

Cole held out a free hand, palm facing her. Before he could speak, Francois exclaimed from a distance, "Bonjour! Bonjour! Comment allez-vous?"

They turned to watch Francois scramble over the ruins of the monastery and approach them. Sufficient light revealed white pants, a pastel green shirt, and a large smile. Nadine followed him at a much slower pace.

"Le Pere Domaine?"

"Oui, oui!"

The two chatted in French. Nadine made it to Cole and they watched, forgotten. After several minutes, Francois turned to them with a broad sweeping gesture and said, "This is Sister Rahel. Of the Order of St. Anthony. The convent is but a short distance through the trees."

Francois made introductions all around. Sister Rahel continued to scowl at Cole and looked with sympathy toward Nadine. Cole asked if they could drive to it and the nun told of a small path through the olive grove that terminated at the convent, and warned him not to damage any of the trees. The nun and Francois turned and began to walk into the grove.

Cole and Nadine repacked the weapons into the Land Cruiser and drove around the ruins of the monastery until they found a trail and followed it, winding among the ancient gnarled trunks. Francois had earlier explained that the Order of St. Anthony had occupied this place for almost seven hundred years.

The small convent nestled at the far edge of the olive grove, its roofline just above the height of the trees. Constructed of brick and stone, it had few doors and a row of windows high on the walls. Over the chapel at one end of the compact building the roof formed a circle, above which a small cross stood and, next to it, a small satellite antenna.

Several chickens meandered about, kept out of a small garden by an undersized fence woven of cut olive branches. Cole parked the vehicle and absorbed the place. Nadine reached across and gently squeezed his neck.

"Well, we made it," she said.

"And without hitting any trees. I wish I could say the same for those bullets." The daylight had displayed several bullet punctures in the body of the Land Cruiser. "This is absolutely nuts, Nadine."

"I know. Let's go check the place out."

More introductions were conducted inside. Sister Rahel made a point of inspecting Cole's back to ensure he didn't carry any weapons. Three other nuns remained; Sisters Sosa, Raca, and Elacha. Sister Rahel explained that Rome had evacuated all but four nuns after the monastery attack several months ago.

"We four were allowed to stay, for which I am most grateful," said Sister Rahel. The other three nodded in agreement.

The nuns fed them a simple breakfast of stale bread and chickpeas mashed with spices. They spoke of events in French and English, focusing on the civil war raging around them.

"It is not necessarily religious in nature," said Sister Rahel. "Factions initially concentrated on fighting the government of Assad. Of course they began fighting each other as well, which drew fighters from France, Russia, Lebanon, Iran, Yemen, North Africa—from everywhere. This created more chaos and death. I will not deny they all have their own version of Islamic righteousness. But much of it represents a struggle for power."

Nadine enquired about life before the war.

"For a millennium we have lived at peace with our neighbors. Assad, and his father before him, maintained that history."

"And now?" asked Nadine.

"We are an easy target," said Sister Rahel. "Yes, some groups have more anti-Christian fanaticism than others, but we are simply convenient. The brothers at the Monastery attempted to maintain relationships with the factions and tribes, but to no avail."

"Why haven't they attacked you?" asked Cole. Their sitting duck situation made him uneasy given this little convent defined their base of operations. He began to think of potential exit route strategies.

"We exist here under the grace of God," said Sister Rahel. "For how long is up to him."

The conversation drifted to gossip from the Vatican, exchanged mostly in French. Cole thought of daylight. No sounds of gunfire or artillery came through the high open windows. They would hunt Moloch during the day. They would also escape back to Turkey during the daylight hours. It appeared their only chance.

The French switched back to English as the conversation moved into the purpose of their arrival. Francois spoke of traveling from the United States to Wales, the murders at the School for the Blind, and foremost their pursuit of this demon. At several intervals during his telling, the sisters crossed themselves. None of the nuns showed any incredulity toward the fact a demon walked among humans. Apparently they occupied such a hellish landscape that the appearance of demons posed few questions. Sister Rahel noted that more than once they had wondered if Satan had not formed his forces in this part of Syria.

The nuns steered the conversation back to the encounter with Moloch at the Cardiff hotel coffee shop, extracting details from Francois. They patted both Cole and Nadine's hands during the description of their personal interactions with the demon. They explained to the Americans that those who survived such encounters were bestowed with special consideration. God had surely protected them.

"Father Domaine, you must summon the power of God to defeat this creature," said Sister Rahel. "You must ask God's protection to find it and most dangerous of all, to approach it."

Francois pinched his lower lip between forefinger and thumb. "Oui. Such is my plan, Sister."

Cole and Nadine remained silent for most of the conversation. Then Nadine began to pry for intelligence.

"Moloch leads a group called al Garal in one of the Dead Cities," she said.

The nuns spoke in a French clamor before Sister Rahel turned to Nadine and said, "We know this group. The worst of the worst. Killing women and children. Wiping out villages."

"How do you know them?" asked Cole. "Or better yet, do you know how to locate them?"

Sister Rahel explained that the convent maintained contact with the local world through the purchase of basic supplies from select merchants. Through these interactions, talk would move to the current situation and the latest news.

"It is blasphemous to think of the situation, but God works in mysterious ways," said Sister Rahel. The tiny woman became angry and spit the location. "They occupy the remains of a village containing the most ancient Church of St. Ageranus. Not a great distance from here. One cries at the thought of such vileness on those sacred grounds."

Nadine opened her leather travel bag and produced a laptop. Cole scooted over to watch her acquire the convent's satellite feed, break through the encrypted security features, and search for the Church of St. Ageranus. A few minutes later she said, "Four miles, almost due west."

"Let's go now," said Cole. "Get him while they all sleep. If they've fought all night, they'll be taking sack time right about now. The element of surprise is on our side. Let's take him down."

He had momentum and their resolve could fade if they waited. They could find Moloch, take care of business, and get the hell out of there all in one day. Nighttime would damn sure bring out the fighting again.

"Américains," said Sister Rahel to Francois.

"Texas," said Francois, a revelation that caused tiny Sister Rahel to raise both eyebrows. The other three nuns looked sideways at Cole and then each other.

"Actually, Cole, this may call for a bit more planning," said Nadine. "Some reconnaissance. Let's get the lay of the land and formulate a more deliberate action."

She had a legitimate point. But he'd formulated a personal plan, one which involved the capabilities of the M-15 and a headshot. He now accepted that no revelations would come from Moloch. He'd come to this conclusion last night on the smuggler's road. This demon had a powerful relationship to the Rockport and Cardiff massacres as well as Martha's death, but Francois's assertion that this creature lied and deceived and perverted rang true. His seething anger and frustration rose to a boil with this acceptance. He didn't take cold killing lightly, but this was different. They were all in a life threatening position and the sooner this got done the sooner they could get the hell out of here. The time for complexities had passed. No answers could be gleaned from this creature, except one.

Let's see how Moloch handles a bullet, he thought. *I can damn sure answer one big question after I squeeze the trigger.*

"I don't mind taking a scouting trip right now," said Cole. "You two stay here."

"No," said Francois. "Let us not forget who shall lead this battle. We shall rest. Last night was tres stressful. We shall rest."

"He's right," said Nadine to Cole. "A couple of hours sleep and we'll reconnoiter."

His head knew Francois had a valid point. They were more formidable as a team. His heart spoke of getting this deadly business done as quickly as possible. His head won out.

The nuns showed each of them to small, sparse rooms. Due to the trauma of the drive, the relief from arriving intact at the convent, and the heavy nature of the breakfast, Cole soon fell sound asleep.

Chapter 32

Nadine woke first. She lay on the cool sheets and reflected on the situation. *This is the most significant experience of my life,* she thought. *Even the gunshots and mortars and artillery, which scared the living crap out of me, seem fitting as part and parcel of the whole package.* The adrenaline rushes, the constant edge, the mere fact they sat in the middle of such chaos lit a fire in her, and it was easy to understand how Check and the other field operatives she'd worked with so loved their assignments.

Ensconced in such a physically challenging place while her internal belief system went through radical changes brought its own element of thrill and fascination. Her relationship with a higher power had changed her. She knew the bullheadedness and a fascination with technology would remain a part of her forever, but now there was the added dimension of spirituality. It gave her insight to how Francois walked through life, and it provided a greater understanding of Cole. He clearly vacillated in the depth of his belief, but she got that. The man had gone through a lot. That didn't let him off the hook for his Lone Ranger BS in wanting to go after Moloch right away, but she'd cut him some slack even on that. He'd obviously changed since they left Turkey and now appeared to focus on some kind of righteous retribution. His simpler approach of just blowing Moloch away had a finality in the current chaos that she understood, but her heart told her it wasn't going to be that cut and dried.

She entered the hallway and heard Cole's light snoring through his door and Francois's heavier snoring through his. She contemplated letting them sleep, but Cole had been right about one thing—it was best to maintain momentum. She woke them both.

Sister Raca made them tea in the small kitchen. Francois lit a cigarette and Sister Rahel slapped an empty tin can on the table, indicating its purpose as an ashtray and her displeasure at his smoking.

"We are a burden, this I understand," said Francois. "And as such, I insist we find a place to eat, away from here, so we may go and return before darkness falls."

Francois had likely given considerable thought to another meal of mashed chickpeas.

"Bad idea," said Cole.

"No, it is an idea of relieving the sisters of our burden."

Sister Rahel stood a few feet away and leaned forward, birdlike, hands on hips.

"You will not starve here, Father Domaine," she said, one eyebrow lifted.

"There is a small village on the back side of our little hill, not one half mile away," said Sister Raca. "It is poor and small but it does contain a tea house which serves food."

Sister Rahel gave Sister Raca a look capable of withering fresh flowers.

"Bon! A nice walk," said Francois.

"Bad idea," said Cole.

Nadine was up for it. "Let's stretch our legs," she said. "It's quiet right now and we'll be back long before sundown." She grabbed her leather shoulder bag and removed a laptop to leave there, keeping the cell phone and electronic tablet in the bag.

Cole lagged behind on the walk down the south side of the convent's hill and turned with regularity to check their backtrack, which drove Nadine a little crazy because a half-mile made for a minor distance, and bad guys were unlikely to pop out this time of day. He packed the .45 in the back of his pants, covered by his shirttails. Francois had said nothing as they stopped by the Land Cruiser while Cole retrieved the firearm. *I'm glad Francois has stopped his commentary on guns,* she thought. *It might be unlikely that we run into bad guys, but not impossible. And dollars-to-donuts Cole can hit what he aims at.*

Two-dozen hovels, most with tin roofs, appeared as they rounded a curve on the hillside. Smoke drifted from several of the houses, goats meandered the dirt streets, and a few old Toyota pickups sat at irregular intervals. A cluster of veiled women stood around the town's well, hand-pumping water into their individual buckets, shooing away flies, and sharing stories. Two old men sat in the shade of a tin-roofed courtyard smoking hookahs, while two young women prepared a meal behind them. Francois strode to this establishment.

The old men stared with hooded eyes as they approached. The women at the well fell silent. The goats, sensing some change, stopped their activities. Francois doffed his Ecuadorian hat at the two old men. They did not change expressions or acknowledge the greeting. Nadine followed on his heels, nodding at everyone although no nods were returned. The whole thing felt like a scene from a spaghetti western. She looked over her shoulder to smile at Cole, but he kept moving those dark eyes with a constant scan.

Several dilapidated tables and chairs were arrayed on the dirt. Chickens scratched the ground around them. Francois ceremoniously removed a large off-white handkerchief and swiped the seats of the chairs as well as the tabletop. Cole and Francois waited for her to sit. Francois then lowered himself, lit a smoke, and placed a US twenty-dollar bill on the table.

"Universal currency, admittedly," he said to Nadine, and looked at the two young women with a quizzical expression.

One of them came over, bowed, and mimicked the act of eating by moving her hand to her mouth and pointing at the twenty-dollar bill.

"Oui," said Francois.

The girl smiled, snatched the bill, and barked an order at her younger sister. Lamb meat appeared and was quickly skewered, sprinkled with spices, and laid on the grill. Moments later, the aroma of lamb kebob filled the small courtyard. Flat bread and a yogurt cucumber dip arrived, followed by a pot of tea and three glasses.

"And so," said Francois, clearly satisfied with himself. "The sisters are children of God, yet they insist on refraining from all God has to offer among culinary possibilities. It of course holds no logic, but I am not one to judge."

Nadine took a sip of tea, stood, and announced her need to freshen up. She started to move away from the table, hesitated, and turned to collect her small shoulder pouch. It was a long held habit of hers and she hoped Cole and Francois didn't view it as mistrust. She'd already confirmed that this little village had cell phone service, and if some critical piece of information showed up or a call from Check came, then it became a matter of immediate access to the rest of the world. Nadine approached the two young women cooking and, after exchanging universal gestures, one of the young women pointed to a doorway off the courtyard.

The barrel of an AK-47 greeted Nadine when she exited the bathroom. Another man roughly slipped a black cotton bag over her head and clamped her mouth, using the cloth as a gag. He whispered a threat in Arabic next to her ear and moved her backward along the hall and out the door. The sun on her skin and the sound of a vehicle starting woke her from the initial shock and triggered a violent struggle. She kicked and flailed with all her strength and caused the man clamping her mouth shut to lose his grip, allowing her to jerk the cotton bag off her head. Before she could call for help, her peripheral vision picked up the wooden butt of the AK-47 driving toward her head. A sunburst of pinpoint lights washed over Nadine's consciousness before oblivion and darkness drew her down.

***

Cole continued to scan the immediate horizon. The women began to talk again at the well. The goats continued to graze on anything with the temerity to grow, several goat bells clanking as the herd moved. Smoke from the hookahs drifted through and mixed with the smell of the grilled lamb. A few flies joined them, darting across the table.

Francois dipped the bread in the yogurt and ate with relish, instructing Cole to relax and enjoy the meal. He provided Cole with more history of the Syrian church, its beginnings after the crucifixion, its survival during the ebb and flow of the crusades and the Arab reconquest, and the changing rulers and ruling tribes.

The lamb kebobs arrived and were set in the center of the table as a communal plate. Nadine had still not returned.

Francois ate with his right hand in the manner of local custom, commenting that the lamb was succulent and highly seasoned. Cole stood and looked for Nadine.

"Nadine!" he called, prompting Francois to tell him all was well and she would return from her toilet duties soon.

Cole headed for the door he had seen her enter. The two young women looked away, a bad sign. He rushed into the small house and saw an empty closet-sized bathroom and another open door leading to the outside. He ran through that portal, pulled the .45 from the back of his pants and cocked the hammer. A quiet dirt road and more shacks greeted him. A beat-up white Toyota pickup rolled away to the south. One man squatted in the bed of the truck with an AK-47 between his knees. There was no sign of her.

"Nadine!" he called again, looking desperately in all directions. "Nadine!"

Francois moved through the back door to join Cole on the abandoned street.

"She's gone," said Cole. His gun hand trembled with frustration and rage. "Just gone."

Chapter 33

Moloch called his fighters to assemble at beginning dusk. They had slept the day away inside their tents, exhausted after a night of hard battle. Their mission to terrorize a village—to slaughter the men, rape the women and children, and burn everything to the ground—had encountered complications. The selected village had just seen the arrival of a larger group of fighters from Iraq with their own personal jihadist manifesto. Moloch's animals had attacked during the night and become surrounded and decimated. They'd fought their way from the village, taking casualties at every step.

Moloch had lost half his scum. This presented only a minor problem. More scum could be recruited from the immediate area. He knew plenty of fanatics from competing armies felt their particular leaders insufficient in their zealotry.

As the remnants of al Garal assembled before him, Moloch picked the wounded who had struggled back to camp after the previous night's battle and had them form a line. They stood in various states of pain and debility. Furious, he swept an arm in their direction. To a man, they collapsed to the ground with raspy breath and blood oozing from beneath makeshift bandages. He pointed a long finger at one of the non-wounded leaders and commanded, "Do it!"

The leader pulled a pistol from his waistband and walked the line of prostrate wounded, one of them his own brother, and delivered a headshot to each of them.

The other fighters watched in silence. A brutal lesson, but they would acknowledge the necessity. Victory at all cost. Wounded men became a liability.

Moloch now addressed his men. "I have a mission for you tonight. It will allow you to recover and refresh your courage."

The fighters nodded, waiting. Several crows shuffled and fought over a human head mounted on a nearby pile of rocks. Their squabbling caused the head to teeter and fall from its perch, rolling among the rubble to settle in the dust. No one paid any attention.

"Apostates of the worst kind. Women of the Book."

The fighters looked at each other and smiled.

"You will prove your manhood. You will prove your manhood many times with each one of these apostate women."

This brought cheers and acclamation from his men.

"You will do so in their place of worship. Let their screams echo from the walls."

More shouts of approval. They knew of this place. The scum could take solace in the fact that no one would be shooting and killing them tonight.

"You will burn this place of aberration to the ground. Throw their bodies on the fire."

AK-47 rifles rose, accompanied by shouts of approval.

"Prepare yourselves. Attack in the deep of night, before the dawn. Purify that place! Purify this entire area! Purify the world!"

Rifle shots and jubilant shouts mixed in a perverted harmony.

This will be done. I will travel afterward, thought Moloch. *My scum will rest and think of me fondly while I am away.* He turned a slow complete circle and absorbed the mountains, hills, and plains surrounding him. *It has been too long since we had such a place. Yes, it has been far too long.*

Chapter 34

Nadine regained consciousness as she bounced in the bed of the pickup. The wet warmth of blood trickling down her scalp and the cotton bag over her head tugged, sticking to the wound. She groaned and tried to remove the bag. A rough boot slammed into her hand, causing her to yelp with pain. The pickup turned and came to a stop. Hard hands dragged her from the truck and she was hustled, stumbling, into an old stone farmhouse.

They jerked the bag off her head followed by a hard slap across her face. Her knees buckled before she recovered and blinked in rapid succession to adjust to the low light. There were seven of them. The small one-room farmhouse showed signs of their extended inhabitance. Sleeping mats lay strewn about the floor, cooking pots and tins scattered on the ground near the corner fireplace, and a lone table occupied the center of the room. AK-47s stood propped against the walls.

A small trapdoor stood open at another corner of the room as the men argued and yelled at each other. One of them slapped her again and shoved her toward the trapdoor. That was enough of that BS, so she pivoted and delivered a roundhouse slap to her assailant followed by a kick to the testicles. The man collapsed. Several of the men howled with laughter at the state of their compatriot, while the others knocked her to the ground and kicked her repeatedly toward the opening in the floor. The opening shone as a refuge; she crawled the last few feet to the hole and dropped in, because whatever was down there would beat the heck out of what was happening up here. Maybe these sons of bitches wouldn't be so damn slap-happy if they had to go down there to get to her. She fell the four feet to the dirt floor. The trapdoor slammed shut.

She lay in a small root cellar. A tiny window slit provided minimal light with the fading day. Nadine assessed her condition. The scalp wound bled again, but the kicks she'd absorbed had not broken anything. The small cellar wasn't high enough to provide standing room, so she crawled over to the slit and looked out at desolate desert and distant hills. Night would arrive soon. She took in the position of the cellar relative to the house. Only the trapdoor lay directly under the house. The rest of the cellar had been dug beneath open ground.

Loud arguments continued above. As the men moved about, dust motes fell from the trapdoor and drifted through the cellar. She used her teeth to rip the tail of her shirt and pull free a small piece of the cloth as she huddled in fear, pain, and rising panic. Her hand shook as she applied the torn cloth to her head wound.

This is bad, this is bad, this is really bad, and if you're paying attention, God, this would be a good time to reach down and pluck me the hell out of here. This is so bad and the cavalry won't be showing up anytime soon, unless Cole somehow saw what happened, but it happened so fast that that isn't likely. God, work some magic because I need it bad.

The arguments got louder and the movements on the floor above became more strident. The trapdoor was flung open and two men dropped into the small space, hunched over, and grabbed her. She fought back with kicks and punches, and bit one of them so hard it drew blood. More howls of laughter came from above as the sounds of battle drifted from the cellar. Two more men, chuckling, dropped into the space and together they lifted her writhing body from the hole.

Bent forward over the table with one man squatting on her upper body, pinning her arms, she continued to fight. Another man ripped her jeans and underwear to her knees, hampered by her kicks and twisting torso. More laughter ensued.

The man squatting on her back maneuvered to pull her arms back, pinning them with one hand while he took a handful of hair and pressed her head into the tabletop. Her mind raced as never before. Her breathing was hard and fast, her eyes wild. One of them sat in a corner, focused on a laptop. He paid no mind to the events around him, muttering and shaking the computer with disgust.

"I can fix it!" she screamed at him.

He looked at her as one of the others dropped his filthy undergarments within eyeshot and then moved behind her. *Oh man, oh man, oh man*, she thought, struggling to maintain eye contact with laptop guy. *Please speak some English, you son of a bitch, because you're it and otherwise this only gets worse and worse and worse.*

"I can fix it!" she screamed at him again.

The man with the computer yelled harsh commands at his fellow jihadists. One or two argued back, but this man was apparently their leader and he barked at them in return. The room became quiet.

"You fix?" asked the leader as he held the laptop and shook it.

"Yes! I fix!"

The leader barked more commands and the others released her. She pulled up her clothing and spit at the man who had sat on her. He slapped her hard while several of the others laughed again, adding a running commentary. The leader yelled at them to be silent.

The shoulder bag lay on the floor, her cell phone next to it, crushed by a boot heel. The electronic tablet sat on top of the leather bag, possibly undamaged, and that could be her lifesaver, although these animals weren't likely to give her much of a chance unless she could show progress on his laptop.

"I need that. To fix," she said to the leader and pointed back and forth between his laptop and her tablet. "I need. To fix."

He nodded and she grabbed the tablet and started it. It booted operational. She slid down the wall near the leader and held a hand for his laptop. He handed it to her and leaned along the wall to watch her activities, pulling an old Russian-made pistol and jabbing it into her bruised ribs.

"Fix," he said.

Chapter 35

He saw nothing to chase, no cries for help, no immediate activity to help Nadine. He shook with frustration.

"It is I, it is I!" cried Francois. "Gluttony. A sin. It is I and my gluttony. Forgive me, mon ami! Forgive me!"

"Shut up, Francois," said Cole as he scanned the village and the horizon. "Please. Just shut up." That lone old pickup had been the only movement, and who the hell knew if it had anything to do with her disappearance?

The light faded and the first gunshots of the night echoed from the surrounding hills. Nadine would hear the same, if she still lived—a thought he pushed back into the recesses. He had to do something. *Think! Think, you idiot. Help her. Work the problem,* he thought.

He fished the cell phone from his pocket and checked the signal. Check had told them that the tap water may not flow or a town's electricity would quit with regularity, but the independently solar-powered cell towers usually kept communications open.

He had three bars. Nadine's phone rang once and switched to voice mail. That wasn't good. He scanned the contact list, hands shaking. At the bottom of the list Wilczek's number appeared.

The CIA operative answered on the first ring and waited for a voice on the other end.

"She's gone," said Cole. "Missing."

The sound of a can's pop-top came over the line, then Wilczek said, "Tell me, exactly, what that means. Do not, I repeat, do not leave out any details."

Cole told him what had happened.

"Go back to the convent. Now," said Wilczek. "It will be dark soon. Get your ass back there. It's where she will go if she escapes."

"Why her?" asked Cole. "Why did someone take her? I don't get it."

"Move, dumbass. I don't have time to give you an operational brief of the area. Go to the convent. Tell the nuns. Ask them to make local calls to everyone they know. Rome put a satellite phone system in there. Meanwhile, I'll make calls. I'm on it."

Wilczek hung up and left Cole with a dead line. "Let's go. Back to the sisters," said Cole. Francois, grim—faced, nodded. They jogged back toward the convent as Francois muttered French to himself the entire time.

Cole and Francois entered the convent and assembled the sisters. Cole explained what had happened. The sisters crossed themselves and prayed, hands clasped at their chests, rosaries dangling. Francois interjected in French to emphasize salient points. Sister Rahel glared at Francois and made a point of asking him if he'd found the village meal adequate. Cole and Francois begged them to make local calls to merchants, friends—just call. Sister Rahel did not hesitate, speaking emphatic Arabic to the people who answered the phone.

The replies to Sister Rahel had a common theme—no knowledge of the kidnapping, at least none people would share. Odds were that Check would get the same treatment. Nadine had disappeared.

Chapter 36

She found the problem with the laptop within sixty seconds—a corrupted secure socket layer preventing connectivity with the cell signal. She muttered and sighed as if it were the most difficult problem one could have with a computer. The leader watched her like a hawk as she worked the keyboard.

"I need some light," she said to him. "Light."

He grunted and instructed one of the men to light a lamp and set it on the floor in front of them. The feeble light flickered, causing their shadows to dance against the wall. Nadine turned to her tablet, briefly locked eyes with the leader, and accessed an old Windows program. She reduced the application to a blue-screen series of DOS command lines. It appeared complex and to the man with a gun pressed against her side just the kind of thing he'd expect a computer expert to do, unless he fell to the level of his fighters, in which case she was screwed.

She ran the tablet's GPS in the background and worked the DOS commands, followed by working the keyboard of the leader's laptop—switching back and forth to give the impression of great, focused effort. The GPS worked. Thank God. Hindered by poor satellite reception inside the walls, it struggled to capture their location, but they sat beneath a large open window and given enough time for the algorithms to work, she could pinpoint their location to within a few yards.

While the GPS acquired satellite positioning data on the tablet, she programmed the leader's laptop to time-out at random intervals and cut the cell signal. She repaired the corrupted secure socket layer and showed the leader his computer now searched for and acquired a signal. The idiot smiled approvingly. Then the signal would vanish, triggered by her random time-out command. She made sure to exhibit great frustration and returned to the tablet as if to check something that might help the laptop.

Positioning coordinates confirmed, she checked her location relative to the convent. It stood less than two miles to the north. Fingers flew as she kept the blue DOS screen visible to disguise the instant message to Wilczek. The message delivered a simple "HELP." She attached the GPS coordinates of the farmhouse to the message and waited. The leader's laptop again acquired a cell signal. The leader's smile changed to a grunt of discontent as the signal failed again at random intervals. Nadine appeared frustrated and she, too, grunted with disgust.

Wilczek responded instantly, indicated by a command line popping up on the tablet's screen signaling an incoming message. She retrieved it from the hidden background, still showing a blue screen.

"I HEARD. WILL SEND CALVARY."

"NO TIME. TAKE IT OUT." She knew this facade could only be maintained for a short time. At some point the leader would get frustrated and he'd turn her back over to the others for their enjoyment. Screw that noise.

"DON'T BE A DUMBASS," replied Wilczek.

She lifted the leader's laptop and connected to a signal again. They both grunted approval. Again the signal died. This couldn't go on much longer. She shifted back to the tablet.

"PLEASE. TELL ME WHEN. I'LL BE OK."

"SURE?"

"YES! YES! YES!"

"STANDBY ONE."

Nadine acted as if she had discovered something important on the tablet and moved back to the leader's laptop. She removed the random time-out, reacquired a signal, and showed the leader. They both watched the bars on the signal icon and waited to see if it would lock in without failing.

Check would be retrieving air assets on his laptop. She'd worked with these assets before. As high tech eagles on updrafts, unmanned Predator drones circled all over the Middle East. Loitering at high altitude for twelve hours at a stretch, their ground operators landed them at remote airfields to refuel and sent them off again. Each drone had two Hellfire missiles, capable of delivery with remarkable accuracy. Several Predators roamed the skies over northern Syria.

It would take just a short while for Check to enter her coordinates, command the program to identify the closest asset, and provide a precise time for delivery of a missile.

"DELIVERY 175 SECS IF NEEDED."

The leader seemed satisfied the laptop now worked. He put the pistol away and tried to take her tablet. She pulled it back, signaled "one more thing" and pointed again at his laptop. He agreed to a bit more time. Then the ignorant bastard would turn her over to his men before either killing her or holding her hostage, only to saw her head off on video. So again, screw all that noise and get ready for the ride of your lives, assholes.

"DO IT! DO IT! DO IT!" she IM'd back.

The drone would veer on a course change at high altitude and feed its Hellfire missile her exact location. She had less than three minutes to get small in that root cellar, and even that might not be enough, although it was without doubt better than the alternative.

"DELIVERY ACTIVATED. GOD BLESS."

It might have been worth trying one more message to Check, asking him to let Cole know what was going on, but she knew Check would refuse; part of the deal was if she died in this effort his association with them would end then and there. She got that, but it still sucked.

She stood, looked at the leader who had pulled the tablet from her grip with finality, and pointed to the trapdoor. "Women problems. I need to go down there."

The lowlife moron didn't understand, so she pointed at her crotch with both hands and said, "Problem. Big problem," and pointed to the cellar opening again.

The leader's face twisted with disgust and he barked the situation to his men, all of whom also acquired looks of revulsion. They argued among themselves, pointing to Nadine, and gesturing madly.

The Predator would be releasing the Hellfire missile right about now.

One of the men grabbed her by the arm, yelling at another man who made a point of gesturing toward her crotch and with great emphasis stated his case. He released her arm and Nadine took the three steps to the opening and dropped in. She got on her hands and knees so they could shut the door. One of the men looked into the cellar, yelled something, and dropped the trapdoor. They argued again as she crawled to the corner furthest from the foundation of the farmhouse, curled into a ball, and counted down what she thought was the remaining thirty seconds. She pressed a fist against her heart as if to control its pounding, got to the count of thirty, and knotted her body even tighter. Her breathing came in short emphatic bursts as she waited, shaking.

In a large, furious flash and thunderclap explosion, Nadine was bounced against the cellar ceiling and pinballed against the collapsing debris. Then all lay quiet.

A jackal yelped from a nearby ravine and the low thunder of artillery sounded in the night. She could see stars. Rocks, dirt, and support timbers lay across her a few feet below ground level. She remained still, listening for the sound of men's voices. Hearing none, she began moving gingerly, her hopes rising. With each small movement she assessed bodily damage, one appendage at a time. Nadine May worked through all her body parts, ascertained nothing was broken, and that by squirming to one side she could escape the hole. She did, and opened her eyes wide in the starlight to see remnants of stone and wooden timbers ringing a smoldering depression where the farmhouse had stood. Her adversaries had been disintegrated in the blast. *Holy shit, Check. Holy shit.*

She decided to wait among the scattered remains of the farmhouse until daylight. The evening's war exploded all around the countryside. Her left knee ached. She flexed it gently as a breeze ruffled her matted hair. One, two, three.

Chapter 37

Cole couldn't sleep beyond a few fitful intervals. He tossed and turned for several hours and ended up outside, leaning against the Land Cruiser and staring at the stars. Artillery explosions rolled across the plains, mixed with the light crackle of small arms fire. Dawn would show in an hour or two. The infinity of the sky and the desperation of the situation highlighted, pretty much more than ever before, how insignificant and puny and useless a man could feel. Nadine was gone, perhaps dead. The normal tranquility of Rockport floated a million miles away and years ago. He didn't know where to go or who to turn to. This entire venture seemed like an endeavor foolhardy beyond belief, and Nadine's disappearance had landed him in a place at the bottom of the well.

Muffled Arabic commands ended his contemplation. Multiple voices came from the olive trees. The noise of snapping ground cover got closer.

Cole quietly opened the back door of the Land Cruiser and removed the M-15 and the shotgun, along with all the ammunition, and carried them into the convent. The .45 remained back in the room. With speed and silence he locked the convent's main door with a large heavy board slid into the braces set on the inside. The thick cypress door, baked hard by the sun over decades, would hold. The other door in the convent's kitchen stood open to the cool night air. Of the same heavy cypress construction, its hinges squeaked when closed, creating a response of heightened conversation from the olive trees. He sealed the door in the same manner as the other.

The high windows, set well above the ground, provided light to the convent but no views. Only a few of the rooms had windows, most did not. One window on each side of the building opened to the common hallway. The building's thick stone and brick walls would handle anything, but the windows created portals.

It was time to wake Francois. Kneeling before a crucifix in the starlit room, Francois glanced over his shoulder.

"They're coming," Cole said with hushed tones. Francois's window stood open.

Francois crossed himself, stood, and viewed Cole with weapons in both hands, an ammunition belt draped over his shoulders. The priest did not ask for an explanation, evidently understanding bad men had arrived to kill them all.

"Get the sisters and move them to the chapel, except for Sister Rahel. We may need her."

Francois pulled on pants, nodded in response, and sped down the hall.

With the weapons and ammunition placed in the hallway, Cole reentered Francois's room, tossed the thin mattress aside, and lifted the simple bed on its end and leaned it against the wall, creating a ramp under the window. He climbed the crude rope webbing that had supported the mattress, peeked over the window, and faced starlit shapes moving from the olive trees to the walls of the convent. He scrambled down and repeated the bed-as-ramp process in his room. By this time, clusters of armed men had collected near the main door. One of them attempted to open the door with the handle, muttered something, and several of them put their shoulders against the stout wood and pushed, grunting with the effort. They weren't budging that door, so he found the next room with a window and repeated the ramp process.

The fighters decided there was no point keeping silent. One of them opened fire on the stout door. The bullets had no effect other than to signal a full-fledged attack.

The shots came as Francois and Sister Rahel approached, both of them instinctively flinching at the explosive crack of automatic fire.

"Pull beds from two of the rooms and prop them below the two hallway windows," said Cole.

They both moved to action without a word. Cole rushed back to the weapons on the floor outside Francois's room and grabbed the M-15, ran to his room to slide the .45 into his pants, and scrambled up the bed ramp. Shouts and random gunfire filled the predawn air. Muzzle blasts and bullets came through the windows on both sides of the convent. These bastards would sooner or later realize their gunfire was ineffective, angled as it was up through the windows and hitting the convent's ceiling. That would drive them to figure out how to climb to the windows and enter. Screams of savagery and yelled commands mixed with the automatic fire.

The ammunition cache was limited, but it might do. Unlike the attackers, he'd keep the automatic M-15 on single shot and focus on accuracy and preservation of the ammunition. Marine Corps training and combat experience now helped him develop a calculated battle plan. Returned fire had to give the impression that more than one person fought back. Fire and maneuver—keep moving. Protect the windows and pray the two doors withstood whatever assault these jihadists threw at them.

An internal switch had gone off, the fears and uncertainties long gone. The situation cried life or death and no middle ground. His Comanche blood surged and he became all fight.

He climbed a bedframe to assess. One of the jihadist leaders stood back and watched his men. Several minutes of random firing through high open windows was proving pointless. This guy would see that unless they could breach the doors, the only viable option lay with them climbing through the windows. At this point, the leader also probably figured they could assault the convent without fear of return fire. That would soon change.

Cole dropped to the ground and ran into the hallway to wrap the bandolier of M-15 ammunition magazines around his waist. Grabbing the shotgun and its small box of shells, he ran to Francois and Sister Rahel who had just finished moving the second bed under a large hallway window.

"Will either of you shoot?" asked Cole, offering the shotgun to Francois.

"No. We cannot," said Francois.

The dark hallway became illuminated at random by outside muzzle blasts coming through the windows, accompanied by battle screams. At one of those moments, Cole viewed Sister Rahel. The tiny woman had donned her habit and stood with fists gripped tight, exuding resolve.

"Will you reload?" asked Cole.

Francois pursed his lips, looked at Sister Rahel whose fiery eyes blazed an affirmative, and replied, "Oui. This we can do."

Cole showed Sister Rahel how to reload the shotgun and sat her against the hallway wall, midway down its length. He planned to manage the M-15 himself, grabbing a loaded magazine from the bandolier around his waist and slamming it into the weapon when needed.

"I'll move from room to room as well as out here in the hallway, firing out the windows. Sometimes I'll use that weapon," Cole said and pointed at the shotgun, "And sometimes I'll use this other one. I want them to think there are several of us firing back."

Francois and Sister Rahel nodded, grim and determined. The outside shots and yells began to diminish. Cole knew what it meant.

"When I pass by here I'll grab the shotgun. Have it reloaded. That's important, Sister. I want to keep a continuous fire. These men will give no quarter. I don't intend to either."

"It shall be prepared for you," said Sister Rahel. "You may be assured."

He paused to listen. The outside fighters had begun to organize, yelling orders at each other.

"Francois, I need you to scout. They will climb through the windows. Probably by a couple of them lifting a fighter to grab the windowsill and climb in. I need you to move as fast as you can from window to window and alert me to any sounds or, God forbid, any of them entering. Got that?"

Francois's expression showed rock hard, battle-ready. "And tell me, mon ami, how I am to alert you?"

"Yell. Scream. Whatever it takes. It's fixin' to get damn loud in here."

"I shall do so. Be most careful. God's strength to you," said Francois.

Cole racked a round into the M-15. "Keep that shotgun loaded for me, Sister. Keep me alerted, Francois. May God be with all of us."

He moved to the bedroom with the most sound outside and climbed the rope webbing of the bed to look below. A dozen men assembled. One of them had slung an AK-47 assault rifle over his shoulder while two compatriots grabbed him by the thighs and lifted him.

Cole could shoot. Military training, years of hunting, and the Aransas County shooting range kept those skills honed. This environment made for close quarters, and the longer rifle bordered on a hindrance. He pulled the .45 from his pants, cocked the hammer, and thought, *Welcome to the dance, assholes.*

The first shot went through the climber's head, the second and third hit the lifters in the chest. He got off one more shot, hitting another in the torso, before the jihadist fighters recovered from the shock of someone firing at them and began to furiously return automatic fire.

Cole leapt off the bed as bullets riddled the window frame and the ceiling of the room. He dashed into the hallway and two doors down, scrambled up on the bedframe and sighted the rifle on the men who still fired at his previous location. Five rapid shots produced five hits, the fighters screaming with pain and anger. He leapt down and saw in the darkness Francois rush out of a room on the other side of the hallway, skid to a stop, and point back toward the room he had just exited.

"They are there!" said Francois.

"Got it!" said Cole.

Francois turned to dash into other rooms. Cole ran by Sister Rahel and tossed the M-15 at her. She caught it and extended her other arm with the shotgun. He snatched it on the run and flew into the bedroom Francois had indicated. Momentum carried him up the bedframe and he had the Mossberg to his shoulder and began to fire directly below.

The shotgun's buckshot devastated the attackers. He fired four times. It made the perfect weapon for this type of firefight. Check's comment about the shotgun flashed through Cole's mind—"For up close and personal." Again, return fire from the fighters hammered the window frame and ceiling of the room. Cole had already jumped away and moved along the hallway.

He ran by Sister Rahel, exchanging weapons again. She began shoving shells into the shotgun's magazine.

Cole fired through another bedroom window, and jumped off the bedframe when Francois yelled from the hallway. He sprinted from the room to see Francois mounted under a hallway window, wielding a bedpost ripped from one of the beds. The invaders lifted a fighter to the windowsill and his two hands gripped the frame. Francois smashed both sets of fingers in rapid succession and caused the invader to fall among his fellow fighters. Cole climbed the bedframe next to Francois and unloaded several pistol shots into the crowd below before bullets filled the space and slammed into the hallway ceiling.

They kept a frantic defense for fifteen more minutes. Cole did not relent with his well-placed shots and the constant maneuvering must have convinced the assailants at least two if not three defenders fired back.

The assault noise below the windows stopped. Chunks of ceiling plaster, hanging, fell to the floor. Both sides of the convent showed groups of fighters standing away from the walls, reorganizing.

Cole knelt by Sister Rahel and checked the shotgun ammunition supply. Less than a dozen shells remained. The M-15 had two thirty-round clips, and the pistol had perhaps five shots left.

Francois knelt with them. "And so," said Francois. "Have they left?"

"No," said Cole. "They're regrouping." He moved to the hallway window facing the olive trees, climbed the bedframe, and took careful aim. The darkness prevented sighting with great accuracy, but one of the fighter's weapons glinted in the starlight and Cole squeezed a shot at the reflected source. A cry returned from the night, followed by more gunfire from the fighters aimed at his window. He moved across the hallway and delivered the same performance to a fighter on that side. The slightest hint of dawn showed from the east.

"If they're smart, they'll stop the random assaults and move on multiple windows at the same time," said Cole, kneeling again with Francois and Sister Rahel. "No way to know if they're smart, but we'll find out soon enough."

"You are bleeding," said Sister Rahel and tore the bottom hem of her habit to craft a bandage.

"It's okay," said Cole. "Some small chunks of rock got blasted from the wall and caught me." He took the proffered bandage and pressed it against his scalp.

"I will need one of those," said Sister Rahel as she pointed at Francois's bedpost club. She turned to Cole and said, "I will reload, of course. But that option shall soon expire." She lifted the box of shotgun shells and rattled it, indicating the dwindled number.

"Oui," said Francois. He moved to one of the propped bedframes and snapped off a post, returning it to Sister Rahel. She gripped it with both hands and swung several times, getting comfortable with its heft. Cole gave a slight head shake and thought, *That's one badass little nun.*

He hoped to hold them off until daylight. There was no guarantee they would stop their assault then, but options expanded with the sun. It would allow him to sight the M-15 at a distance and maintain fire if they backed off again.

"Alright. We keep doing what we've been doing," said Cole. "Sister, forget loading this weapon. I'll take it with me." Cole poured the remaining shotgun shells into a front pocket. "If they coordinate their attack and go after multiple windows at the same time, I need each of you to focus on different sides of the building. I'll back you both. Yell for me. Use those clubs. Smash fingers. Let's hope they come after these hallway windows. If they focus on the rooms, it's liable to be damn tough moving fast enough between them."

The attackers focused on the rooms. Initially the three held them at bay. Cole kept moving, and caught glimpses of Francois clocking several of them on the head as their upper body struggled over the windowsill. Sister Rahel would climb a bedframe, raise her club high, and wait as a hovering hawk for fingers to appear. Cole several times delivered a headshot to an attacker in the process of dropping into a room. Carrying all the weapons from one spot to the next, he'd leave either the shotgun or rifle at the doorway as he entered.

It began to get desperate. Screams of anger and barbarity came from the attackers as they threw themselves at the windows on both sides. At one point, as Cole flew along the hallway, he saw a room where a fighter stood, his AK-47 at the ready, while another one followed and dropped to the ground behind his fellow fighter. Cole slammed to a stop and shouldered the shotgun, killed the first one, pumped what he thought was the next round into the chamber, and heard the empty click of the firing pin when the trigger was pulled. The surviving fighter had already moved his weapon from the sling position on his back and squeezed off rounds at Cole, shooting from the hip. The bullets hissed past as he dropped the shotgun, reached into his back belt, and whipped out the .45. A snap shot spun the attacker and a second, better aimed shot finished him off. Yells from his side of the hallway brought him running into the next room, where Francois teetered on the top of the bedframe and grappled with a fighter who was attempting to enter the room. A .45 caliber bullet popped back the head of Francois's adversary. The sudden lack of struggle with his opponent caused Francois to tumble off the frame and onto the floor. The window filled with the next attacker, who swung his AK into a firing position as he squatted on the windowsill. Cole took aim but the pistol's action stood locked open, out of ammunition. The barrel of the AK-47 had begun to swing in his direction when Francois rushed past him and smashed the fighter's face with the bedpost. The blow sent the fighter tumbling back through the window and onto the ground.

Cole snatched the M-15 from where he'd left it at a nearby doorway, calling to Francois over his shoulder, "Thanks!"

"It is nothing!" said Francois, fire in his voice.

Cole had to get back to the rooms on the other side of the hallway where Sister Rahel patrolled. He slapped the pockets of the bandolier around this waist, identifying one more clip of ammunition. Maybe thirty-five rounds total remained. It might do. It would have to.

He found her in the second room he looked into. She stood wraithlike on the top edge of the bedframe ramp and pressed against the wall next to the window, the large bedpost club held with both hands high above her head, waiting. The predawn light made visibility better.

She turned to Cole, released a hand from the club, and held up a finger for silence.

"It is something," she said.

Cole edged over to stand beneath the window and listen. The sound of scattered gunfire came, but not directed at them. Quick, violent screams followed. A strange crushing or crunching sound carried in the air. Then all stood silent.

Sister Rahel, perched above him, shook her head with an expression of bewilderment. He crossed the hall to find Francois. The priest stood in the hallway under a window opposite Sister Rahel's side of the convent.

As Cole approached, gunfire commenced again but, as on the other side, not directed at them. Yells and commands mixed with short, abrupt screams. The peculiar muffled crunch repeated again and again. Then silence.

Cole and Francois looked at each other, both quizzical.

"Let us see," said Francois as he moved to the propped bedframe.

Cole joined him. They climbed and, shoulder to shoulder, peeked over the windowsill. The new dawn brought just enough light to see. Bodies lay everywhere, and blood pooled beneath fatal bullet wounds. It was a horrible sight.

Many of the bodies lay with broken necks and crushed skulls. These dead men had no bullet wounds. The rope webbing on the frame squeaked below them. Sister Rahel climbed and hoisted herself between the two men's shoulders. She gasped at the carnage before her.

Cole picked up on movement at the edge of the olive trees. A man moved among the tree trunks, giving quick glimpses of his gray tunic and pants and long gray hair tied in a ponytail.

"There!" he called as he pointed out the window. "There, Francois! Do you see him?"

Francois squinted into the faint light. Several seconds later he said, "Oui. I do see."

"That's him!" said Cole in a hushed and frantic tone. "That's him! The man from Rockport!"

Francois remained silent, intent on catching glimpses of the figure.

A softly righteous voice came from behind both men. "Oui. I know who he is."

They turned to Sister Rahel, their faces inches from hers.

"You've seen him before?" asked Cole.

"No. But I know who he is. It is Michael."

They lost sight of him among the trees as he moved west.

Chapter 38

Cole removed the cypress crossbar from the main door, observed the splintered wood where the attackers had fired multiple rounds to no avail, and walked outside. Francois followed. They picked their way through the bodies, Cole still carrying the M-15. He stopped to inspect the bodies he hadn't shot—those with their necks broken or heads crushed. Francois did not join this activity. Sister Rahel retrieved the other nuns from the chapel and stopped short at the door. She turned and marched into the kitchen, found the convent's phone, and began calling, her voice in French carrying to the two men.

"Who's she talking to?" asked Cole.

"She shall ask several local villages to come remove the bodies. She stipulates that she will pay well to the ones arriving first."

Clearly the bodies would not remain on her hallowed grounds.

Cole and Francois walked away from the convent and sat on ancient stone steps at the edge of the olive trees. The sun had begun to heat the day. The birds called and made a racket from the grove of trees, bringing a small sense of normality. The smell of pooled blood wafted by, even at this distance.

Francois lit a cigarette and said, "We must find the Mademoiselle."

Cole exhaled loudly, the adrenaline rush from the battle only now abating. "Yeah. I know. I have an idea where to begin." He swept his arm in the general direction of the strewn bodies and fought back a sudden urge to retch. "More of those crazy bastards are likely wherever we look."

"Oui. This is so."

"Let's get the vehicle and drive. Begin at the village where she disappeared. Run concentric circles, stopping at every village and hut we find. Many of them speak French, so you can question them. Along the way, I'll buy more ammunition."

Neither man moved, taking this time to regroup before they leapt into the next endeavor. The first of the dilapidated pickups struggled up the hill to the convent. They watched the driver go and talk with Sister Rahel while the driver's workers loaded bodies into the back of the truck. They would have a busy day.

"Howdy, boys."

Both men jerked around to see Nadine a few steps away, walking toward them, covered with dirt and a portion of her hair matted with dried blood. Her face had scratches and contusions and she walked with a slight limp. Cole's mouth dropped open.

She put a hand on each of their heads for just a moment and swung a leg over Cole and planted herself on his lap. She held his head with both hands and kissed him hard.

Too shocked to respond, Cole sat with eyes wide open and hands on her wrists. He began to chuckle during the kiss, and rolled into full laughter. She pulled back and joined in. The sound of her laughter caused the body workers to stop and stare. Francois squirmed as he sat, beside himself.

"So, bucko, how was your evening?" she asked Cole.

"Semi-tough. How 'bout yours?"

"About the same."

They both roared, hugged, and kissed. Then both were knocked onto their sides and off the stone steps and on to the soft earth as Francois crushed them with his weight. He lay on top and held each of their heads in a hand while he delivered kiss after kiss to both. Loud, smacking kisses. He gave kisses to their cheeks, kisses to their heads, and kisses to their mouths. Cole and Nadine continued to howl with laughter.

***

After they recovered and wiped away the tears of joy, they retired to the convent where the sisters served a simple breakfast in the kitchen. All the nuns latched on to Nadine, hugged her, and wiped her face and arms with wet cloths. They cleaned and treated her scalp wound. Cole received the same treatment. Everyone averted their eyes from the scene through the kitchen door of local village men performing cleanup activities. Sister Rahel asked Francois if the porridge provided sufficient sustenance or if he would prefer to venture into town to eat. Francois responded by leaning back and lighting a smoke.

Nadine told of her kidnapping in broad terms. She skipped the attempted rape and explained the explosion as something Check had mysteriously managed to pull off. Cole gave her a lifted brow at her obfuscation of what had clearly been a drone missile, but here and now wasn't the time to get into that and besides, it felt so damn good to be alive and with her friends. *Holy mackerel,* she thought. *By the looks of things, Cole must have opened up an entire drum of whup ass last night.*

As she talked, she remembered she needed to call Wilczek, so she borrowed Cole's cell phone. He answered after two rings.

"Check. It's me. I'm alright."

"Thank God. Where are you?"

They talked with short, tight sentences. She explained she thought it best to lay low until dawn and walk the few miles back to the convent.

"One hell of a firefight at the convent last night," said Wilczek. "I couldn't help. Close quarters. The cowboy and priest all right?"

She assured him they remained in good shape. Wilczek demanded she head for the Turkish border. She told him the team had not made a decision on next steps but would keep him informed.

"You're being a dumbass," said Wilczek.

"Yeah. I know."

Wilczek insisted she communicate once their plans became finalized. He promised to help in any way he could and signed off with a gruff, "Call me."

Nadine asked about the firefight at the convent. Francois and Sister Rahel explained as best they could. Cole declined to elaborate. She made a mental note of his reticence with a commitment to talk through it with him later, for both their sakes. Killing was a bad, bad deal in anyone's book. While she internalized her actions of calling in the Hellfire missile as some remote life-saving action—like the cavalry showing up—the bodies strewn around the monastery somehow felt more personal. *Maybe it's always been that way,* she thought. This face-to-face killing, in her eyes, should not remain a private matter for Cole to reconcile on his own. And, just maybe, her remote killing shouldn't either.

The night's violent tale ended with the sighting of the gray-haired man Cole had seen in Rockport. Sister Rahel again declared her knowledge of this person. The other sisters crossed themselves. Francois smoked and watched her and Cole, grinning like the Cheshire cat. That irked her a little, but nothing could overcome the joy of being alive and surrounded by love.

"So what do you think?" she asked Cole. "What does it mean?"

Cole apparently knew the answer, but slowly turned his coffee cup on the wooden table with a checked-out stare.

"Cole?" she asked again.

"He's heading toward Moloch," said Cole. "Due west, wasn't it? Just a few miles?"

"Oui!" said Francois as he slammed a hand on the table. "Why could I not see this! We must depart!" He stood, hands on hips, waiting for them to leap up as well.

Cole never took his eyes off the coffee cup. He likely felt torn, what with mounds of dead bodies not fifty feet away from where they sat and now urged by Francois to immediately agree to put them—and especially her—back into harm's way.

"Cole," she said, gripping his arm. "I'm fine. This is a weird and different space right now, I know. I just missed getting my butt blown up and you've been fighting and killing all night. And right now, outside that door, people are tossing dead bodies into pickup trucks. So, yeah, it's all pretty much otherworldly. It blows me away, too. But that's not the point." She turned to address Francois as well. "The point is we're still alive and we're here and, well, let's finish this thing."

The coffee cup stopped its slow turn. He placed a hand on hers and squeezed, nodded to Francois, stood and said, "Okay. Let's go get the sumbitch."

Chapter 39

They loaded the Land Cruiser, prepared to depart. Other than several new bullet holes, the vehicle proved operational. Hugs and private prayers passed between everyone. Nadine felt intense sadness at their departure. Sister Rahel told Cole he did not need his weapon, for a much more powerful force accompanied them.

"I know, Sister," Cole said. "And Francois is capable of channeling that power. I just want this firearm along to make sure."

Sister Rahel snapped her head toward Francois and back to Cole. "I am not speaking of Father Domaine. You have an archangel with you! Fear nothing."

Nadine navigated using the small GPS Wilczek had given her. Without doubt, it held sidebar transceiver capabilities she wasn't supposed to be aware of, which was ridiculous because right now, since they were in motion, Check would be popping a warm Diet DP and following their progress. Surely he didn't think her that dense.

The track they followed had no other traffic. They passed several herdsmen tending their goats. No one waved. War had taken a respite, the only sound coming from the tires on gravel and rock. They traveled slowly. She gave course corrections as they moved from one crude track to another. After several miles, Cole's cell phone rang. He didn't bother to answer and handed the phone to her, saying, "It's probably Check."

"You're going to a Dead City. The one with the ruins of the St. Ageranus church," said Wilczek when she answered.

"Hi, Check. It's okay," she said. "And can't a girl get a little privacy? I'm stunned you would know such a thing."

"Yeah, I bet. That particular Dead City lies two miles ahead of you," said Wilczek. "What the hell are you doing?"

"We think Moloch's there," said Nadine.

"Fine. Stop and let me level the place. You skirt by it and head to the highlands. Turkey is twenty miles west by northwest. I'm downloading alternative routes into your GPS now."

She held up a hand, signaling Cole to stop. He rolled another thirty feet, halted, and kept the engine running.

"I love you, Check," said Nadine. "I mean it. You saved my life. You cared. But this can't play out like that."

"The hell it can't! You can achieve your objective by letting me handle this! Mission accomplished and get your butt to Turkey."

Nadine looked first at Cole and then in the side mirror at Francois in the backseat. "I'm sorry, Check. I really, truly am."

"It's the damn cowboy, isn't it?" asked Wilczek. "Some lone ranger crap where he has to personally take this guy out. Put him on the line!"

"I'm not going to do that. Please listen," said Nadine. "This has to be done at close quarters. For a variety of reasons, none of which I can explain right now. It's all of us, Check. We all need this."

A long pause ensued. "I thought the three of you would have run out of them by now," he said.

"Run out of what?" asked Nadine.

"Dumbass pills. You must have had one hell of a stash when you flew into Turkey. I'm talking about a seemingly inexhaustible supply."

She smiled. "I do love you. Now, leave us alone for just a bit longer. Please."

Wilczek hung up without a reply. Nadine made a chopping motion with her hand toward the road ahead and said, "Aller!"

Francois squeezed her shoulder from the backseat.

They drove for another mile and a half. Cole stopped the vehicle and turned off the engine. "Let's approach on foot. I don't want him to hear us coming."

"Oh, I'm pretty sure he already knows we're coming," said Nadine, remembering the three extra cups of coffee in Cardiff.

Francois left the Land Cruiser, smelled the air, and stood resolute. He adjusted the snakeskin belt over a juniper-green tunic. She and Cole waited. Francois reached back into the vehicle and produced a robin-blue kaffiyeh, the traditional Arab scarf worn as a headdress. He draped it around his neck, flung one of the tag ends over a shoulder, and began that bowling-ball-lean-forward walk. She realized that this situation probably was his bailiwick, and you absolutely had to admire the guy, fearless with his own funky style. They kept silent and followed the priest.

Cole chambered a bullet into the M-15. *I get it, Cole,* she thought. *But the smart money has to lie with Francois.* They were back in a spiritual realm and Cole needed to understand that, although a little firepower gave her some comfort.

A light breeze stirred the dust-like sand. Their feet crunched on shards of ancient rock. Ahead they saw remnants of walls, low and crumbling.

Crows hopped along the tops of the walls and pecked at objects they could not discern. They walked another hundred paces before Cole moved into the front and ducked behind one of the walls. He signaled them to follow.

"I'll scoot closer and have a look," Cole said. "Y'all stay here."

"No!" said Francois in an urgent whisper. "I am fully aware of your intentions. You waste your time and endanger us! We shall move closer and I shall address him!"

Nadine knelt with them.

One of the objects on the tumbled walls they hadn't been able to see a minute ago now became obvious. It wasn't hard for her to visualize their own heads occupying the same spot.

"He did it in my town!" said Cole, also with a heightened whisper. "Murdered my people!"

"This is not apropos!" said Francois. "He has killed for centuries, you may be assured! This does not pertain to your town, your people. You truly hold such a mentality?"

"What about Martha? What mentality should I have about her? Ignore it?"

Their voices became louder. "Shut up!" said Nadine. "Both of you! Or else just shoot off flares and ring bells so he'll know where we are!"

They sat in silence. Cole and Francois glared at each other. She knelt on one knee facing them. "Hold hands," she said.

The two men breathed heavily, filled with frustration. Nadine extended a hand toward each of them. No one moved.

After a long pause, they extended hands toward her. She grabbed both. "Now each other. Complete the circle. I mean it."

Francois extended his other hand to Cole. Cole leaned the M-15 against the wall and clasped hands with his friend.

"Alright," said Nadine, softly. "This is the end game. We can't go into this pissed off at each other. Think about where we've come from and how something, somewhere, for sure looked out for us, and how the power we generate through mutual love and respect can only help. Please, for God's sake, stop acting like teenagers and focus."

Francois followed with a Latin prayer, and repeated it in English. "Saint Michael the Archangel, defend us in the battle, be our safeguard and protection against the wickedness and snares of the devil; may God rebuke him, we humbly pray; and do thou, O Prince of the heavenly host, by the power of God, thrust into hell Satan and all evil spirits who wander through the world seeking the ruin of souls. Amen."

Cole stared into the priest's eyes and added, "Nadine's right. Let's go kick some ass, Francois."

They squeezed each other's hands, let go, and shared a look of grim commitment. Cole gripped his weapon and checked the safety. Francois watched and rolled his eyes.

A scream of unworldly proportions washed over them—a scream which filled the sky with anguish and rage and dread and hatred. It permeated the air and scattered the crows and caused the earth beneath them to quake. Adrenaline coursed and the hair on Nadine's neck and arms stood at attention and goose bumps covered her skin. They all gripped the ground in reflex, dug fingers into the dusty soil and looked wildly at each other.

Next a starburst blast of crystalline white intensity bleached the whole area of any color. It echoed across the foothills and rumbled down the ravines. It tumbled several of the stones on the wall down onto the three. They became temporarily blinded by the flaring light and reached for each other, panic-stricken. They clasped bodies as their breath came with desperate gasps. Then all around them fell quiet.

Cole unraveled from the pile-on first. "Check and his damn drones," he said, rubbing his eyes. "He could have killed us!"

Nadine rolled away from Francois and blinked wide-eyed. "No. I have close personal experience with those," she said. "No. This was a clean blast. Pure."

Francois slumped against the wall, wiped his eyes with the kaffiyeh, kicked a stone off his foot, and stood. A returning breeze moved a lock of long hair across his forehead. He stared toward the source of the blast.

"It is over," he said. "The demon has been sent to the pits of Hell."

He held on to the stone wall for support and moved around it, stopped, and fell to his knees.

"How do you know?" asked Nadine. Francois did not answer and continued to stare into the distance.

Cole stood, halted to steady himself on the wall and extended a hand to help her stand. They walked the few steps to Francois and looked to where he focused. The ancient remains of the Church of Saint Ageranus no longer displayed the dirt and grime and blood and campfire soot of centuries. The remains now shone, pure and white. In the center of the ruins stood the gray-haired stranger. His long hair no longer tied back, it lay across his back as the breeze sent several strands floating over him. His shoulders slumped and his head hung with exhaustion. He stood still as a statue, frozen.

Cole lowered a hand to Francois's shoulder and dropped to one knee. Nadine placed her hand on Francois's other shoulder and dropped to a squat, hugging her knees with her other arm. All was real and time did not move.

The timeworn man slowly turned his hanging head toward them and cast a look both spent and benevolent. Then he vanished.

A wave of sadness swept over the three, palpable and shared. They were alone again.

"Did you hear what he said?" asked Nadine.

"Yes," whispered Cole. "He said 'realize.' I heard it as if it was spoken in my ear."

"No," said Nadine. "He said 'faith.' Clear as day."

They stayed in their cluster, each lost in wonder. They felt cleansed, free. A desert dove whistled over their heads, bending in flight among the ruins.

"Soutenir. Sustain. This was my message," said Francois, his voice trembling.

They stayed in their awestruck position, united, for several more minutes. Francois stood first as the other two released their hold on his shoulders. "And so," he said. "We should depart. This American friend of yours—this Check—can guide us through his device. It is day. Let us depart from this savage country before the light fails us." He employed his distinctive rolling forward gait toward the vehicle, humming a French tune. Cole and Nadine followed, holding hands.

It was over. All the pain, horror, doubt, confusion, and fear lay behind them on the snow-white remains of this Dead City. All had changed and the world spread before them with a shared mindfulness.

Nadine called Check as the Land Cruiser moved west. He promised to stay with them and communicate at regular intervals.

The three talked on the cautious drive with slow, easy tones—still awash in their experience. The day appeared calmer and their souls at peace. The scene they'd left had a reality of such clarity it would stand forevermore a part of their being. The aftermath now took on a surreal quality.

"I have faith," said Nadine as she looked out the window, counted boulders in series of threes, and saw beauty among the rugged moonscape terrain. "It has grown so much over the last week. It's amazing. And it's not just an expanded faith. It has grown roots. Deep roots."

Francois reflected and relaxed. "It is an affirmation," he said. "To continue my path. My quest. Even with such strong faith I had doubts. This I admit. I am but a man." He paused to light a smoke. "I am humbled. Yet fulfilled. I sit, in this most uncomfortable of conveyances—must you consistently hit the larger of these rocks, mon ami?—oui, sit here filled with awe over what has happened."

Cole smiled and looked at his friend in the rearview mirror. He remained cautious, with a firm grip on the wheel and a vigilant eye on their surroundings. When Nadine announced they had just crossed the border into Turkey everyone began to relax.

"I do realize, now," said Cole. "I realize I will always have questions. There will always exist things, events, happenings, I can't explain. I realize God is not fathomable. We are too small. Maybe that's why he gives us the small miracles. The daily miracles. It's something we can grasp. Like love. Something we can hold onto."

"Like love," said Nadine as she smiled and gazed into the distance.

"Oui. Amour," said Francois. "It is what binds us. It is all which is good."

They drove another minute before Nadine spoke. "Athos, Porthos, and Aramis."

"The Three Musketeers," said Cole, chuckling.

"Oui," said Francois. "Magnifique."

Cole's chortle escalated. Nadine joined in. Her voice rose to a crescendo as she howled with laughter. Francois began to giggle and shook his head until he, too, escalated to a loud joyous laugh. Tears coursed down all their faces.

Chapter 40

They waited for their flights at the Istanbul airport. Francois would depart for Rome, Cole and Nadine to Houston. Francois insisted they order champagne. Cole relaxed and thought of getting home to Rockport. The slow rhythms of a Gulf Coast town pulled hard. Nadine and Francois carried on an active discussion about the Trinity.

"So this Father, Son, Holy Ghost thing," she said. "Does it run in series or parallel?"

Francois sipped champagne and lit a smoke. "It is most unfortunate I cannot answer this, cher," said Francois. "It is not for my lack of knowledge, be assured. It is simply that I do not understand what you are asking."

Cole watched and listened with bemusement. He would miss their interactions.

"Dynamic relationships," said Nadine. "Are they linear and hierarchical or do they act as independent agents?"

"These things are not mechanics," said Francois. "It is not the assemblage of a computer program. It is God, Jesus Christ, and the Holy Spirit."

"Yeah. Got it. Thanks for the definition," said Nadine. "Now, how do the moving parts interact?"

Cole noticed her suspended foot tapping the air in threes, the tempo increasing. He made a call to Jeeter Johnson.

"I'm heading home, Captain," said Cole.

"Did you get the SOB?"

"Yep. It's over," said Cole.

"Good. Get your butt back to Texas, son. I'm glad you got him. Long damn odds from where I'm sittin'. Well done. Nadine and the priest?"

"Everyone's fine," said Cole. "And the powers-that-be should be happy, from the Vatican on down."

"Hell, that didn't matter near as much as you not getting your ass shot off. Call me when you get to Rockport."

"Will do, sir. Jeeter. And by the way, you were right. Nadine May is pretty amazing."

"Yeah, she is. Don't tell her I said that. Travel safe, Cole."

Francois and Nadine continued their discussion, travelers moved about, and flights were called in Turkish, French, and English. Soon it came time for Francois to depart. They exchanged hugs, kisses, and tears.

"Stay in touch, Francois," said Cole, extending his hand. Francois brushed past the hand and wrapped Cole in a bear hug and kissed him on both cheeks.

Cole hugged back, adding, "Be careful. Bon voyage, mon ami."

Francois laughed and said, "Yes. I shall. And your French is much improved, my friend."

Nadine and Francois hugged for a long time. Both shed copious tears. When they pulled apart, Nadine rested her hand on his cheek. Francois held her hand and kissed it, and pulled away. "Au revoir, cher. Au revoir."

They watched him move toward his gate, leaning forward and rolling with intent.

***

Once airborne on the flight to Houston, Nadine curled her legs beneath her and shifted to face Cole.

"What do we do?" she asked. "You and I."

Cole reached for her hand. It was inevitable this topic would appear once they became situated on the plane. "How about we start with a date? Dinner and a movie. Maybe a nice steak. Then anything you want to watch."

Nadine smiled, apparently satisfied. "I'd like that." She shifted back to face forward. "You're not plain vanilla, Cole. Anything but."

"What?"

"Nothing. Dinner and a movie. A date. I'd like that a lot."

The End

Thank you for reading *Evil Runs*!

To tell a good tale. It's a simple and valid answer when the question pops up, "Why do you write?" At the end of the day, it is to tell a good tale.

I hope you enjoyed the experience, and thank you for joining me.

Many readers have asked, "What's next for Cole, Nadine, and Francois?" Admittedly, I've become infatuated with these folks and what might be the next adventure.

Well, the next tale is already underway and I'll keep progress updated on my website.

Meanwhile, I would love to hear from you. I can be contacted via:

www.vincemilam.com

or

vincemilambooks@gmail.com

Finally, I need to ask a favor. If you're so inclined, I'd love a review of *Evil Runs*. Whether you loved it or it put you to sleep—I'd just appreciate your feedback.

Again, thank you so much for dedicating the time to spend with me, Cole, Nadine, and Francois.

Sincerely,

Vince Milam